TEN BELOW ZERO

WHITNEY BARBETTI

"Squeeze, Squeeze, squeeze"
xo
Whitney

For Sona, who thinks she's ten below zero. Sona, you have the warmest soul I've ever known.

awna byenna

"Joy came always after pain."
— Guillaume Apollinaire

Chapter 1

A single text message changed my entire life.

Unknown: This is Jacob's friend, Everett. He said we should meet.

Ten words. Two sentences. And yet, it was the beginning of my entire life as I knew it, though I didn't know it when I first read the words.

It was also a wrong number. But I didn't tell him that, the mysterious Everett. My friends, or more appropriate, roommates, had just left me alone, so I sat in my apartment, wearing a sweatshirt that was three times my usual size and paint-splattered yoga pants. My face was completely free of makeup and my hair was in a bun on top of my head, a style that could not be accused of being fashionable in any magazine.

My night suddenly had an extra option thrown into the mix. Normally, my nights consisted of the same things: books, people watching from my balcony, studying, or working my shift at the restaurant. I was never chosen for Friday or Saturday nights. No one I knew would call me "outgoing" or even merely "friendly." My shifts were usually breakfasts and early lunches, when the customers were too hung over from their all night partying to bother with engaging conversation. They were less likely to dwell on the scar on my face, or the one on my arm. My scars weren't something I particularly enjoyed talking about over eggs and coffee. But a text from a stranger was something that didn't happen every day. Or any day, really. The only people that texted me were my roommates and it was always to pick up their drunk asses. As they had walked out the door this evening, Jasmine had even told me she expected me to be available to pick them up. And why wouldn't they count on me? I was dependable. I didn't party. I spent more time inside the apartment than out of it and I never ever had plans. Granted, Jasmine took advantage of my lack of social life and I let her. Tonight, though, when she'd blown the insincere kiss at me on her way out, I'd been angry. Which was new for me.

So I cradled the phone in my hands, rubbed a thumb over the words on the screen, and made a decision. To be reckless.

Me: Sure. Where? When?

I sent the reply before I could talk myself out of it.

It was dangerous behavior, especially for a twenty-one year old girl, but I always played it safe. I'd never broken curfew, I'd never snuck a guy into my room, I'd never gotten wasted, I never so much as straddled the line into rebellion. I was practically puritanical in my behavior. When I'd turned eighteen, all bets were off. And then, after being attacked in the middle of an abandoned parking lot, I'd crawled into a hole of indifference.

Which was probably why my roommates took advantage of my ability to pick them up from whatever hole in the wall they'd needed rescue from. I didn't have a life. I didn't do things. I didn't have plans and I most certainly didn't meet with strangers on a whim. I went to my anthropology classes. I worked. I hid in my room.

I tapped my fingers on my desk, willing his reply to come. And then I suddenly wondered if he even lived in this area. My new-found sense of spontaneity could be short-lived, depending on his reply.

I didn't have to wonder long.

Everett: The Brick. Nine?

Being the shut-in I was, I quickly woke up my laptop and Googled The Brick, sighing in relief when I saw it was four blocks away from my apartment. I wouldn't even have to drive. I could run home if I wanted. I was forever thinking practically. Practicality: killer of dreams and fun. And I was practicality's most valuable assassin.

Me: See you then.

I stood up and stretched, staring at my drab closet, hoping for inspiration. Just as I started to walk to the closet, my phone vibrated across the desk.

Everett: What will you be wearing? I need to know who to look for.

I looked down at my current ensemble. This wouldn't do. I bit my finger as I contemplated. Inspiration came to me in an instant and my fingers flew across the on-screen keyboard.

Me: Look for the girl who doesn't belong.

His reply came quickly, and seemed warmer than his earlier texts.

Everett: Now I'm really looking forward to meeting you.

If I smiled, I would have then. But I didn't smile, not ever.

I whipped the sweatshirt over my head, sliding the yoga pants off immediately after. And then I strode across the hall into Jasmine's room. We didn't have explicit rules about sharing clothes, probably because Jasmine knew I'd never have an occasion to wear something that wasn't from my usual drab wardrobe. But I opened the doors to her closet and stood back, admiring the bevy of options that greeted me. Four years earlier, I had worn clothes very similar. Less fabric and more skin. My hands caressed the hangers longingly. I caught sight of my left arm and pulled it back, as if it had betrayed me. The scar that ran from my elbow to thumb was a reminder of why I wasn't a Jasmine anymore.

I grabbed the pale pink strapless dress from the hanger. I'd seen Jasmine wear it once. It was fitted to the body, with tiers on the skirt that reminded me of a mermaid's scales. I remembered Jasmine hadn't liked it much because her chest has spilled out of the top. Thankfully, though I had ample cleavage, no one would accuse me of being busty.

I ran out of her room as if I'd be caught and slid into the dress once I'd arrived in my room. I couldn't wear a bra with it, but that didn't matter. I didn't have a full length mirror in my room because I'd never needed one, so I walked barefoot down the hall to my other roommate's room. Carly was much nicer to me than Jasmine was. But she related more to Jasmine and spent more nights living it up with Jasmine at the local bars, so I was often left alone, which didn't bother me in the least. In fact, I thrived in the loneliness. Carly could have treated me the same way Jasmine did and I still wouldn't care. Mean or nice, it made no difference to me. Sometimes Carly's niceness was as annoying as Jasmine's meanness.

I walked to the mirror on her closet door and looked in. The pale pink color of the dress was pretty against my snow white skin.

My eyes traveled up my reflection until they hit my face. I'd need to do something about the messy bun on the top of my head. And maybe makeup too.

I raided Carly's supply of makeup, darkening my bright blue eyes with kohl liner. I smudged it around my eyes, creating a smoky eye. When I stood back to look at my reflection, I was reminded of my first year after leaving foster care, when I didn't leave my bedroom without a full face of makeup. I shook the memory away and hesitantly rubbed some concealer across the scar that marred my left cheekbone. It was angry, raised off the skin from my lips, up my cheekbone, and into my hairline. I let my fingers graze over the ridge that cut into my pale skin and in my reflection I saw the scars on my arm and face aligned parallel. Before my brain delved into the black hole of that memory, I pulled my hand away and turned my face to get a better look at the scar on my cheek. The concealer I'd applied had only highlighted its prominence on my face.

I took a tissue and rubbed it away, preferring to show the tender flesh than to cake it with liquid lies. After sliding some simple studs in my ears, I walked into the bathroom and brushed my hair out.

The bun had given my long brown hair some volume, the ends curled out just a bit. I wore it with a part down the middle and let it hang without any extra effort. By the time I'd left the apartment, it was nearly nine and I'd knew I'd have to hurry.

The sound of laughter greeted me as I hit the sidewalk and I looked around, shivering from the fear that snuck up in an instant. What was I doing? I didn't do this. I didn't leave the apartment at night ever unless I was picking up my roommates. And I certainly didn't walk anywhere at night anymore. My hands gripped the small purse I'd slung across my body. I'd packed my phone, my ID and credit card, lip gloss, and a knife. All normal, except for maybe that last one. I carried a knife with me everywhere. After being at the wrong end of one four years earlier, I knew just how deep they could cut.

I walked briskly down the sidewalk, thankful that the sidewalk was packed with people spilling out of bars for a smoke. Fifteen strangers was less scary than one.

What felt like a few minutes later, I stopped, standing right outside The Brick. Or, what I assumed was The Brick. Sure, the neon sign above the metal door stated its name, but the building did not exactly live up to it. It was concrete and steel, and a total dive. But I'd committed to this moment and had no desire to turn around. I pulled my phone out of the purse and looked at the time. 8:59. I nearly applauded myself on my promptness before I realized I probably should have shown up fashionably late.

The bouncer carded me before letting me walk into the bar. It was one long room. Narrow. A long, black lacquered bar glistened under the dimmed red lights, running the length of the room itself. On the opposite side of the bar were a bunch of pub tables. It was quiet. The only noises came from the bartenders setting thick glasses on the bar top, or the hushed din of conversation. I stepped a bit more into the bar and heard the dulcet tones of something resembling blues music from the speakers that hung over the bar.

Remembering why I was there, my eyes traveled over the handful of couples that occupied the pub tables and deduced they were not who I was looking for. My eyes moved to the bar, taking in the lone patrons who sat there.

There was an older man, who looked halfway to a deep sleep at the end closest to me. I safely assumed he wasn't Everett. I noticed a couple suits and narrowed my eyes, but passed over them when I saw a woman sidle up from behind me to sit between them. If I didn't have a purpose for being here, I would be very interested in watching their exchange.

I saw a few lone stragglers and a couple middle aged women before my eyes landed on him. I almost didn't see him, as his head was bent down while he played with a lighter. He sat near the very end of the bar, alone, with a short glass of amber liquid in his free hand. His hair was ink black, thick, and overlong. I could see a spackling of facial hair on his face, though it looked more like he hadn't shaved in a couple days than a legitimate beard. I couldn't see his face easily from the dim lighting so I moved slowly down the bar in his direction.

As I approached, I took in his clothing. Black jeans, black belt, black dress shirt. Over the back of his chair was a black leather jacket. A man in black.

I took the seat next to the man in black and set my purse on the bar top. The bartender walked my way and I kept my eyes trained on him as I felt the eyes of the man to my left focus on me.

Out of my peripheral vision, I saw the man in black's eyes slide down my body and I resisted the urge to squirm in my seat.

"What'll you have?" the bartender asked, bracing his hands on the bar across from me.

I raised my head to look over the man in black at the bottles that lined the wall. "Gin and tonic please. Extra limes, too."

The bartender nodded and moved away. I set my phone on the bar top and then reached in my purse to pull out my credit card. And then I turned my gaze towards the man sitting next to me.

The first thing I noticed was his bright eyes. My own blue eyes were bright, but his were a frosty blue-green, unnatural looking with his black hair and thick black brows. His forehead scrunched up before he tilted his head. "Sarah?" he asked tentatively.

The bartender returned with my gin and tonic and I slid him my card. "Do you want to start a tab...Parker?" the bartender asked, reading my name from the card.

I turned my gaze to him and nodded. "Please."

"I guess that answers my question," came the voice beside me.

I turned my head back in his direction. "Oh?" I asked, coolly.

"I'm waiting for someone," he explained, swirling the liquid around his glass absent-mindedly.

"Someone named Sarah?" I asked, turning to look straight ahead.

"Yes." I felt him turn his eyes to me again and take in my appearance. He was seeing the side of my profile that showed off my scar, but he didn't seem put off, or disgusted by it.

I turned my face to his and stared at him, directly in his eyes. His eyes didn't waver from mine, not for a second. I felt something stir within me and blinked rapidly in surprise. I couldn't name it. It startled me. It wasn't fear or annoyance: those were the only emotions I felt with any real strength. I guessed it was attraction. When he tilted his head a bit, my suspicion was confirmed. It was lust. There was something about the way he looked at me. When he spoke, he commanded my attention. And it was then that I felt the familiar emotion: annoyance. I did not need to feel lust for this complete stranger.

The man next to me was handsome, in a rugged way. His face wouldn't be accused of being pretty or soft; his face looked like it'd lived through the effects of the sun, the torture of grief. The faint lines around his mouth suggested he knew how to smile, and did it often.

The only line on my face was cut with a knife.

I forced the muscles in my face to relax. He certainly was attractive, and in another lifetime I might have flirted heavily with him. But I was different now. I made a habit of studying other people, of watching them live their lives. That was how I lived mine - through study, not through experience.

I sipped my drink and looked around the bar. "I guess she's not here yet."

He sighed and ran an impatient hand through his hair. "Guess not." He glanced towards the entrance and tossed back the rest of his drink. He seemed a bit fidgety. Nervous, maybe? I watched his hand play with his glass. His other hand flicked on the lighter repeatedly. Click, click, click. I felt my throat go dry.

I turned to my drink again. The bartender had placed a pile of sliced limes onto a cocktail napkin next to the drink. I brought one slice up to my lips and placed the fruit between my teeth, pulling the peel away as I ate it.

After placing the third peel onto the napkin, the man in black, who I'd deduced was Everett, looked at me. "Are you actually eating those?"

I nodded and swallowed. I licked my lips on impulse and I didn't miss the way his eyes followed the movement of my tongue.

When I said nothing, he watched me eat the fourth slice. He'd turned his body more fully to face me and watched me in disbelief. "Isn't that...sour?" he asked. He looked like he wanted to gag.

"Yes." I shrugged. "So?"

I ate the fifth one while he watched me, enraptured. I felt uncomfortable under his scrutiny. I was usually the people watcher; no one ever paid attention to me.

When I finished the sixth one, the bartender placed another napkin of slices next to my mostly-full drink. "Thank you," I said without a smile. I rarely smiled. I wasn't sure how to do it genuinely. I wasn't depressed. I just wasn't emotional.

"It's rude to stare, you know," I said matter-of-factly to Everett as I started in on the additional slices.

He shook his head. "I've never claimed to be anything else. And I've never seen someone eat limes like they're apples."

I furrowed my brow. "Neither have I. Especially since the peel of an apple isn't thick like it is on a lime." I placed the peel on the napkin and looked at him. "And besides, apples are disgusting." I didn't put much feeling in what I was saying, which probably made me sound monotone. I turned to look at him again, my eyes tracing his face. Under his bright eyes were dark circles, making the ice blue of his eyes look even brighter. From the dark circles to the lines on his face, it was obvious he was tired. And something about that attracted me. I liked seeing imperfections; I liked that he wore a bit of exhaustion on his face.

He shook his head, as if in a trance, and turned to his phone. He seemed agitated. "Is Sarah late?" I asked. I felt the corner of my eye twitch and I brought my hand up to touch it. I'm sure surprise showed in my eyes. The situation was amusing, that I knew. But I didn't expect my face to react.

Everett blew out a breath and raised his glass to the bartender, the universal gesture for a refill. While the bartender poured his drink, Everett's fingers flew across the screen before he set it back down on the bar.

I bit my lip nervously. A second later, my phone vibrated across the bar's surface, the noise deafening in our silence. I watched Everett halt in bringing his refilled drink to his lips to look at my phone. It was lit up from the incoming text message notification. He scrunched his brows together and took a sip of his drink.

I took a leisurely sip of my own drink and then carefully placed it on the napkin, smoothing the corners, before picking up my phone. "Excuse me," I said, turning my body away from his.

Everett: Are you still coming?

I felt Everett's eyes on me, so I replied quickly, uncomfortable with such singular attention.

Me: I'm here. Hi.

It was all I could come up with.

I turned back around and set my phone on the bar, picking up another lime slice just as his phone dinged and my text filled his screen.

Everett looked at it and looked at me. "You're not Sarah, though?"

"Nope." This time, I did squirm in my seat. I hadn't exactly thought this part out.

"Was your name ever Sarah?"

I raised an eyebrow at that. "No." What kind of question was that?

"I'm…" he started, running a hand through the mop of hair on his head. "Confused. Yes, confused. I was expecting a Sarah."

"Well," I said, taking a delicate sip of my drink. "You got a Parker instead."

"Is this a joke? Jacob told me he was giving me Sarah's number."

"Who's Jacob?" I asked, nonchalantly.

For the first time, a flash of white stretched his lips. "You're not Jacob's friend, are you?"

I took another sip of my drink and placed it on the napkin. "Probably not." *I don't have friends*, I added to myself.

"Did I text a wrong number?" he asked, leaning back to get a better look at me.

"If you were expecting a Sarah, who is Jacob's friend, when you sent that text, then yes, my number was the wrong number." It was said with a slight bite of sarcasm, but I controlled my features, maintaining the aloofness I was projecting.

"Well, why didn't you say something when I said, 'This is Jacob's friend, Everett' in my first text?"

I shrugged and swallowed another lime. "I figured you thought your friend Jacob was kind of a big deal and that I should be expected to know him." It was a lie, but it sounded funny.

Everett took a sip of his drink. The moment right after he swallowed he laughed, a short sound. "And you decided to come along? To meet me? I could have been a crazy serial killer for all you knew."

I visibly trembled. My hand nearly dropped the lime peel I pulled from the lips and my throat closed up, causing the fruit I was swallowing to nearly come back up. I knew my alarm was at what he said, not fear that he was what he suggested he could be. Serial killers didn't dress all in black and drink whiskey in bluesy bars. They lurked around corners, in the dark, preying upon those unaware of their presence.

I knew my reaction to his off-hand remark had registered with

Everett because he seemed uncomfortable. I tried to break the tension.

"I was bored," I blurted out.

"Come again?"

I took a sip of my drink and let the gin cool the nerves that flared up, before I swallowed. "I came along because I was bored." I set the drink down and turned towards him, sizing him up. "And my status has not changed."

I watched as Everett let that sink in. It was a bitchy thing to say. But I was socially awkward, stilted from my self-imposed loneliness. Words could bite. When I spoke to strangers, I wanted my words to have fangs.

He took a sip of his whiskey, his eyes guarded. I couldn't read him as easily as some other people and that frustrated me. We sat there at the end of the bar, our eyes locked on each other as we contemplated what to say.

He set his glass down on the bar and rubbed his thumb over his upper lip. His gaze never wavered, never slipped from mine. My mind flooded with thoughts; I couldn't quiet a single one of them.

"Why did you really come?" he asked, his voice just barely above a whisper. Something about the way he said it made my leg want to bounce up and down. I decided I wanted him to say it again.

"What did you say?" I asked, leaning closer. The space between us became nonexistent a second later, when he wrapped his hand on the back of my chair and leaned in closer, close enough to brush his lips against my ear. I felt an uncontrollable need to cross my legs. My breathing became shallow, my heart rate picked up and I couldn't help the flood of desire that overtook my body.

"I said," he started, his breath warm from the whiskey, "why did you really come?"

I felt trapped. He had completely enclosed me and his voice… why was I squirming? Without a second thought, I stood up, grabbed my clutch and phone and took off out the door.

I ran down the sidewalk, my heels catching in the impressions of the worn concrete. I fell a handful of times as I ran blindly towards my apartment, ignoring the cat calls and stepping into the street to avoid plowing into groups of smokers gathered along the sidewalk under the street lamps. Smoke wafted in my face and I remembered a piece of the memory I suppressed. Smoke was a comforting smell to me, but every time I smelled it I was brought back to my body lying on the asphalt, a voice urging me to wake up.

They said that scent was the strongest sense related to memory and I believed it. It dredged up memories that I tried to ignore.

As soon as I stepped into the apartment and slammed the door, I vomited into the kitchen sink.

Chapter 2

Around 1:00 a.m., I was lying in the center of my bed, on top of the covers, still wearing Jasmine's dress. I had vomit in my hair and on my face. I didn't care. My mind was still processing what had happened.

My phone buzzed on the nightstand. Jasmine and Carly were probably ready for me to pick them up.

Instead, I was greeted with a text from someone else. It was a photo of my Visa and a short message.

Everett: Want this back?

I felt something finally: the annoyance I was so familiar with. But why did he have my credit card?

Me: That's stealing.
Everett: Nope. I paid for your drink and fourteen limes and the bartender asked if I was your boyfriend and I told him yes.
Me: That's lying.
Everett: Yep.

The annoyance within me flared to a burn. And yet, something about this amused me.

Me: I did not have fourteen limes.
Everett: Well, that's how many I was charged for. I didn't lie

about that part.

Me: Oh, and you are not my boyfriend.

Everett: Thanks for clarifying. You've still not answered my question.

Me: No, I don't want it back. Please, buy yourself something pretty at Tiffany's. On me.

Everett: Wow, ten minutes of conversation and you can read me like a book.

Me: I don't think it was ten minutes of conversation.

Everett: Are you always this contrary?

Me: I'm not contrary.

I settled back into my bed. The side of my lip twitched again. It was the oddest sensation.

Everett: Do you always run like a bat out of hell from bars?

Me: I always run from strange men.

Everett: Meet me for breakfast tomorrow. You can repay me for the fourteen limes with a greasy breakfast fit for a hangover. Wear tennis shoes, so you can run away with more grace this time.

Me: I'll wear heels.

Everett: Of course you will. Schmidt's. 9 a.m.

Me: Fine.

My reply was reluctant. Did I really want to have breakfast with him? I weighed the pros and cons and decided I would. More out of curiosity than anything else. He couldn't be as scary in daylight. He'd stand out, in his black clothing, like a cartoon character.

Another text came through.

Jasmine: Can you come pick us up?

She included an address. My annoyance flared up again. I suddenly remembered I was wearing her dress. I wasn't going to change.

I showed up to the unsuspecting house fifteen minutes later. I'd thrown my puke speckled hair into a bun, washed my face and brushed my teeth before leaving the apartment. Jasmine and Carly were sitting on the curb, waiting for me in the dark. Carly was alternating between barfing in the street and hiccupping. I assumed the latter was causing the former. I sighed and opened the door to the backseat, pulling a grocery bag from the floor and hastily handing it to Carly. Jasmine was more sober than usual and eyed me carefully after we'd settled Carly into the seat.

"Is that my dress?" she asked, accusation thick in her voice.

"It is," I confirmed, belting Carly in. I stood back onto the curb and looked at Jasmine with challenge, willing her to say something, anything. She squinted at me in the dark, as if she couldn't figure me out.

In the end, she shrugged. "You can have it."

"Good," I answered. "Because I'm pretty sure there's puke on it."

The alarm clock blared at 8:30 a.m. but I was already awake. After returning from picking up Carly and Jasmine earlier, I'd fallen into the shower and numbly scrubbed off the puke. It was how I dealt with situations that brought up unwelcome memories. I turned my mind off. A therapist had told me it was common for those who had been through traumatic experiences to block the memories, to make themselves numb to avoid feeling.

The problem was, I didn't have to make myself numb. I just was. My brain swam in Novocain. I walked through life, straying from potentially dangerous situations. If I was even the slightest uncomfortable, there was no question of fight or flight. I'd always fly. I didn't care, I didn't let myself soak up anything. I relished the numbness.

I was emotionally bankrupt. That's what a therapist had told me, when I told her how little I felt. Emotions were always vague, fleeting little things. I felt them in small spurts, similar to how one might feel a drop of water hit their skin and wonder if it would start raining. Except for me, it never rained.

So why did I agree to join Everett for breakfast? I wasn't sure. Not even in the slightest.

I walked into the bathroom and turned on the light, squinting a bit as the fluorescents chased away the dark. I'd slept poorly, though that wasn't unusual. I didn't care much for sleep. I found no solace, no rest, in sleep.

I started brushing my teeth when I looked up. My reflection told a story of a pale-skinned girl, with circles under her eyes so dark they looked like bruises. My hair was a frizzy mess from laying on it while wet. With my free hand, I gathered up the hair and left the toothbrush in my mouth to enable my other hand to tie the mess into a bun on top of my head.

When I departed my room, Carly was in the kitchen making scrambled eggs.

"Hey," she said while piling eggs on a plate.

"You're up early." It was my usual greeting. Though I much preferred Carly to Jasmine, I still wouldn't say we were close in any sense.

Carly gulped a glass of orange juice, nodding. She was wearing an oversized tee that hung to her thighs. "I feel surprisingly good after last night." I recalled all the puke and then was reminded that my car was likely a mess. Carly flipped her black hair over her shoulder and looked at me quizzically. "What's that look for?"

"My car is a mess." The mild annoyance crept in. Annoyance and I were quite familiar with each other. Especially when it came to my feelings for puke all over my upholstery.

Carly's face fell. "Oh, shit, I'm sorry. I'll clean it up after breakfast."

"I have breakfast plans." I wasn't sure why I told her, but it caught her attention. She turned to me with a knowing grin.

"A date?" she asked, seemingly hopeful.

I nearly shuddered. "No. Someone did me a favor and I guess I owe him pancakes now."

Carly's grinned, but after perusing my clothing the smile slipped from her face. "Are you wearing that?" she asked, gesturing with her spatula.

I looked down at myself. I was wearing stretched out yoga pants and an oversized sweatshirt, my usual attire. I shrugged when my eyes met hers again. "Yeah."

Her eyes practically doubled in size. "No," she emphasized, dropping the spatula on the counter and turning the stove off a second later. "You are not wearing that. And your hair?" she looked at the mess on my head, her face pained. "Come here," she insisted, dragging me down the hallway.

Thirty minutes later, I was walking down the sidewalk towards the pancake restaurant. Carly had forced me into coral and navy colored dress with navy heels. She'd made my bun look less like a nest and had even swiped some makeup on my face, hiding my dark circles. I felt out of place, which fit the situation, as I wasn't sure what to expect.

My hands started tingling when I made out the sign on the side of the building, trying not to focus too hard on the people milling about on the sidewalk, the few that stopped to give me a second glance.

I was finally feeling more than annoyance: I was feeling longing. For my stretched out yoga pants.

I'd told myself on the walk to the restaurant that something was off the night before, the night we met. There were millions of other men in California. What was so special about him? It was the liquor or the spontaneity that messed with my brain. I didn't feel things. Lust didn't grip me like a vise, twisting me inside out with desire. That was irrational. That was not me.

My eyes tracked the man in black on the sidewalk. I couldn't explain how I knew it was him, but I did. And then he turned.

My eyes betrayed me the moment they met his. They refused to break contact and a moment later, my equally traitorous heart stuttered in my chest. He was walking across my path, head turned in my direction while I stood, a statue on the sidewalk. I vaguely registered the jostling by other pedestrians, rushing to their destinations.

He stopped his path and angled his body to face mine, his eyes pinning me in place. The entire world kept moving around me but I was seconds away from my heels forming roots into the concrete.

He walked towards me, confident in his stride. My heart stirred in my chest and I knew, without hesitation, that this man would destroy me. The thought made me breathless. With fear and expectation. More prevalent than those, however, was desire. What was happening to me?

When he reached me, my breath came back loudly, as if I'd been startled. He cocked his head to the side, looking me up and down. "Going somewhere?" he whispered.

The foot traffic jostled us a bit, so he reached a hand out to steady me, his hand touching the bare skin of my arm. The touch sent a little shock and I glanced down, disorientated. I noticed his shoes then. My mind blanked.

"They say the first thing you notice about someone is their shoes, but that can't be true because I just barely noticed yours." The thought flew from my mouth without provocation. I looked up at him, a little embarrassed. A smile curled one side of his lips and his eyes crinkled. He still looked tired.

And why did that last thought send me into a land of inappropriate visions?

"I didn't notice yours either," he admitted. He stepped back and looked down. "Hmm," he murmured.

I blinked rapidly. Were we really talking about our shoes? "What?"

"You did exactly what you said you'd do."

It took a moment for it to click. "I couldn't find my running shoes," I answered.

"Hopefully you won't need them this time," he said, pulling gently on my arm to lead me to the restaurant.

"Where's my card?" I blurted out.

Everett looked at me as if I'd wounded him. "Breakfast first," he insisted, his head angled to me, his hair in his eyes.

I'm not sure what it was about my face that made him laugh at that moment, but he did, and the sound reached into my belly and teased the desire that lay there in wait, like a snake waiting to strike. How was it possible that he looked the same in the daylight, with the morning sun lighting up his features, drawing more attention to the lines around his eyes and mouth? And why couldn't I stop looking?

"I'm not hungry," I said as he led us to a booth in the back. I kept my eyes averted from the other patrons as some of them looked at us. What did they see when they looked at me? Were they admiring the dress or fixated on my scars? I hadn't bothered hiding them this morning.

And on that thought, I looked to Everett as he gestured with his hand for me to have a seat in the booth. Why hadn't he mentioned anything, asked about my scars?

He took the seat across from me and asked the waitress for a coffee before looking at me.

"Water," I answered.

After the waitress walked away, Everett broke eye contact to open up his laminated menu, perusing the available options. He didn't say anything as his eyes glided across the menu. He made little hums here and there, nodding as if in deep thought about waffles and sausage links.

He lifted his eyes to mine. "What are you going to have?"

"Nothing."

"You'll have something." His eyes didn't waver. I squirmed a little and crossed my arms over my chest.

"No."

His eyes narrowed, but not in anger. More like in contemplation. The waitress returned with our drinks while we were engaged in an unannounced staring contest.

She wrote down Everett's order and turned to me. Before I could open my mouth to answer, Everett interrupted. "Key lime pie. And if you have extra limes, could you toss those on her plate, too?"

"Sure thing," the waitress cooed before sauntering away. I watched her departure with fake interest, trying to avoid looking at Everett. His gaze on my face made my skin itch.

"I said I wasn't hungry," I finally said, smoothing out the skirt of my dress.

Everett picked up his cell phone, black like his clothing, and glided his fingers across the screen with one hand while he poured creamer only into his coffee.

"That's very rude, you know," I said. My eyes tracked his hands, admiring the way he poured the creamer to the very top without overfilling.

His eyes shot to mine in an instant, one black chunk of hair hanging over his forehead in front of his left eye. "I never claimed to be anything else." A repeat of his line the night before.

He didn't smile. Instead, he stared at me. His eyes didn't glide over me. They were completely focused on my own. I felt the challenge that they insinuated.

"You need a haircut."

That incited a small smile from his lips. "According to you?"

I squirmed a little in my seat. "Well, actually yes. And the general population."

Everett arched an eyebrow. "Oh, really?" he asked, leaning forward on the table. "Have you surveyed the general population on the matter of my hair length?"

He was teasing me. My eyes tightened with annoyance. "Of course not. But the general population keeps their hair at a length that can manage a semblance of a style."

He rubbed his chin in contemplation. I could nearly hear the rasp of his fingernails against his scruff. "Are you saying my hair is not styled?"

I sipped my water and let the liquid cool my tongue. "Yes. It looks like a rat made a bed on your head." It was a lie, but it had its intended effect.

His eyes opened up then, fully, startled. "Now that is a rude thing to say."

I nodded. "I never claimed to be anything else," I said, throwing his words back at him.

Everett leaned back in his booth and, while staring at me, he ran his fingers through his thick, black locks, pushing them away from his face. In doing so, he exposed his forehead. Immediately, my eyes found the line that followed his hairline. It was faint, white, and clashed with his deep olive complexion. I knew it was a scar, even though it had faded a bit, and there was a small dent off the center of his forehead. I felt something spark within me then. Something more than mild annoyance. I met his eyes and saw the words he didn't speak. *We both have scars.*

I didn't realize my finger was brushing the one on my arm until I saw his eyes glance down. I hastily pulled my arm back and under the table. I wished fervently I'd worn something with sleeves.

"Why haven't you asked about my scars?" I said without thinking.

He sipped his coffee, making a quiet slurping sound. His eyes held mine the entire time. He pulled the cup away from his mouth and licked his bottom lip before setting the cup on the table. He pushed one hand up his forearm, pushing up the jacket sleeve. He pushed it past his elbow before bringing his hand back to the table. My eyes darted between his hand and arm. I knew that whatever he was doing, it was deliberate. His hands rested on the table top in front of us, veins raised under his knuckles. And while I stared at his hands, he turned the exposed arm over, bringing the underside of his wrist up for me to see.

The first thing I noticed was the scars. Beneath the sprinkling of hair they sat, little white and red circles, tracking the paths of his veins up to his elbow.

"Why don't you ask me about mine?" His voice startled me, breaking my concentration on his skin.

He was exposing his scars to me. I tried to summon up embarrassment, but instead I felt relief. We were on the same playing field. Where my scars were jagged and angry, the result of an attack, his scars were deliberate, repetitive. I yearned to learn more. I blamed it on my compulsion to study people. I didn't truly care about Everett. But exposing scars that were normally hidden was as honest as nudity, if not more so.

But I barely knew him. So I didn't bother answering his question.

He pulled his sleeve down, hiding the circular scars that covered his arm like confetti. He leaned forward on the table, pulling me under and into his presence. "How did you get your scars?"

I sipped my water again, my throat going dry at having his full attention upon me. Before I could answer, the waitress set our plates on the table in front of us. Everett pulled back, the spell was broken.

I looked down at my key lime pie. It was dyed an unnatural bright green-blue color. I pushed the plate away from me and took the bowl the waitress had set down, filled with lime wedges. As I brought the first one to my mouth, I felt Everett's eyes on me and I looked up. He hadn't even picked up his silverware yet. He just stared at me. In the daylight, his eye color was so light it looked as bright as the color of the fraudulent pie.

I took a bite of the lime while holding his gaze. He shook his head and cut into his stack of pancakes. I watched as he drowned them in syrup and tried to keep a scowl from forming. His pancakes would be soggy and gross before he had time to finish them.

He took a bite and met my eyes again. With his mouth full of pancake, he raised an eyebrow at me and gestured to my bowl of limes.

"What?" I asked, confused.

He swallowed and sipped his coffee. "Are we going to take turns watching each other take one bite of food?"

I wasn't embarrassed that he caught me staring. As I'd mentioned before, not much affected me. Feelings were like a rich piece of cake: too much made you sick. My indifference was like a comfort blanket. I wrapped myself up in it and kept myself from feeling. Life was easier this way.

So why did Everett make me feel different? Was it the clothing I wore? Was this a costume, the heels, the dresses? When I put them on, did I subconsciously become another me? It was a bit unsettling and I swallowed my bite of lime with discomfort.

I watched him eat another bite and lick the sticky syrup from his lips. He had nice lips. They were wide, not too thin, with a pointed cupid's bow at their center. Around his lips was his several-days-past-five-o'clock shadow.

"Do you have a job?" Apparently, his presence lowered my guard, and I spoke more freely than usual.

Everett nodded and ate two more bites of pancakes before answering. "I do. But I don't work in the summer."

I ate another lime, contemplating. "What do you do?"

"I work with middle school students."

"Teaching?"

He ate the last two bites and settled back in the booth, getting comfortable. "No."

I noticed he didn't elaborate. As I was finishing my last lime wedge he asked, "Do you have a job?"

"Yes."

He took a sip of his coffee, again making that soft slurping sound. It distracted me. "What do you do?"

"I'm a waitress."

Everett pursed his lips, seemingly finding this information interesting. When he didn't say anything, I bristled. "What?"

He shrugged and reached into the messenger bag he'd brought with him. He pulled out a small green notebook. I watched him flip open the lid and write something, careful to keep it from my view. I narrowed my eyes.

We sat like that for a couple minutes, me glaring at him while he scribbled some words onto paper. When he was done, he put the notebook back and looked at me again, as if nothing had happened.

"That was not polite," I said, still glaring.

"Ah, another way to say, 'rude'. Good job. I'm sure you'll find several synonyms for me."

For some reason, that seemed to only further infuriate me.

The waitress dropped off the check and Everett reached into his wallet. He slid my credit card across the table top to me and before I could put it with the check, Everett was out of the booth with his messenger bag and walking to the cash register.

I sat at the table for a moment, wondering if this was goodbye. Was I supposed to walk out the door and be on my way back home?

I stood up and brushed my hands down the front of the dress before walking towards the door. I passed Everett as he paid and stalled a minute, deciding at the last second to wait for him before exiting the restaurant.

Everett turned around and opened the door for me, so I walked back outside on to the sidewalk.

"Thank you for breakfast," I said, awkwardly teetering on the sidewalk, trying to keep away from the foot traffic.

"That wasn't breakfast for you, was it? If so, I am disappointed. All you ate were some limes."

He was facing me, our bodies just inches apart to keep from being separated by the people passing around us.

"I wasn't hungry."

He stared at me, eyes unreadable. His focus never wavered, despite the many people that bumped us as they moved along the sidewalk. "When you do feel hungry," he started, his voice lower than before, "what do you prefer to eat?"

I swallowed thickly. "I like cheeseburgers, with extra cheese." Almost as soon as the words were out of my mouth, I wanted to take them back. As if he read my mind, I saw the side of his lips lift up ever so slightly.

"You ask for extra limes, extra cheese..." he started, staring at me, breathing in the space that I breathed. "What other extras do you like?"

My mouth went dry at that. His voice was warm, smooth, like chocolate fondue. "Extra space," I whispered. "I like extra space." I backed up a step, praying for balance.

He regarded me for a minute, looking out of place wearing all black under the bright sun. "Did you walk here?" I didn't answer, just stared at him as if he would eat me alive – which he probably would. I took another step backwards and glanced over my shoulder.

As if he knew I was slipping away, he held a hand up to halt me and stepped forward until we were breathing the same air again. Being this close to him was like holding my breath under water. Exhilarating. Dangerous, if I didn't come up for air.

"Parker." It was the first time he'd said my name. I met his eyes again, the clear blue-green of them mesmerizing. "Do you want to go to lunch later?" A second after he said it, he winced. Did he, too, experience that quick kick of regret the moment words left his mouth?

I still didn't answer. I think we both knew the answer to his question. I backed up again, ready to leave, but his next question stopped me.

I chewed on my lip as I contemplated. The question he'd asked before in the restaurant, the one I hadn't answered, popped into my head. "Morris Jensen," I said.

Someone bumped Everett in their rush across the sidewalk, causing him to bump into me. I saw Everett's face morph in an instant as he turned and glared at the impatient pedestrian. And as just as quickly, he turned back to me again. Anger furrowed his brow and thinned his lips. There was a fire in his eyes that I found captivating. "What did you say?"

"Morris Jensen," I repeated. "That's how I got my scars."

I couldn't tell you why I told him. Maybe because I wanted to tell someone, even if it was a mostly-stranger. Especially since I didn't plan on seeing him again.

"Goodbye," I said awkwardly, turning around and walking towards the apartment.

Ten steps down the sidewalk, I braved a glance back. Everett had moved to the exterior wall of the restaurant, his body shadowed beneath the awning, as he wrote in the notebook I'd seen earlier.

I watched him scribble words down, leaning against that wall, cloaked in the harsh shadow. And then his face lifted and he stared at me, his light eyes piercing in the dark.

I did this often, staring at people, watching them do day-to-day things. But never so openly, so brazenly. I enjoyed watching mannerisms, quirks, or the moment a person made a decision, let that decision wash over their face, tighten or relax their muscles. I liked predicting their next movements, probably because I'd been blindsided by the person who had irrevocably changed my life. Morris Jensen.

But Everett held my stare. It was intense, but curious. An animal observing its prey.

Quickly, I spun on my heels, somehow maintaining my balance, and hustled down the sidewalk to the apartment complex.

That afternoon, I cleaned out my car and left the windows open to air it out. I was soaked in sweat by the time I'd finished and took advantage of the quiet apartment to take a leisurely shower.

When I jumped out of the shower, I was startled by Jasmine busting in the room. I hastily wrapped a thick towel around me and stared at her as she plopped down onto the toilet.

She looked at me coolly, daring me to say anything. Jasmine, while not close to me in any sense of the word, knew things. Things like how much I guarded my privacy and how I was an avoider of conflict. She regularly took advantage of both of those things at the same time, like she was doing at that moment.

"You have another bathroom." It was said quietly, as I always spoke around her. The apartment boasted three bedrooms and two bathrooms. Luckily, I'd been given the master bedroom, which came with its own en suite bathroom. It was luck more than anything else, after living in this apartment for three years and being the only remaining roommate from the original group that had first moved in here years earlier.

"Yeah, Carly's in there. She's sick." Jasmine stared at me with eyes too big for her face, but the look she held was sharp, conniving. To say we didn't get along would be like saying that grass is green. It was obvious to Carly and to any one of Jasmine's boys that she paraded in and out of the house. I didn't hate her, but she seemed to hold some kind of contempt for me.

I stood there, inches from her as she used the toilet. We stared at each other while the water dripped from my face onto my chest. We were at a standstill. She would expect me to leave the bathroom, but I decided I didn't want to.

"Carly said you had a date this morning."

My eyes narrowed. Annoyance. Carly, while sweet and unassuming, had a big mouth. Instead of answering Jasmine, I pinned her with a stare.

Jasmine finished and stood up, yanking her shorts back on. She smiled at me, an unfriendly smile. Her blonde hair fell around her shoulders like she'd just come from a salon. It was the kind of hair that people envied. Blonde, soft, full of body. Luckily, I felt nothing but annoyance for her. She was a rash that wouldn't go away, itching at my skin with her stares and words.

"Was he cute?" she asked as she washed her hands, using too much of my soap and splashing water all over the mirror.

"I don't know." It was honest. He wasn't a man you'd see in any model magazine. He was tall, in shape, with piercing eyes and a quick tongue. His hair was too long and he didn't seem to like colors that weren't black, but he still called to me on a deeper level. A level that was unnerving and, let's just be honest, annoying. As I mentioned, I felt annoyance often. It was the other emotions that were tricky, slipping through my fingers like oil.

"What's his name?"

I picked up the hand towel after she finished drying her hands and wiped up around the sink and the mirror, roughly, hoping she'd see what a giant pain in the ass she was. Not like that did me any good. If anything, it seemed to widen her malicious grin, her pearly whites sparkling with gleeful animosity.

Instead of answering, I carefully pushed her out of my bathroom and then continued pushing until she was out of the bedroom completely. She resisted a little, but she was no match for me with her skinny legs and little body fat.

"Why are you so weird?" she asked right before I calmly closed the door in her face.

I hesitated a moment. "Why do you care?"

She narrowed her eyes a moment, as if considering my question. "I don't," she finally answered, before spinning around and walking down the hall.

It probably should have hurt my feelings, but since I didn't have any, I felt the usual – indifference.

Carly had moved in shortly before Jasmine, but they both hadn't been here a full year yet. Carly and I got along a bit better than Jasmine and I did, but I still felt nothing about it one way or another. Years of bouncing around foster homes had enabled me to not care about making a connection to anyone. And the scars I'd earned from letting my guard down reminded me that other people were dangerous.

I wrapped the towel tighter around me and grabbed a second towel for my hair. I took a seat at my desk and booted up my laptop.

I checked my bank account first before I started paying my bills. My waitressing job paid most of the bills, but I was fortunate to have my rent and schooling paid for with grants and scholarships, as I had emancipated from the foster care system when I was eighteen. I had one more year of college left before I would be on my own, but I had a well-padded savings account from my settlement with Morris Jensen.

I suppose I should feel like that money was tainted, dirty, and came at the cost of permanent scarring. My lawyer had kindly mentioned the money would more than cover any plastic surgery I desired, but the fact was that I didn't want surgery. And I didn't care where the money came from. I'd been forced into shock from the experience, so far into shock that most of the experience was still out of focus in my memory. A therapist had suggested I never came out of shock. She'd warned that the moment I came out of shock, when I fully grasped the entire situation, it would be traumatic and I would likely have a hard time coping.

I knew that was partially why I took comfort in my lack of emotion. The longer I existed without being ruled by emotions, the safer I was from what I had subconsciously buried in my memory.

As far as Morris Jensen went, I didn't specifically remember a whole lot. I knew what the doctors and police officers had told me. They'd asked me, when they'd caught him, about the bullet in his stomach. But I didn't remember the entire event. I remembered flashes. I remembered the dark, the screaming. I remembered tires squealing, the radio blaring. I remembered the crack I'd heard when my head had bounced onto the asphalt, the smell of oil and fear. Most of all, I remembered the smell of fear, tinged with blood and sweat. And if I closed my eyes and concentrated, I remembered the moments after, when I'd been completely changed.

Chapter 3

Three years earlier

The doctors told me I had fought him hard. The blood under my nails was being carefully scraped by a very nice woman who tried distracting me with a story about her granddaughter. But my attention was focused on the social worker who was standing in the doorway, trying to keep the detectives from questioning me.

"She is too emotionally fragile to deal with questions right now."

I was puzzled by that. I didn't feel fragile. I was in pain, sure. Physical pain from the cut on my face, the skin stretched with stitches to cover the gaping hole in my cheek. The eight-inch cut on my forearm was quite painful as well. But maybe the social worker saw the ripped skin and torn tissue and assumed that she saw me. I was much deeper than just flesh wounds.

"I'm fine," I said, my finger nails being picked clean underneath the harsh fluorescent lighting. The detective with the brown eyes looked at me with a sort of weary hope. As if I was his last obligation before he could go home and crawl into bed with his wife and wake up with his kids to cartoons. One last thing to cross off his list before he could go home, crushed with the safety of being a family man. The thought made my lips curl.

The social worker looked at me like I was out of my mind. Which, really, I was. I had no idea what had actually happened, so I knew I couldn't provide the sort of details the detectives would want to know. But I wanted nothing more than to be gone from here, gone from the eyes that stared at me either dispassionately or sympathetically.

The detectives moved around the still shocked social worker and took my answers. They took photos of my arm, my face, my hands, and my back. I gave them clothes I'd been wearing when I was brought to the hospital.

As I signed my discharge paperwork, the officer bagging my clothing asked, "Do you have anyone we can call?"

"No." My finger ran over the bandage on my arm absently.

"No one?" The social worker asked as she handed me a few pamphlets that I folded and stuffed into the pocket of the sterile scrubs I'd been provided.

"No," I repeated flatly. I didn't need to be reminded of my loneliness. No parents, no siblings, no friends. I belonged completely to myself.

When I walked out of the emergency entrance, I turned the corner around the building and stopped short.

There was a small woman leaning up against the wall, only visible thanks to the parking lot lights that shined on the area around us. I knew her as the woman who'd saved me, who had brought me to the hospital and called the police.

She blew out the smoke she'd just sucked in from her cigarette, tossed it on the ground and stomped out the lit end before walking towards me. The air around her smelled of smoke, which I normally detested, but the smell was safe to me. It was the smell that roused me from consciousness on the asphalt.

"They let you out?" Her voice was deep, smooth, sexy – like red wine. Her hair was bright red and her green eyes were lined with thick black liner. She wore an oversized leather jacket, white jean shorts that were ripped at the hem, and ass-kicking knee-high black boots.

I nodded, my eyes over traveling her. She was a few years older than me, and had the overall impression of a total hard ass.

"You hungry?" she asked without waiting for me to answer, walking across the parking lot and whipping out a key from her pocket. A small sports car parked illegally flashed its lights and she wrenched the passenger door open.

She didn't look at me for confirmation and really, she was my best bet. I had left the hospital intending to get a cab, but arriving at my apartment alone was not appealing to me. So I followed, climbing into the seat next to her as she fiddled with her phone before tossing it on the console. Every movement of hers was graceful, but violently so. She was a small package of smoke and mystery and currently the only person in the world who knew what happened to me. And with that, a thought occurred to me.

"Did the police question you?" I asked as she whipped out of the makeshift parking spot and flipped on her headlights.

She shook her head and glanced at me as she looked at the side mirrors. "I don't talk to cops."

"Why?"

"Because they want to know my business." She exited the hospital parking lot and shifted the vehicle, increasing the speed on the main road. "I have to deal enough with them in my line of work, so I heartily avoid them when I'm not working." The keys hanging from her keychain jingled, the various items hanging from it glittered from the car's interior lights.

"What's your name?"

I snapped my eyes up to her face. "Parker."

"Do you want to die tonight, Parker?" she asked, shifting into a higher gear.

I didn't know what to say, but fear seized my muscles, and I stared at her, terrified.

She looked over at me and muttered, "Jesus. Your seatbelt." She inclined her head towards the buckle that lay empty. "Buckle up."

As quickly as it had come up on me, fear left me just as fast, though a little bit sat stubbornly there, not trusting this woman. I buckled my belt in haste just as she whipped around a corner, not bothering to stop for the light. Granted, it was just a couple hours before dawn and there was little actual traffic, so I didn't feel terror like I would have if it had been rush hour.

A few minutes later, we pulled up in front of a twenty-four hour department store. I looked out the window, confused.

She was already out of the car and walking towards the entrance, so I had nothing else to do but clumsily follow after her, in through the automatic doors and into the air conditioning. Summer was unbearably hot in California, even in the early hours of the morning.

I followed her into the women's clothing section while she rifled through a pile of jeans. "What size are you, Parker?"

"Eight," I answered immediately. "Why? Wait, I have clothes

at my apartment."

She looked at me beneath brows that were dark like her eye makeup, impatience simmering just beneath the surface. "Yeah, and you live forty miles from here. I'm hungry. And your hospital attire is going to kill my appetite." She tossed a pair of jeans over her shoulder before walking purposefully towards the tank tops.

"I don't even know your name," I protested, though that seemed like something I should have asked before climbing into her car in the first place.

"Mira," she mumbled, holding a tank top in front of me to check the size.

"How do you know I live forty miles away?"

"I checked your wallet while you were unconscious." She spun around and pushed her way through the racks of clothes to the check out.

"But you didn't remember my name?" I asked, blindly following behind.

"I wasn't looking for your name when I found you, I was trying to figure out where you lived," Mira replied as she tossed the clothes on to the checkout belt.

"Why?" It seemed like an odd thing to worry about.

"I told you, I don't like cops. If we'd been close to your address, I would have called an ambulance and waited, figuring a cop would give you a ride home from the hospital." The cashier stared at us as we spoke. Mira spoke with truth, but with a heavy hand of impatience too.

When the total rang up on the register, Mira whipped out some cash and paid for the new clothing.

"I could have paid," I protested meekly. It was futile. Mira was a hurricane and I was along for the ride.

Mira took the change from the cashier and walked towards the exit, once again not waiting to see if I was following. She stopped at the restrooms and pushed the bag of clothing into my hands. "Get dressed. I'm hungry."

I walked into the restroom with my bag of clothing and took a second to breathe. This had been the most traumatic and also the craziest night I'd had in my entire life. Five hours earlier I had awoken to a woman's smooth voice, my head resting on warm pavement. I remembered little of what had transpired, except that I'd hurt, everywhere.

I opened my eyes and turned towards the bathroom mirror. It

was my first time seeing my face. I walked a few steps closer to the mirror and turned my face to get a better look.

The scar on my cheek cut into my hairline. A nurse had shaved part of my head to make the gash easier to sew back together. The skin around the cut was red, angry, and bruised too. There was a bandage over the stitches. I had to keep the area dry for a week. One of my eyelids was raw from road rash, and the eye itself was swelling quickly.

At that moment, I remembered the reason I was in the bathroom and I quickly changed while in one of the stalls, sliding on jeans that were looser than I expected. I winced while pulling the tank top over my head, feeling the material gently brush the abrasions on my back.

On my way out of the restroom, I tossed my scrubs into the garbage and looked for Mira outside of the restroom, soon realizing that she was gone. Instantly, disappointment and loneliness bloomed in my heart. I quickly shut the feeling down and strode towards the exit, not sure what to do or where to go, but knowing that I was on my own.

Except I wasn't. Just outside the entrance was a waft of smoke and sure enough, Mira was there smoking a cigarette and running her fingers over her phone. I watched her for a moment, watched how she sucked in the smoke from the cigarette before she blew it out in a small stream. Her eyes caught mine and she pocketed the phone before striding towards me. "Let's eat," she said before taking two long pulls from the cigarette. She dropped it and stomped out the lit end before stalking back to her sports car.

Twenty minutes later, she pulled into a diner just off the freeway. Before she could open her door, her phone rang. I sat in my seat, unsure of what to do as she answered.

"Yeah," she said. It was an unusual way to answer.

After a moment she said, "I'm at Paulie's." She glanced at me for a minute. "I have a mouse." I trained my eyes to look out the windshield, feeling embarrassment at being privy to her conversation. I quickly looked at the dash, noting it was nearly five in the morning. "Not sure what I'm gonna do yet, Six."

Six? Was that someone's name?

"Hey, chill out. It's fine." A second later, I heard a loud voice on the other end of the phone. "God damn Six, I just want a fucking cheeseburger. How about you take a nap, shower off your shit mood and then call me, okay?" And with that, she hung up.

She pocketed the phone and exited the car, so I followed as was usual for us.

As we were being seated, all I could think about was Mira, the mystery she was. Who was Six? And why would going to sleep at 5 AM be considered a nap? It was a relief to have something else to think about other than what had happened to me seven hours earlier.

When the waitress came over to take our orders, Mira took the menu from my hand and shushed me when I tried to protest. "Two cheeseburgers and fries. Extra cheese on the burgers. And a couple Cokes."

The waitress sauntered away and Mira turned her attention to me. It was the first time she'd really looked at me, to my knowledge, and I squirmed a little in my seat. "Okay, Mouse. I have a feeling you're gonna argue, so this is what's going to happen. You're going to eat a burger and fries so that I can give you something for the pain you're going to feel tenfold when you wake up. You're going to crash on my couch and then once we've both had a good bout of sleep, we'll go from there."

I didn't know what to say. I didn't think arguing would make a difference, except further annoy her. "Can I ask you a couple questions?"

She narrowed her eyes, turning the whites into slits. "Depends." She shrugged off her leather jacket and then waved a hand at me. "Go ahead then, I can see the wheels turning in your head already."

"Where do you live?"

Her eyebrows raised at that. "In a house. Next question."

We both knew she evaded my real question. But I continued. "What did you see when you found me?"

Mira's head fell back to the booth behind her. "I was waiting for you to ask this one. I saw a car fishtailing down the road. Don't know why I bothered to follow it. And then I saw a door open and saw you tuck and roll out of the car. I had to slam on my brakes to avoid hitting you myself. The other car stopped, a man got out and I got a shot off before he decided not to stick around."

"What? You have a gun?" I'm sure my eyes were wide with shock. Mira rolled her eyes.

"Keep your voice down, won't you? Yes. I carry." Mira looked around and seemed satisfied that the diner was mostly empty. She stood up and turned around, lifting her tank top up a few inches to expose the holster that sat against her lower back. A black revolver rested, snug in the holster. She pulled the tank top back down and sat in the seat again before continuing. "After that, I checked your wallet and checked you for internal injuries. You were mumbling and whimpering, kind of squeaky like. Then I poured you into my vehicle and dropped you off in a wheelchair at the ER."

I remembered that. I remembered looking at her, shocking red hair. Remembered feeling the heat of her leather jacket against my skin while she repositioned me in the wheelchair, the smell of smoke as she'd pushed me through the doors and into the waiting room.

The waitress dropped off our sodas before returning to the kitchen. I sipped mine as I contemplated my next question.

"Why are you helping me?"

I knew instantly the question made Mira uncomfortable. She scratched the skin at her wrists, not looking at me at all. I took two long sips of my soda, not expecting an answer, until she spoke. "Because I've been you before. A mouse."

"I don't want you to feel like I'm an obligation."

"But that's exactly what you are," she insisted. "Don't feel shame for it. If I didn't want to help you, I wouldn't have stuck around after dropping you off at the ER."

It annoyed me that I was this stranger's obligation, that I would owe her something. But before I could protest, she interrupted me yet again. "Parker, listen. I'm not good at…" she paused. "Talking. I'm shit at it. You heard me on the phone with my boyfriend. When I don't want to talk, I hang up or I just stop. I don't waste words. I don't hold hands or braid hair or anything a normal woman would probably do for you. I'm a fighter. I'm better with fists than with words and I want to help you. Because I've been where you are, and someone picked me up and showed me how to fight. You're a fighter too. I saw it on the pavement, when you were covered in blood that wasn't all yours." She took a sip of her soda, not bothering to use the straw. "I need to give it some more thought," she started. "But you're alone and there's nothing worse than that."

That stung a bit, but it was the truth. I guess I was more transparent than I thought.

"You walked out of the hospital alone. You didn't call anyone to come rescue you. So I'm not here to rescue you. I'm here to rehabilitate you."

After that, our food arrived and we spent the meal in silence.

Cheeseburgers with extra cheese turned out to be just what I needed.

Present

After paying my bills, I slipped into some running shorts and a tank top. I was out the door a minute later, headed down the sidewalk towards my school.

I was never a runner before I met Mira. My idea of working out had been dancing at the club or raising my hand for another drink. But Mira had pushed me, pissed me off, and forced me to be strong. So now I ran almost every day. I ran the four miles to campus, grabbed lunch from a food cart and ate in the park nearby so I could indulge in my favorite pastime: people-watching.

When I made it to campus, I heard my phone go off. I plopped onto a bench and pulled it out of my arm band.

Everett: You never answered my question about lunch. That was rude of you.

My lips twitched.

Me: I never claimed to be anything else.
Everett: And now you're stealing my words. You definitely owe me lunch.

I hesitated. Yes, for some strange reason, I wanted to see him again. There was something really peculiar about him, and his scars had piqued my interest. But it was completely unlike me to engage with someone, least of all a man, in a one-on-one setting.

Me: Fine.

Chapter 4

Thirty minutes later, I was sitting in a booth, waiting for Everett to show up. I was still wearing my workout clothing, soaked in sweat from the run to the apartment to grab my car.

I was finishing my second glass of water when the door to the restaurant jingled. I lifted my eyes and watched as Everett strode towards the table.

He slid into the seat across from me before signaling for the waitress to come around. Our eyes met and my chest tightened. It'd only been a few hours since I had last seen him, and yet seeing him again was feeding an ache that squeezed in my chest.

"Is it safe to assume you're wearing running shoes now?" he asked.

"I am."

"So I better be careful of what I say, so you don't run again?"

I shrugged and sipped my water. "I'll probably run anyways."

Everett leaned on the table. I inhaled his scent, which I could only describe as cool water, though in theory, water didn't have a scent. "Do I intimidate you?" he asked, one eyebrow raised.

I was sure I frowned slightly. "Not exactly. I just don't make a habit of talking to people."

Everett stared at me until the waitress came around. "A cheeseburger. With extra cheese."

I lifted my eyes to his. He was watching me for a reaction. I controlled my features to stay calm. When the waitress walked away, I spoke again, "They don't make it as good as Paulie's does."

"Paulie's?" he asked.

I shook my head, signaling that I didn't intend to speak that aloud. "Why did you want to meet up again?"

"I was bored."

I glared at him. "That's…"

He smiled, his first real grin. "Let me guess what you were going to say: Rude. Yes, Parker, I am in fact very rude. And unless you've already forgotten, you said the same thing to me last night."

My mind flipped back like a book to when I admitted I'd gone to the bar to meet him out of boredom.

"Sorry I ruined your date last night."

Everett cocked his head to the side and eyed me curiously. "It wasn't a date. And even if it was, you didn't 'ruin' it."

"Your text message made it sound like a date."

"Did it?" he asked, running his fingers over the scruff on his chin. "Well, it wasn't."

"Then what was it?"

"That's none of your business."

My eyes snapped from watching his fingers on his chin to his eyes. "It was just a question."

"And you don't answer all of mine. So why should I answer yours?"

I sat back in the booth and crossed my arms over my chest. "What questions?"

"Why did you really come to the bar? It would have been easier to just reply, 'wrong number.'"

I blew out a frustrated breath. "I had nothing else to do. And I wanted to change things up a little bit."

"You were right when you said to look for the girl who doesn't belong. You couldn't have looked more out of your element."

Something about his words bothered me. The tone was neutral, but it felt like a dig. I responded the only way I knew how.

I gestured to his clothing. "Well you look like you belong at a funeral." It was an immature dig, but it was the only one I could come up.

Everett laughed humorlessly. "I probably do."

I furrowed my brow, confused. "What does that mean?"

"Nuh-uh," he said, shaking a finger at me. "My turn to ask a question."

I bit my lip to keep from arguing. Why was he bothering me so much?

Everett watched me with fascination. When he seemed satisfied that I wouldn't say anything else, he settled back in his seat. "So," he started. "Morris Jensen."

I was already regretting telling him. "What about him?"

The waitress delivered our burgers and left without a word. Everett's eyes hadn't even glanced at the burgers. "I looked him up online."

I ran my tongue over my teeth, waiting for more. "So?"

Everett took a bite of his burger and chewed, his eyes never leaving mine. I popped a few French fries in my mouth, nervous from the attention.

"He's going to trial in a few months."

"So?" I said again, with fries in my mouth.

"Nice manners." His smile looked mischievous and I found myself more nervous from him looking at me than us actually talking about Morris Jensen.

"Are you going to testify?"

I swallowed. "No." It was the answer I always gave.

Judging by the look on his face, it wasn't the answer Everett expected. "Are you joking?"

I took a bite of my burger and shook my head. After swallowing, I answered. "No. I'm afraid I'm bad at jokes."

"You are the sole survivor of a serial killer and you aren't going to testify against him?" Everett looked angry and his voice had raised several octaves.

I was really annoyed now. He read a few articles online, so what. He didn't know anything. And he assumed too much. "I said no." I glared at him, daring him to say another word about Morris Jensen, so I could run from the restaurant.

Everett calmed down and called the waitress over. "I'd like a beer please. Whatever you have on draft is fine."

I chewed my burger in silence. Everett finished his beer and ordered a second one before he'd even finished his burger.

When I'd finished my burger, Everett was on his fourth beer in less than an hour. I stared at him before asking the question that was bouncing around my mind. "Do you usually drink this heavily at lunch?"

Everett whipped his head up and looked at me. He hadn't glanced at me since he received his first beer. I noticed his eyes were tired, sad, and called to me on an emotional level. Whatever the emotion was, I couldn't name it. It was foreign, an intruder.

"I'm an alcoholic, Parker. I drink this heavily all day long."

The words stole my breath. He said them without preamble, as if he was as disappointed in himself as he expected me to be. What stuck in my mind the most was that he said them at all. He barely knew me. Most of the alcoholics I'd known growing up never owned up to it and denied it even after their second DUI.

"Are you driving?"

"I'm an alcoholic. I didn't say I was an idiot." The bite of his words fell flat for me and I ignored them.

"How did you get here?"

"I walked." Everett held his head in his hands and sighed, as if the weight of the world sat on his shoulders.

"I live two blocks from here. I can give you a ride home." I didn't know how functioning he was as an alcoholic, but for some reason I felt responsibility in making sure he arrived home safe.

"Okay," he agreed quietly, slumping further in the seat. "Sure."

I paid the bill and had Everett follow me out of the restaurant. We walked to my car in silence. He told me his address and I plugged it into my GPS. Ten minutes later, Everett was asleep in my passenger seat.

When I pulled up to a small house in a quiet neighborhood, I turned off the engine and turned my head to look at Everett. His elbow was propped up on the window, his head resting in his hand. He looked calm when he slept. With his face relaxed and his eyes closed, there was nothing intimidating about him.

The sleeve had slipped down on the arm that rested on the window, so I was granted a better look at the scars on his arm. Many were faded. Most had become white, years old. There were a handful of newer scars that had little red dots in the center of them. They were needle scars, I knew that much.

I leaned over my seat, looking closely at the scar along his hairline. His head in his hand forced some of his hair up, giving me a better view of one end of the scar. It too was white, faded. There was a small dent in his forehead just beneath the scar on one side. Brain surgery of some kind, I knew.

Being this close to him, I was able to breathe in the cool rainwater scent that mingled with the scent of leather. His lashes were long, black, thick. He had laugh lines around the corners of his eyes and a nose that had been broken once before. It was a handsome face, a sturdy face. And I couldn't help but wonder about it, about him.

As if he had sensed my closeness, his eyes opened in a flash and met mine. I stared at him, holding my breath. His breath washed my lips with warmth and I gradually opened my mouth to allow air in. Everett closed his eyes and breathed in deeply. "Mmm," he murmured.

He was smelling me. As I'd smelled him. Lust burned bright and I closed my eyes.

A second later I heard the passenger door open and I opened

my eyes, watching Everett climb out of the car.

"Thanks for the ride, Parker." He walked up his steps, his gait slow and a little wobbly.

I waited until he was on the other side of his red front door before I let out a breath and put a hand over my heart. It was raging, out of control.

I drove away and finally named the emotion that had taken up residence beside my heart: sadness. Inexplicable sadness.

Late Monday morning, I arrived at the restaurant ten minutes early for my shift and started taking breakfast orders. It was an odd hour to eat, which meant business was slow as usual. That was fine by me. My mind was still wrapped up by the day before and what had happened. I wasn't sure how I felt about Everett and his admission. I wasn't sure why I cared. And most of all, I wasn't sure why I felt sad about it. I didn't feel sadness. I didn't get close to people on purpose. I didn't want to feel anything for anyone else, and I didn't want to carry the obligation of caring. The only person I had ever cared for was Mira.

I hadn't heard a word from Everett since I dropped him off. I didn't expect to, after all. I didn't even know what it was that we had been doing. All of it was confusing. It was too much.

I was so wrapped up in my own thoughts that I didn't look up at the patrons that were seated in my section until I heard my name being said as I pulled out my order pad.

"Parker."

I whipped my head up and came face to face with Everett. I blinked several times, wondering if all my thoughts had conjured him up, if this was a mirage.

But no. He was there, with clear eyes and a frown.

Why was he frowning?

I slid my eyes to the person sitting in the seat opposite him. She was in her mid-twenties, with long blonde hair and bright blue eyes. She looked like sunshine. She watched Everett looking at me with great interest before looking at me as well. A little frown formed her lips and I was suddenly overcome with the urge to laugh. My lips twitched. Even her pout was pretty. I slid my eyes back to Everett. He was wearing a bright blue tee and jeans, looking nothing like himself. And both of them were frowning at me.

"What can I get you?" I didn't know what else to say.

The blonde woman looked at Everett with concern etched into her face. "Ev?" she asked.

Ev. It didn't fit him. Not that I had any authority on what "fit" Everett. But these blue clothes and this sunshine woman, and her stupid nickname for the man in black did not fit at all.

Everett looked away from me and turned to his breakfast companion. "Sorry, Charlotte. Um. Coffee, please." He didn't look back at me, instead focusing his attention on his hands.

Charlotte looked concerned but spared me a quick glance. "Tea, bag out."

I turned away and walked quickly back into the kitchen. My hands shook as I poured his coffee and my mind raced. Was Charlotte his girlfriend? Why was he wearing colors? Why was he frowning at me?

And more importantly, why did I care?

I nearly dropped the glass coffee pot as my hand shook with the fearful realization that I liked Everett. I rarely, merely, tolerated people, but Everett? I actually liked him. More than I had liked anyone in years. A creative string of swear words flew through my mind, annoyance replacing the palm-sweating fear.

I poured cream into Everett's coffee and then I poured hot water into a second mug and left a tea bag on a saucer. I took a breath and returned to the table, trying my best not to show how badly I was shaking. I placed the coffee and tea cup on the table and stayed longer than I should have. To be fair, it was both Everett and Charlotte's reactions that made me stay.

Both of them stared at Everett's cup. Charlotte looked at me and cocked her head to the side. "Who are you?" she asked. There wasn't any animosity in her face, just curiosity.

My eyes darted to Everett who was still staring at his coffee cup. What were they staring at? I brushed my hands down my apron, trying to dry my sweaty palms.

"C-can I get you breakfast?"

Charlotte stared at Everett before looking at me with a plastic smile. Her smile only made me more nervous. "Give us a few minutes, hun," she answered.

That was all I needed. I spun around and walked into the back, all the way to the walk-in freezer. I didn't stop until I had walked fully into the small room, until puffs of cool air surrounded me. I flung my hands out, shaking them in the cold air, annoyed with myself, with my body's reactions.

"Hey," a voice barked. I turned my head to the freezer door. My manager, Doris, stood at the entrance, hands on her hips. Her white apron was stained with grease and her gray hair was piled high on her head, under her hairnet. "What are you doing in here?"

I put my hands in my apron and walked back out with my head down, avoiding eye contact. Doris was a force to be reckoned with, impatient and unforgiving.

I walked back around to the entry from the kitchen to the restaurant, taking a peek at Everett and Charlotte. Everett was still looking at his coffee. I could tell Charlotte was speaking to him, based on the way she was leaning forward across the table top, her hands inches from his. Her long blonde hair shielded her face from view, but I could clearly see Everett's. His brow was furrowed. He had one hand in his hair, his arm propped on the table. I wondered then, about Charlotte. She had to have seen his scars. What did she see when she saw them? And in what ways had she'd seen them?

The thought made my stomach roll with nausea. I was angry with myself for worrying. I had no ownership over Everett. The feelings that were battering my head didn't belong inside me. They were poison, corrupting the indifference I adopted.

"Table ten is up," the hostess said, coming up behind me and pointing to the elderly couple she had just seated.

"Thanks," I muttered, before looking back at Everett. Ice blue eyes met mine. He was staring at me. He tilted his head to his coffee, holding my gaze.

Cream. I'd poured cream in his coffee before giving it to him. He hadn't asked for cream. But I'd remembered from when we had had breakfast the day earlier. And I'd taken it upon myself, though subconsciously, to add the cream.

A small smile stretched his lips, as he watched me struggle with that realization. What right did I have to do that, to remember how he liked his coffee? It felt intimate. The simple act of bringing him coffee the way he liked it had implications of how well I knew him. No wonder Charlotte had looked at us with confusion.

I saw Charlotte's head turn to follow Everett's gaze and I spun around, knocking into another waitress with arms full of plates. I bit down on the swear word that begged to be released from my lips. Luckily, the waitress held onto her plates, because just behind her was Doris, an impatient look on her face. I knew what that face meant.

I blew out a breath and walked to table ten, walking past Everett's table on the way. I took the drink orders for table ten, aware of Charlotte's penetrating gaze on me. My skin itched and my legs begged me to run.

Instead, I turned around and stopped at Everett's table. "Have you decided on food yet?" I pulled out my order pad and tried to play cool.

"Pancake stack. Extra bacon," Everett ordered, leaning back in his seat, watching me. I met his eyes for a moment. They were sad. And suddenly, I felt it too. But it was just a drop. I didn't embrace it. "Please," he added, his voice just a little lower. My breath caught.

"Egg white omelet. No cheese. Vegetables on the side. And I

don't want the potatoes it comes with. Can I have fruit instead?" Charlotte's voice forced me from looking at Everett. I blinked at her. "Fruit?" I asked dumbly.

Charlotte looked at me with eyes narrowed. "Yes, fruit. Do you have fruit?" She spoke slowly, as if I was missing the brain cells required to understand her.

I shook my head, though my thoughts were still clouded with Everett. "Uh, yes. I'll go put that order in," I said, turning around.

"Parker," Everett's voice stopped me. Slowly, I turned around again and lifted my eyes to his. "Can I have another coffee please?"

I nodded and spun around, walking back to the kitchen. I grabbed the coffee pot and hesitated only a moment before grabbing a bowl with single serve creamers and headed back to the table.

I set the creamer on the table and poured more coffee, keeping my eyes trained on the cup and not on Everett. But it was futile. I watched as one of his hands reached for the bowl of creamer, plucking two containers from right under my hand. As I topped off his coffee, his hand brushed mine.

My eyes quickly sought his and he stared at me again, as if willing me to read his mind. The thought was equally exciting and terrifying. I walked stiffly away from the table and filled the drink orders for my other table.

When I was back in the kitchen, I put in the order for table ten and waited, my eyes glancing back at my tables, lingering on Everett's. I couldn't help it. I felt compelled to watch him. He saw me and picked up his phone, his fingers moving across the keyboard. He looked back at me again and set his phone down.

A moment later, my pocket buzzed. Doris had a strict no-cellphones policy, but everyone checked theirs anyway. With half the employees being college students, it was only natural that they would steal a minute to check our phones.

I rarely checked mine, mostly because I had no need to. I had no social media accounts to maintain and just five contacts in my phone. No one ever needed to talk to me; if I heard from someone it was for a favor – like Jasmine.

I looked around for Doris's beady eyes before stealing away to the bathroom. Once I checked that the stalls were empty, I pulled out my phone.

Everett: I liked it better when you poured the cream for me.

I clenched my jaw and debated replying. I hadn't heard from him since I'd dropped him off at his home. But I didn't want to lose control of myself, and I knew talking to Everett was a slippery slope to my undoing. So I ignored the message, tucking the phone into my pocket, and returned to the kitchen.

I delivered Everett and Charlotte's breakfast without any incident and poured Everett more coffee. By the time they asked for the check, I had poured him a fourth coffee and he was out of creamer containers. I looked at the empty bowl and debated grabbing more, but I shut the thought down and walked back into the kitchen.

Everett looked at his coffee and at the empty bowl before looking at me. It was like we were both speaking the same silent language. He smiled, a real smile, and picked up his phone again. And my pocket buzzed.

I stole away to the bathroom once more, pulling out the phone.

Everett: You know I take creamer with my coffee and you deliberately refused to bring me any.

Guilt crept in and I was suddenly annoyed – with myself. A change of pace. That changed when I received the next text.

Everett: That's rude, you know.

I bit down on my lip, feeling it tremble, as if tempted to smile. And then the door to the bathroom opened.

Charlotte stood before me and seemed unfazed by my presence in the bathroom. That's how I knew she was expecting to find me. Her long blonde hair was thick, curled slightly at the ends. Her face was hard, her eyes narrow.

"How do you know Everett?"

She didn't waste any time. I turned to the sink and started washing my hands, rolling up my sleeves, exposing the scar. I looked at the scar a moment before answering. "I don't." It wasn't a lie.

I looked up in the mirror and saw her reflection staring at my back. "You do," she insisted, crossing her arms over her chest. It emphasized her large chest. As if I needed further proof of her desirability.

I rinsed the soap from my hands and shook them, letting water splatter across the sink. I pulled down a couple paper towels and dried my hands before wiping up the splatters. I could taste her impatience in the air. It was insufferable.

I threw away the paper towels and looked at her pointedly. "No, I don't." And then I walked out of the bathroom, back to the kitchen. I stayed hidden this time, not peeking around the corner at Everett while we played our staring contest game. When I figured he had paid for the check at the cashier by the exit, I peeked around. He was indeed gone, with Charlotte. That knowledge sank in my stomach, holding me still. It was lead. And I didn't want it.

I walked to the table to clear the plates and found a $50 bill under Everett's plate. Under the bill was a note, torn from what looked like a notebook.

Parker,
I'm sorry about yesterday. Some of us have scars that aren't meant to be seen.
Dinner tonight. My house. Six.
Everett

My stomach flip flopped as I read that. "Some of us have scars that aren't meant to be seen." That part was honest, heartbreakingly so. And those words touched me with their truth.

I tucked the note away and finished my shift, unable to keep my thoughts from straying to Everett.

Chapter 5

That night, I sat in my bedroom, staring at the note sitting on my desk. My eyes strayed to the clock several times as I debated what to do. Jasmine and Carly had already left for the evening. It was their understanding that I would pick them up from whatever mess they'd fallen into. I hadn't been asked. But Jasmine had laughed at me on her way out. "See you at one! Or two, or three, or whenever we're ready."

I hadn't corrected her, but I hadn't acknowledged her either. I had two choices: sit in the apartment until I received Jasmine's text or go to Everett's.

My eyes strayed to the clock again. 5:45. I was really pushing it.

At 6:00, my phone vibrated across my desk. I picked it up.

Everett: Fashionably late is still late.

I had never been so completely undecided in my entire life. Stay or go?

Ten minutes later I was standing on his doorstep. Before I could knock, the door swung open. Everett had changed from his earlier clothing. He was wearing black jeans and a black tee shirt. My eyes traveled to his arms unwillingly before I looked back up at him.

"Sorry I'm late," I said as we sized each other up.

"No you're not," he replied, stepping aside and holding a hand out for me to come in.

"How do you know?"

Everett closed the door behind me before gesturing me to follow him down the dark hallway into the bright kitchen that waited through a doorway.

"Because I don't think you were planning on coming."

I swallowed. "I wasn't."

Everett nodded and walked to the fridge while I took in his kitchen. It was warmly colored, lots of reds and golds, with splashes of modern influence in the stainless appliances and the small lights that hung over the kitchen island. I took a seat at one of the bar stools while Everett pulled a bottle of white wine from the fridge.

He held it towards me and I nodded. He poured two glasses before handing one to me. I watched him hold his glass and couldn't stop the words that slipped off my lips.

"Should you be drinking that?"

Everett raised an eyebrow and proceeded to sip. "Just did," he replied after swallowing.

I played with the stem of my glass. "But you said you're an alcoholic."

"I did. And I am."

I looked at him, confused.

"I'm not a recovering alcoholic, Parker. I know what I am. A lot of alcoholics are in denial. I'm not. I know it's one my many weaknesses."

I was still confused. And my face must have made that clear. Everett sighed and set his glass down, on the other side of the island from me.

"I'm an alcoholic, but I've no desire to be otherwise."

"Why not?"

"I didn't fall into alcoholism the way some people do, the people who are desperate to get out but feel themselves slipping away. I am completely in control of myself."

"Except when you're drunk." The words were bitter on my tongue and I pushed the wine glass away. It was a small move, but one that Everett noticed.

"Yes. Fortunately, I don't make a habit of getting drunk in the company of others. I get drunk at home, alone, so the only danger I am is to myself."

"You were drunk yesterday. I had to drive you home."

Everett looked down into his glass. "Yes, I was. I'd say I'm sorry for that, but then I'd be lying."

"And you don't lie?"

"No."

We were staring at each other now.

"Ever?"

Looking at me square in the eyes, he shook his head.

"Why not?" I took a large swallow of my wine. I was tiptoeing into dangerous territory.

"You've told me that I'm rude, Parker." I nodded, confirming that. "I am. I'm rude because I don't conform to society's belief that white lies are inconsequential. I don't believe in hiding behind words that aren't truthful. I'm an impatient man. I don't beat around the bush. If you ask me something, I won't lie to you."

I let that sink in. "You lied to the bartender. You told him you were my boyfriend."

Everett looked surprised. "You're right, I did. I guess you're a bad influence on me."

"I don't believe I influence you at all."

"Oh, but you do," he insisted.

"How?"

"You bring out something in me."

"Is that something rudeness? Because if so, then I agree."

He nodded, nonchalant. "I don't say things I don't mean." He took a sip of his wine, finishing it off. "Take this wine glass for example. If I had poured milk into it and told you it was wine, would you be upset when you took the first sip, expecting the bite of fermented grapes and getting milk instead?"

"I like milk."

Everett fought a smile. "I do too. But I also like to know what's coming. It all boils down to control." Everett grabbed the bottle of wine from the fridge and came around the kitchen island, refilling my glass. His arm was stretched alongside mine as he poured. Inches. That was all that separated us.

He was standing beside me, so I sucked in a breath and turned to face him. He was looking down at me. His hair was long in the front, drawing attention to his eyes, which were searching mine. He leaned down on the island, bringing our faces closer together.

His eyes searched my face, slowly. And then his lips parted. "I like control, Parker." His words were a thick whisper, moving the air across my lips.

I licked my lips. "Why?"

"Because," he whispered, his air warm on my wet lips. He moved his arm slightly, so it was now touching mine on the granite countertop. I felt the heat from his arm ripple up my own arm. It was a shock; his touch was an electric wave, moving through me with his closeness and his words. He brought his face closer to me and my body hummed. "I need it," he whispered, his other hand coming up to my hair. I felt his fingers touch my strands, but I kept my eyes trained to his. "I want to control the things I can't control." He pulled a chunk of my hair towards him, playing with it. "There are a lot of things in my life that are out of my control. Big things. Bad things. So when I can," he said, leaning in, "I grip control like it's my lifeline. I don't surrender control." His lips were hovering over mine. "Ever." My chest heaved heavily, the breaths coming in short and fast. My heart beat loudly, the blood thrumming in my ears.

And then he pulled back. "I have cancer, Parker."

My heart stopped for a minute, restarted. A moment later, my breath caught up. I'd been underwater, slowly, gracefully gliding with his words. And then I was thrust back to the surface, sucking oxygen into my cramped lungs. And I was without words.

Everett watched me go through the series of reactions. The lust that burned a fire across my body had been doused with reality.

"A brain tumor," he continued.

My lips were open, but no sound came from them.

Everett broke eye contact and sipped his wine. "It's a good bout, too. Strong." He raised his hand and tapped his forehead. "The bastard is hanging out right here."

He was being nonchalant about it, drinking his wine and leaning back on the counter. A million thoughts rushed in at once.

"Are you doing chemo, radiation? Or whatever it is they do?"

Everett set the wine glass down and moved to the other side of the island, grabbing an oven mitt and opening the oven door. "No. Just waiting."

"Waiting?" I asked. "For what?"

I watched him pull lasagna out of the oven and set it down, pulling off the oven mitt. He looked at me, an eyebrow raised, as if annoyed that I didn't get it. "To die."

It was a slap. A viciously cold slap of truth. "Is it inoperable or something?" I was trying to understand what he was telling me, so I could wrap my head around the fact that he was waiting to die, and was nonchalant about it.

"No, I'm sure it is. But I'm not interested." He grabbed two plates from the cupboard. "Do you want to eat here or in the living room? I rented a couple movies."

I threw my head back and looked at him like he was out of his mind. My anger burned bright, like a candle that had been doused with gasoline. "Are you kidding me right now?" I asked, standing up from the kitchen island. Everett set the plates down and looked at me wearily, waiting for me to rant.

"You were just leaning into me like you were going to kiss me and a second later you're telling me you have a brain tumor and you're not going to operate, and in that very same breath you're asking if I want to eat on the couch and watch movies with you?"

He pursed his lips. "Yep. That's about right. Except for the kissing part; I wasn't going to kiss you."

Whiplash. That was the best way to describe the current situation. I forced the kissing part from my brain and concentrated on the rest. "Why aren't you operating? Why aren't you doing anything about it?"

"Because Parker, this isn't my first rodeo. I've had this same cancer before." Everett walked around the counter to me. "This," he said, exposing the scar along his hairline, "is my every day reminder. I fought this cancer for three years when I was a teenager. And then I spent another three years rehabilitating. I was homeschooled, a loner, a sick nobody." He thrust his arms in front of me. "I was pricked and prodded and I spent years stuck in a bed or rehabilitating." He put his arms down. "I fought for a long time. And I'm tired. I'm tired of fighting. The cancer is there, even worse than before. The odds aren't great. And I'm okay with that. I'm okay with my life. I'm okay with death."

Fury narrowed my eyes. "What does that even mean? Who can be 'okay' with that?"

"With death?" he asked. "Easy. I am okay with it. There's no other way to say it. It is what it is."

"What does your family think?"

"Don't be stupid, Parker. What do you think they think?" He shook his head at me, growing impatient. "They want me to fight it again, of course they do. But this is what I want. I need to have some kind of control over my life. So this is it."

"This is it?" I asked, gesturing around. "Being an alcoholic and waiting until your time's up?" I couldn't say why I was enraged, but I was. It was none of my business, and normally I would bathe my brain in indifference. But something about this was so completely wrong. I couldn't help but speak my mind.

"This is it," he confirmed. He grabbed a serving spoon and looked at me. "Everyone is going to die, Parker. You're going to die, I'm going to die, we're all going to die. And I want to leave this world with a little dignity. I want to spend the rest of my life, no matter how much is left of it, doing what I want. I don't want to die in a bed, in a hospital, after fighting a losing battle. I want to die peacefully."

I realized I was standing from my earlier outburst, so I sat, calmly. "How much time do you have left?"

Everett served up a heaving spoonful of lasagna. "That's the beauty of this situation – I don't know. My doctors don't know. The type of cancer I have is a ticking time bomb. I might live a while, a long while, or I could die tonight."

I heaved out a heavy breath, worn out from my anger. The emotion had grated on me, raw and dangerous. I settled down. Not back into indifference; there was no way I could feel indifference again around Everett. But I was settled. That was the best way to describe it. My emotions were neutral.

"Please don't die tonight."

Everett laughed and pushed a plate towards me. "That would be keeping with the picture you've painted of me, wouldn't it? It would be poor manners for me to drop dead into my lasagna."

It was uncomfortable to laugh about, but I felt compelled to ease the tension I'd created. "Yeah, and that would not be a dignified death either."

Everett chuckled softly. "I want control, Parker. I don't want to have an expiration date. Who wants to know when they die, really? I don't want to dwell on my death. I want life. I want to put my hands into all the life there is and let it flood my senses, all of them, all at once." Everett hadn't moved from behind the other side of the island, and yet I felt his words as if he'd whispered them directly in my ear.

"It sounds like you have a plan," I said, swallowing a sip of wine.

"I do. I leave this weekend."

"For where?"

"Eventually, I plan to get to the Grand Canyon."

I picked up my fork, took a small bite of the lasagna. "And then?"

Everett took a bite, swallowed. "The Four Corners."

I took another bite. "This is good, Everett."

"Extra cheese, Parker."

I bit my lip. How could I go from feeling indifference, to lust, to anger, to calm, to wanting to smile within just a few minutes? I looked up at Everett, watched him chew.

"Where else?"

Everett shrugged, took another bite. After swallowing, he continued. "I'm going to visit ghost towns, weird attractions, and whatever else I feel like." My heart picked up pace. There was nothing more intriguing than the idea of visiting an abandoned city, devoid of people. Unchanged, trapped in time. The fact that you could step back into time and see an intimate part of someone else's life hit the happiest place in my soul. Which was to say, the only happy place. The place that I kept hidden, the place that found enjoyment in the small luxuries I indulged in.

Jealously flared up. I bit the inside of my cheek.

"What?" Everett asked.

I lifted my eyes to his. "I didn't say anything."

"Sure you did. Just not with your voice." His eyes glittered under the light. Their cool color was warm with what I assumed was excitement for his upcoming adventure. For the first time in a long time, I longed. Not just for the prospect of traveling, but for connection. I actually wanted to be around Everett. I wanted human connection. And I wanted touch. I wanted his touch. I wanted his hands and his lips, and his skin against mine.

When I was around Everett, I forgot why I avoided it all.

I got up from where I was sitting and walked around the island. This was an experiment. I normally lived life through observation, not through experience.

This would change that.

Tentatively, I walked to Everett. He watched me carefully, with eyes that seemed to sense my intentions. He dropped his fork and turned to me, opening to me.

With all the courage I had, I stepped closer, until we were a breath apart. And then I rose up on my tiptoes and pushed my lips to his.

What I'd intended to be a quick meeting of lips turned into a devouring of lips, of eyes. His hand immediately found the small of my back and pressed, pushing me further into him. I pulled back and looked into his eyes. There was a fire in his eyes that made my heart skip, tumble, and fall in my chest.

He looked at me like he was starving. And perhaps he was. So I fed his hunger with my lips, pressing them along his jaw line, kissing each laugh line. And then my lips found his and he sank in. Our teeth clashed. My hands gripped the fabric of his shirt tightly.

I felt his fingers thread through my hair and then I felt the tug as he pulled the hair, bringing with it a delicious sort of pain.

And then I pulled back and heaved a breath. Tears pricked my eyes in an instant. I turned away, towards the kitchen island, and held my breath, squeezing my eyes shut.

Everett didn't let me collect my thoughts. In an instant, he trapped me against the kitchen island. I couldn't look at him.

I felt shame wash over me. And fear. And a thousand other things. With my eyes shut, I wished them all away. Imagined them as drops. Sliding away. Six breaths later, I turned towards the body at my back, opening my eyes and finding Everett's.

"You're trapping me," I said. I let annoyance seep into my voice.

"Yep."

"Move."

"Make me."

I gritted my teeth and pushed against him. He was strong. But every man had an Achilles heel, right where their legs met. I raised my knee and pushed gently against the area I knew would cause him to back off. "Move," I said again.

Everett smiled, a wicked smile, but stepped back. Despite conceding to me, he seemed proud of himself. I couldn't figure out why.

I moved away.

"Are you running again, Parker?"

My back was to him. I looked over my shoulder. "Not yet." I sat back in front of my forgotten lasagna. "I'm hungry."

Everett was still smiling. It was annoying.

"So," I said, before taking a bite and letting the explosion of tomatoes and spices play on my tongue. I swallowed. "Who's Charlotte?"

He lost his smile. "No one," he answered, before taking a bite of his food.

"I thought you said you don't lie."

He looked up at me, under thick black brows. "I don't. She's no one of consequence to me."

I didn't know how to feel about that. I swallowed some wine and set the glass down, playing a finger around the rim. "How do you know her?"

"I fucked her a time or two."

I was mid-sip and nearly choked. I put a hand over my mouth and swallowed uncomfortably. The image of Charlotte, long angelic hair and pretty mouth hung in my thoughts, taunting me. I shouldn't have let it bother me, but it did. And damn it, I was annoyed.

"That's blunt," I finally said.

"That's what I am."

"Also, you're kind of an asshole."

"Yep," he agreed. "But why do you think so?"

"Because you reduced her to someone you 'fucked'. I feel sorry for her."

"Yeah, well don't. And I'm not reducing her to anything; that's all she was. It was a mutual agreement. And a disappointment, for us both."

"She acted like a jealous girlfriend when she followed me into the bathroom."

Everett seemed surprised by this information. "Well she shouldn't. I don't even like her."

I felt like I was intruding on something very personal and looked down at my plate, playing with my fork along the plate's rim.

"But you have breakfast with her?" Suddenly a thought hit my mind. "Were you...with her last night?" Just saying the words made my stomach churn. Acid burned my throat. "Never mind," I quickly added. "None of my business, sorry."

"Do you want it to be your business?" He'd lowered his voice. The hairs on my arms stood on end. "And to answer your question, no. She's a work colleague. She's taking over some of my end of the school year stuff before I leave, so we met up to discuss things."

I looked up, caught him leaning across the counter. His hair had flopped over one eye, but the other was trained on me. "You work with her? Every day?"

Everett leaned back and signed, working a hand through his hair. "I did. This is my last week of work."

"For the summer?"

"For forever. I'm done. I cashed out my retirement."

Our earlier conversation came back to mind. He was a ticking time bomb. "And you're just going to live on the road? For how long?"

He took a bite of his lasagna. "For as long as I want." He gestured to his house. "This is paid for. My car is paid off. I have no financial obligations." Everett picked up his wine glass, smiled down at the pale liquid. "I'm free."

I envied him. To have the passion, to live your final days the way you wanted. To not feel suffocated with emotions, emotions you purposefully deprived yourself of. To be free. I closed my eyes and imagined it myself.

"You could do it too, you know," he murmured, interrupting my thoughts. I snapped my eyes open.

"What do you mean?"

"Go on the run. Leave your problems for a little while. Be carefree."

I shook my head. "No."

"What do you have stopping you?"

I thought about that for a second. The answer was obvious to me: nothing. So I lied. "I have to support myself. Being a broke college student doesn't afford me the luxury of being carefree."

"Broke, really? You spent all that money already? I find that hard to believe."

I snapped my head up. "What are you talking about?"

Everett smiled behind the wine glass. "Your settlement."

I breathed in through my nose to calm the anger that had turned me cold. "How do you know about that?"

Everett set his wine glass down. "Google. I told you I'd searched the internet for Morris Jensen."

My hands formed fists. "That's none of your business." I pushed my plate away. "I can't believe you invaded my privacy."

"First of all – believe it. I don't give a damn about anyone's privacy. And secondly, I didn't invade your privacy. All the details of your accident are on various websites, as is your settlement information. You shouldn't have told me your business if you didn't want me to know." He took the last bite of his lasagna and grabbed our plates, moving them into the sink. "Besides, I find it hard to believe you blew all that money. Your car is a junker. You aren't superficial. You don't dress in fancy threads. You don't care about your appearance. If you'd spent that money, you'd have fixed that scar on your face first."

The anger was escalating. "You're an asshole."

Everett looked over his shoulder and narrowed his eyes before he turned around to face me. "Yes. I am. I call it like I see it. And I see a girl who hides behind her hair, who doesn't give two fucks about her looks. You think no one notices you. You think you can sit back and watch everyone else and they don't get to watch you. But guess what, Parker? You are hiding in plain sight. I see you. I see the parts you don't want anyone to see."

He stepped around the island and cornered me again. My heart started fluttering manically in my chest and I stood up on my tiptoes as he invaded my breathing space. Everett narrowed his eyes on me. "You're ice cold. You don't let yourself feel. You don't care about anyone, not even yourself." His face came to the side of mine and I gasped, the heat of his face on mine causing tiny flutters that slid across my skin. "In here," he said, pushing on the skin above my heart, "you're ten below zero. And you're closer to death than I am."

He pulled back, looking at me with a mixture of anger and sadness. And then he walked away. "You can let yourself out, right?" he called over his shoulder. I heard his steps thunder up the stairs to the second story, so I did the only thing I could do. I walked out the door.

Chapter 6

I sat in my car, parked in front of his home for several minutes. My mind tried processing all that had happened while my heart throbbed in my chest.

This was why I didn't connect with people, why I stood on the sidelines and stared. I didn't want this, to own any feelings. Especially feelings that hurt. I didn't want pain. I didn't want any of this.

After heaving a sigh, I turned the key in the ignition. Nothing happened. I tried again and still nothing. Everett was right about one thing: my car was a junker. It was built years before I was born, and then had been stripped and welded with parts from another car. It was a salvage title, and a huge pain in the ass at the most inconvenient times. It was one of the reasons I was annoyed all the time.

Everett was also right about something else; I had all that money. Sitting in my bank account, going nowhere. And I didn't care about anyone, not even myself.

Thinking that caused a small prick of pain in my chest.

I tried turning the key in the ignition again. Not even the slightest noise came from the engine. I laid my head on the steering wheel, suddenly overcome with all that had happened this evening.

It pissed me off – Everett had pissed me off. Even with the scar that marred my face, people didn't notice me. I hid in the corner, or in the shadows, observing. I didn't live, not really. And Everett was dying. But he was more alive than I was. That's what he had meant, when he'd said I was closer to death than he was. It was true. And that meant a lot of what Everett had said, though harsh, was true. Asshole.

It was annoying that someone who had only met me a handful of times had figured me out this quickly, had told me to my face what he'd observed. I was the observer of other people. People didn't observe me.

So it was with that anger that I stepped out of my car and slammed the door shut.

That anger fueled my feet up the steps of his concrete walkway, up the steps to his front porch. That anger powered the knocks that my fist rapped against the door.

Everett took his sweet time coming to the door. When he opened it, he looked unsurprised to me standing on his porch. "Forget something?" he asked, sounding bored.

"Yes," I said, stepping into his space. I put a hand on his chest and pushed him until he took a step back into his house. "You're an asshole."

"I am," he confirmed. I was still pushing against him while he backed up into the house. Once I was fully in the house, I slammed the door shut.

And then I pounced. A breath later, I was in his arms, lips clashing against his. He supported my weight in his arms, my legs wrapped around his waist. I felt my back hit the wall, but I didn't care. My senses were full, overflowing with this, with Everett.

I felt him groan into my mouth and I brought my hands up to his hair, pulling on the hairs that curled at the nape of his neck. I pulled, hard, and squeezed my legs around his waist.

"Fuck," he growled against my lips, pulling back and

slamming me against the wall again. I took a breath when he'd released my lips. I didn't inhale much oxygen before his lips fell onto mine again. His hands wrapped around my waist and he squeezed, hard enough for me to turn my head away and gasp for air.

"What is this Parker?" he asked, pressing his forehead against mine as he blew ragged breaths across my lips.

I struggled for air, but my body was lit up like a firework, waiting to ignite. "If you have to ask, you're an idiot."

I heard his soft chuckle. And then he pulled me from the wall and walked me to the living room. His lips caught mine again, keeping my attention on him and not on the room he'd carried me into.

I felt my back hit the couch cushions before he came down on me, pressing me into the softness. I felt like I was sinking, into the couch and into heady desire. It was scary, letting these emotions control me, consume me, but my body was stronger than my mind. So when Everett lifted my shirt off my head, I helped him remove his.

He inhaled in between each kiss he peppered down the center of my chest. When he reached the button of my shorts, my body trembled. I reached a hand down to unbuckle them, but his hands stilled on mine.

"No," he whispered. He pulled my hands to his lips and kissed the knuckles of one hand before laying my hands on my chest.

I heaved a breath and my entire body shook. It was like being on the precipice of hell. And I badly wanted to fall, to let Everett fall with me.

So I did.

My hands reached up and found his bare chest. In the darkness of the living room, I made out something tattooed along his ribcage, but it was hard to figure out what it was.

All thoughts left my head the moment Everett's hand reached into my shorts, pushing past the brief barrier of underwear and touched me. I couldn't help it; I bucked.

His free hand grabbed my hip and squeezed reassuringly, while his other hand stroked me, stoking the fire that was burning me up. He was gentle at first, and I whimpered – wanting a million things, all at once. I felt my body climbing and I reached up, desperate to grab hold of anything. It ended up being his jaw. I pulled him down, curling my nails into his jawline as his lips descended onto mine. I felt the bite of his facial hair and suddenly, it was sensory overload. His fingers on me, inside of me, his lips gracing my jawline, his teeth nipping my earlobe, his free hand pushing and squeezing my hip. I descended into madness, into bliss, within what felt like seconds.

When my breathing slowed and my heart settled in my chest, I turned my face away. What the hell had just happened? I couldn't dare look at Everett, so I swallowed hard, clenched my jaw.

There was silence between us, as if we both couldn't believe this had happened in just a few moments. He'd essentially kicked me out and then I'd barged my way back in.

I didn't want to identify the emotions that swept over me. I sat up and found my shirt, tugging it over my head. I stood up and buttoned up my shorts, all the while keeping from looking at Everett.

My hands trembled on the button and I squeezed them into fists to still them.

"Parker," Everett started, but I interrupted him.

"No," I said, putting a hand up, letting my hair spill down and shield my face from his.

"No?" he asked. I felt his hand touch my arm and I immediately yanked it away from him. Regret. That's what I was feeling. I didn't want to name it, but it sat within me anyway, flowing in my veins, keeping my eyes from his.

"No," I repeated. "This was a mistake. You. You aren't good for me." The words were hard to say, but they came unbidden from my throat. "You're an alcoholic, you're dying, and you're not very nice." The words, though true, weren't why he wasn't good for me. But I wanted my words to cut deeper than a knife. I wanted to hurt Everett. Because in making me feel all these things, he'd hurt me. He'd cut me deeper than Morris Jensen ever had.

I whipped the door open and ran.

I hadn't slept. I'd fallen into my bed while the night replayed over and over in my mind. It was like walking through a nightmare, on repeat. And the feelings lingered. They weren't drops that I could numb myself to. They were real, true feelings. I didn't want them.

Around sunrise, I stood at the kitchen sink in the apartment, taking desperate bites of leftover, cold pizza. I used my fingers to push in the pieces that hung out of my mouth, trying to fit where there was no room. That was when I felt the first tears. They ran from my eyes so steadily that my hands were drenched, my mouth capturing some of the salty tears while I tried to swallow the pizza. The lump in my throat wasn't from improperly chewed pizza; rather it was suffocated regret. I was using food as hate, punishing myself with my mistake.

I threw the remnants of the pizza onto the counter and hacked out what was in my mouth into the sink. What the hell was I doing? I used my hands, furiously pushing the pizza down the garbage disposal as the sobs wracked my body. I gripped onto the edges of the sink, hung my head, and let the regret pull me under.

Why did I always do this? Why did I purposefully hurt people? And why was it bothering me now? Pain was growing inside me like a weed. Ugly, twisted, the roots curling around whatever I let it touch. And I'd let that pain take root in someone else. Why? I couldn't say. Maybe it was less lonely to know I wasn't the only one hurting. He'd hurt me, so I wanted to hurt him.

I ripped off a few paper towels and mopped up my face before staggering out of the kitchen and collapsing onto the sofa. I threw an arm over my eyes to block out the sun that shined stupidly through the windows. Why hadn't my roommates closed the blinds? Half the time they wandered into the apartment just as the sun was making its way across the kitchen. When I didn't give them a ride from whatever hell hole they walked in to, that usually meant they were out until early morning. Carly and Jasmine were often loud and still inebriated at dawn, their legs unable to carry them to their respective beds. The sofas served more as beds than actual places to relax. It was usually why the sofa usually had a slight scent of booze.

I turned my face from the microfiber, gagging at the scent of stale, sweet-smelling vodka. As if I'd dreamt it, I heard the key being jammed into the lock on the apartment door, and high pitched giggles interrupting the calm of the morning.

"Which way does it turn?" The voice was loud and felt abusive to the air around me. Like the sound of a cymbal clapping in my ear. The giggles erupted again and I heard the sound of something falling in the hallway. Judging by the sounds of clattering, I'd guessed it was a purse. I heard, "Shit!" yelled in between laughter and the sound of something heavy collapsing against the door.

I knew my roommates well, better than they knew me. After all, my favorite hobby was observing other people. I didn't engage in reckless behavior – my incident with Everett not included – I didn't do anything that was fun but also dangerous. I didn't just toe the line of caution. I hid under it.

So when my roommates fell into the door while it swung open, I just watched. I'm sure some would see my behavior as odd, bordering on creepy, but I was fascinated by human nature. And my current view featured lots of legs and wild hair.

Jasmine caught my eye first. She towered on her hot pink heels. Her white shorts were short enough to be viewed as beach wear and covered in stains. Her pink and white sequined tank hung off of her like it had been stretched within an inch of its life and finally gave up. Her bright white teeth flashed against her tan skin as she fell onto the floor on her back, heels cracking against the wood floor. Her long blonde hair was a mess of tangles all around her. I barely made out the sparkle of a tiara that was worn haphazardly in the giant mane of hair.

Carly was doubled over, holding her stomach as the laughs rolled off of her body. Flinging her purse down, she laughed so hard I half expected her stomach to slide out of her mouth and onto the floor. Where Jasmine was my polar opposite in personality, Carly was the in-between. Her current outfit of flip flops and jeans was something I would have chosen myself, more for comfort than style. But Carly compromised with Jasmine on the top – a deep v-neck tee that was orange. Not the kind of orange you'd see in the produce section, but more like in the tropics. It too was covered in stains.

I watched them quietly from the couch until Jasmine rolled onto her stomach and pushed the hair from her face when she spotted me. She squinted at me and propped herself up on her elbows. "What's wrong with you?" she slurred. She looked like a drunk princess, with the tiara crooked on her head and her makeup smeared.

I wrinkled my forehead in confusion. I was lying on the couch like a normal person while she looked like she'd been dumpster diving, and there was something wrong with me?

Before I could answer, Carly turned her attention towards me and cocked her head to the side. "Are you okay?" she asked, walking closer to me. It was then that I remembered the tears that had come on so suddenly. Self-consciously I turned my face away from her scrutiny.

"I bet she stayed up all night studying instead of partying with us, Car," Jasmine said, dismissing me instantly. I'd never been more thankful for her incorrect assumptions. Jasmine groaned and placed her hands on the ground as she pushed herself to standing. She wobbled a bit before grasping the column that separated the dining area from the kitchen and pulled her shoes off. "I'm surprised I didn't ruin these," she said loudly.

Carly collapsed on the end of the couch, just next to my feet and let her head fall back against the cushion. "That was so fun," she said, eyes closed. I watched her lips tilt up in a small smile. She sighed.

Jasmine wobbled into the kitchen and opened the refrigerator. "Here, Car," she said, grabbing a bottle of orange juice. "Drink this."

It was my bottle of orange juice. And instead of pouring the juice into glasses like a civilized human, Jasmine lifted the bottle as if she was going to drink directly from the opening.

"Hey," I barked, relaxing into the annoyance I felt. I embraced the annoyance. "That's mine. If you want some, ask. And if I say yes, use a glass."

There was complete silence. I looked at Carly who was staring at me like I had multiple heads attached to my body.

"You grew some balls, Park?" Jasmine asked, holding the jug of orange juice halfway to her mouth.

I was normally closed off, avoiding confrontation like the plague. And yet, I'd just told Jasmine off for the first time since I'd met her.

I stared at her, glaring. It was too early in the morning and I was far too sleep-deprived to deal with this. I didn't want to think about the fact that I was also a mess of confusing emotions. "Use a glass, Jasmine."

She narrowed her eyes at me, a small smile playing on her lips. Jasmine often looked at me like this, as if I was a toy she liked playing with. Except there was nothing innocent about it. She was going to test me, I knew it. A moment later, she lifted the jug towards her mouth, eyeing me defiantly.

Before I knew what I was doing, I stood up and walked towards her. I raised my hand, causing Jasmine to flinch. And then I smacked the orange juice out of her hand. It fell to the tile and exploded, spraying orange juice spectacularly all over the cabinets and floor.

Shock registered in an instant. Had I really just done that? Judging by the look on her face, Jasmine was just as shocked as I was. She looked to Carly and my eyes followed. Carly sat on the end of the couch, hand over her mouth, her eyes as wide as saucers.

I walked away then, towards my bedroom, leaving them with the mess. It was immature, sure. But I didn't want to face them, to hear their questions – unspoken or otherwise.

I slammed my door, hard enough that it rattled it on its hinges, and collapsed on my bed.

When I awoke around noon, I had a text on my phone. It was a picture of my car.

Everett: Want this back?

I chewed on my lip for only a moment, my finger hovering over the reply button. Instead, I hit the button I knew I should: Delete.

I logged into my email and registered for fall semester classes at the local college before shooting Mira a quick email. Mira and I, though different in appearance and attitude, shared the same thought about phone calls: no thanks. The only way we communicated was via email.

Mira,
I'm starting fall classes in two months. Do you want to meet for lunch at Paulie's sometime?
Parker

Clearly, I was as loquacious via email as I was in person.

While I pulled my hair into a ponytail, Mira's reply came through.

Mouse,

No can do. I'm out of state. I'll let you know when I'm back in California.

M

Mira was the closest thing I had to a friend, though we never connected the way two women engaged in a normal female friendship did. We didn't go to the movies or to dinner. We played with knives and tried kicking each other's asses. But it'd been a long time since we'd done either.

So I couldn't help the tiny drop of disappointment. Instead, I embraced the annoyance. It furrowed my brown, straightened my lips. I wore annoyance really well.

I closed my email and stood, walking to the window to look out. My car was missing from its usual parking spot. I'd have to figure out what to do about that. Call a tow, probably. I sat on the bed, facing the window and fell into memories from the night before.

While I stared out the window, I heard a knock on my door. Before I could call out, the door opened and Carly stepped into my bedroom. "Hey, Parker. Can I come in?"

"You already are," I replied, matter-of-factly.

Carly looked at me confused, so I rolled my eyes and gestured with my hand for her to come all the way in. "What?" I asked.

Carly shut the door behind her and approached my bed, wringing her hands together over and over. "Are you okay?" she asked, hesitantly sitting on the corner of my bed.

I shrugged. "Yeah."

Carly tucked a lock of her dark hair behind her ear and looked at me. She looked unique. Her mother was Swedish and her father was Chinese, lending her a really different look. Asian features mixed with green eyes and freckles on her nose.

"I feel really bad about earlier. Jasmine was drunk."

I rolled my eyes again and stood up, crossing my arms in front of my chest. "If you're excusing her from her behavior because she was drunk then she must be drunk all the time. That wasn't anything unusual for her, Carly. She's a selfish bitch. She sees me as toy." I suddenly felt like I'd said too much. And judging by the look on Carly's face, she agreed.

She slowly stood up from my bed and looked down at the ground. "Well, I'm still sorry."

"Don't be. I made the mess."

"I cleaned it up," she offered, looking at me hopefully. Sometimes she looked at me like she was a puppy desperate for attention or affection. I think that's why Jasmine had such a hold over her. Jasmine was a leader, and Carly was very much a follower.

"Well then I'm the one who's sorry," I replied.

"Jasmine refused."

"That's shocking," I deadpanned.

Carly threw back her head, sending curls in every direction as she laughed. "I know, right?" she said between laughs. She smiled at me and left my room a moment later.

Chapter 7

I went for a run before stopping sooner than usual and heading back to my apartment. I couldn't turn my brain off, so I wallowed in my room the rest of the day. I alternated sitting on my balcony, but found no enjoyment in my usual activities. My thoughts kept drifting to Everett, but I kept my phone off, so I could avoid the temptation of seeing if he texted.

The following morning, I was working my shift at the restaurant. Doris was especially grumpy, so I did my best to stay out of her way. I ducked behind the counter, behind the cooks, anything to avoid her wrath.

There was something about me that deeply bothered Doris. Her husband had interviewed and hired me himself and ever since she'd made my cheap nametag with her label maker, Doris had made it her mission to watch me. Waiting for me to slip up.

I was ringing up a customer's check when Misty, the hostess for that day, walked up to me.

"Who's the babe at table ten?"

"What?" I asked, not really paying attention. I had to apply a discount to a portion of the customer's bill and the computer didn't seem to have the option I was looking for.

"He asked to be seated in your section. Tall, dark, scarily handsome? Ring any bells?"

I whipped my head up so fast that I felt a pop in my neck. My eyes scanned the tables until they landed on him, sitting at table ten and staring at me with his icy eyes. His journal was sitting on the table in front of him and he was wearing his trademark black clothing.

I couldn't help the heat that warmed my core at the sight of Everett. Knowing what had happened when I'd last seen him, my heart skipped a couple beats and my mouth went dry.

"Boyfriend?" Misty's voice pulled me from my inappropriate thoughts and I shook my head, tearing my eyes from Everett's.

"He's no one," I answered, and focused my attention on the computer again.

"The way he's looking at you makes that hard to believe," Misty said, in her annoying little sing song voice. It was as if anytime I felt a foreign emotion, I reached out, desperately, looking for something to be annoyed about. Annoyance was safer, comfortable. Thanks to Misty, my heart rate was slowing and my brow was now furrowing.

"Yeah, well he's a guy. They all look at us like we're a piece of meat."

Misty's gum popped in my ear. *Keep it up, Misty*, I thought. I enjoyed being annoyed.

"Oh my God, he's coming over here!"

There went my heart again. I kept my eyes focused on the computer, though out of my peripheral vision, I saw him approaching, a tall force of black clothing.

"Parker," he said. I bit my lip and tried to ignore him. His voice was like his drink: smooth, warm like whiskey. I could get drunk off his words.

He was so, so bad for me.

"Parker," he repeated. "Do you make a habit of ignoring your paying customers? That's..." he didn't finish his sentence because he knew he didn't need to.

Hell. My lip twitched. Without moving my head, I glanced up through my lashes.

"I'll get your drink order in a minute," I said, trying to seem like my attention was on the computer, when it was actually completely on Everett.

He leaned forward, bringing his hands up to clasp on either side of the computer table. "You already know what I want, Parker."

I heard Misty squeal a little next to me before I shot her a look. She winked at me and then scampered away. I finally looked up at Everett.

He looked tired. He always did. But the lines around his eyes were deeper, the shadows under them more pronounced. His hair was in its usual messy, glorious state and his lips were in a firm line. He looked more than a little impatient.

It annoyed me that he dared look impatiently at me. He was the one who'd kicked me out, and then let me back in. Then he'd helped himself to the pieces of my soul I unwillingly gave.

And plus, he'd reminded me that I had a conscience and made me feel things that were uncomfortable. The feelings he'd instilled in me were like wearing a wool sweater that had been washed and dried hot; they were itchy and they didn't fit.

"What?" I asked, mirroring his impatience.

"We need to talk."

I felt my jaw tick. "Nope."

"Yeah, actually we do." A second later he gripped my forearm in his hand and all but dragged me outside of the restaurant.

"You're going to get me fired."

"Do I look like I care?" he asked, exasperated. We stumbled together off the concrete stoop, onto the sidewalk. The air was annoyingly crisp and the street was mostly deserted. I finally turned my eyes to Everett.

"I don't know why you would care," I said, crossing my arms

over my chest.

"Don't be a brat, Parker. What the hell was that last night?"

I looked away, to the right, showing him the side of my face that was scarred. And then I shrugged, feigning indifference. "I need to get back inside before I lose my job."

"Fuck your job. You don't care about it. Why invest even a second of your life in things that don't make you happy?"

I gritted my teeth. "Not all of us have the luxury you do, Everett." I didn't speak his name often. Speaking it now felt personal. My stomach rolled.

"What? The luxury of knowing you're dying? Some fucking luxury. Sorry for that." It was the first time he seemed upset about dying and I couldn't stop the trail of my gaze over him. He stalked away for a second, the sound of jingling coins and the smell of rain swirling around him. And then he turned back and pinned me with his icy eyes before stalking towards me.

I couldn't help my body's reaction. The way he was approaching was thrilling. My heart sped up and my lips opened in protest. But before I could utter a word, his lips were on mine, hungrily devouring them, devouring me. His hands held my face tightly; he held me as if he was afraid I'd run.

He pulled back and breathed hard. His nose was pressed to mine, our lips still touching. I was terrified to open my eyes, so I just held on to his arms.

"You are wasting your life," he whispered. "Why did you fight so hard to live so little?" He drew in a breath and then blew it across my face. I felt his fingers touch my scar and I flinched. "You fought, Parker. You are a fighter. But right now, you're a coward." He pulled away. "Open your eyes." I did. His eyes were hard, his eyebrows drawn together. "What are you afraid of?"

"Parker," a voice came from the door. I pulled away from Everett and reluctantly met Doris' eyes. She stood on the stoop we'd fallen off of, hands on the hips hiding under her greasy apron. "I don't pay you to lock lips. Get in here."

I ran my tongue over my teeth. And then I looked at Everett. There was a challenge in his eyes, to prove him right – to prove I was wasting my life working a job I didn't enjoy, living a meaningless life. To continue working, to continue breathing in the indifference.

I looked at Doris again. "I quit."

"No you don't. You're fired."

A smile threatened. I looked at Everett and then at Doris again. "Great."

"You sure showed some balls," Everett said on the walk home. My hands were tucked into my apron as we moved down the sidewalk.

"Why does everyone think an act of bravery is merely a male trait?" I huffed.

"Would it be better if I said you showed some ovaries?"

"Not funny – and no. It would be better if you said nothing."

"Ouch." Everett said, exaggeratingly holding a hand over his heart. "Your Native American name would be She Thinks She Wounds With Words."

That annoyed me, as usual. I narrowed my eyes. "Your Native American name would be Man With Unkempt Hair."

"You can do better than that," Everett said, bumping into me from the side. I walked further out of his reach. "You did a number with your words two nights ago."

My mind had replayed my words to him over and over, on a continuous loop. "It was the truth. You appreciate the truth."

"I do," he nodded. "But what you said? It didn't bother me. You'll have to try harder than that to hurt me."

"Why would I want to hurt you? I don't care about you, one way or another."

He clicked his tongue. "Parker, I thought we'd established that

I preferred the truth. You're not very good at the lying thing."

This conversation was elevating my annoyance with each one of his comments. "I barely know you," I protested, careful to keep my voice even. "You're just some guy who hangs around me like a lost puppy."

"And yet, you met me at the bar. And you came to the restaurant the next morning, and you came to me for lunch later that day. And then you came to my house for dinner the next night. Who's chasing who, Parker?"

My jaw was clenched so hard I was sure I was going to crack my teeth into tiny bits. I was unused to conversation, especially with a man who made me feel. It kept me off balance. Cloaking myself in indifference was impossible around Everett. I stopped suddenly and turned to him. "You're an asshole," I said, looking him square in the eye. "Just because you say things that are true, it doesn't make you an admirable person. Some people need to hear a lie."

Everett motioned his hands in a circle. "Tell me more; tell me all of it, Parker." He looked amused, patronizing. And it only made me angrier.

"You dare to call me a coward, when you're the one who is giving up on life. How dare you tell me how to live, when you're dying?" My voice had raised several octaves, but I wasn't done. "You're dying, Everett. Wake up." I pushed a finger into his chest. "You're a drunk, you don't value the women you sleep with, and you stick your nose in business that isn't yours."

Everett walked towards me, invading the few feet that had separated us. "So let me get this straight. You think I'm an asshole. Yep, I am. Get over it, sweetheart." He took another step towards me. "You say I'm not admirable because I tell the truth even when it hurts. I agree. But," he said, his voice lowering, "I don't care. I don't tell the truth for admiration. I tell the truth because lies hurt more. Lies wrapped up in pretty words don't benefit anyone in the end." He stepped closer and I backed up. "And you don't know a thing about me, to say I am giving up on life. I spent years of my life fighting this disease. I wasn't living, not really. And now I am living and I'm dying." He stepped closer and I stepped back once again. "Don't you dare criticize how I am spending the final days of my life when you're not even living." He brought a hand up and pulled on the hair that lay on my chest. "I am a drunk. You're correct. But Parker? I always value the women I sleep with. Charlotte and I are over. We never even really began. And before you assume how I treated her, maybe you should get both sides of the story."

He tugged the hair hard enough to pull me closer. "I value women, Parker. But you don't. You don't value anyone."

It hurt, the way he spoke to me, the way he invaded my space. But I refused to look away. I met his eyes and stared back. Indifference felt like another planet to how Everett made me feel, and there was no way I could pretend he didn't affect me.

"And I don't stick my nose in business that isn't mine. You gave me the key. Did you expect me not to open the door? Not to find out about Morris Jensen?"

I didn't know what to say.

"Listen," he continued in the silence. "You think you hurt me with the things you say? You don't. Nothing can hurt me. That's the beauty of my death sentence."

He was only making me madder. It bothered me that he could hurt me and I couldn't hurt him back. "Why are you so focused on me then?"

Everett smiled and looked down at my hair in his hand. He twirled one of the waves around, twisting it and letting go. "Because I'm a self-serving bastard. Don't get me wrong, I want to help you. But I also want to hurt you. I want to break you. I want to see you live." He looked back at me. "I'm stuck on you, unfortunately. And my conscience won't let me leave this earth seeing you live so half-heartedly."

I sucked in air. I couldn't breathe. "What if I like the way I live?"

"Ha," he laughed humorlessly. "That's just it – you aren't living. And if you liked this life, you wouldn't have asked me that question. You'd have told me to fuck off."

"Fuck off."

"Too late now. I'm stuck on you. Which means you're stuck with me."

I slapped his hand from my hair and turned, walking down the sidewalk away from him.

"Not running away from me this time, Parker," he said, catching up with me.

"Go away."

"No."

He made me angry. I wanted to hurt him. "I don't even like you!" I yelled, turning to him, my fists balled with rage.

"You don't have to like me." He grabbed one of my fists and brought it to his chest, pulling me close. "But something about me gets to you. I can hear it in the noise you make when I get close to you. I see the look in your eyes, a combination of desire and fear."

I tried pulling my hand from his, but he held tight. I yanked harder and he reached out, grabbing my other fist and pulling them both into him, pulling me so we were inches apart. I stopped fighting. "What do you want from me?" I asked, defeated.

"Come with me on the road trip." There wasn't even a moment's hesitation.

"You barely know me," I protested.

"You barely know me," he replied.

I shook my head. "Why?"

"I want you to."

I furrowed my brow. "That's it?" I asked incredulously.

"Yep. Men aren't complicated creatures, Parker. And we mean what we say. So come on, humor me. Come on the road trip. If you want to return home at any point, I'll buy your plane ticket."

I fidgeted. I couldn't help it, but I did want to go on this road trip. And a bigger, scarier, part of me wanted to be around Everett as much as possible. If he thought he could make me value my life, maybe I could make him fight for his. Both were a losing battle, but the words fell from my mouth a moment later. "Okay."

"Okay?" he asked.

"Yeah, fine."

"Whoa, don't sound too thrilled, please." He let go of one of my hands and I brought it to my chest, self-consciously. "Just promise me something," he said, a laugh on the edge of his voice. I looked at him and cocked my head to the side in question. "Don't fall in love with me."

I laughed. For the first time in years, I actually laughed. It sounded rusty and maniacal. But I actually laughed. My eyes bugged out of my head and I slapped both hands over my mouth.

Everett was looking at me curiously. "That sounded like a dying cat."

I cleared my throat and removed the hands covering my mouth. "That wasn't very nice."

"Yeah, well, your laugh is fucking awful."

"Don't worry, I'm in no danger of falling in love with you."

He nodded. "Good."

We resumed walking when a thought suddenly occurred to me. "Wait. Do you have a reliable car for this road trip? Mine is, well, not reliable."

Everett scoffed, "Like taking your car was even a remote possibility. I don't think you can even actually call that piece of shit a car."

"It is a car."

"Don't you mean 'cars'?"

I narrowed my eyes. "Yes, actually, it's two cars welded together. It still runs."

"Really?" he asked.

I kicked a pebble on the sidewalk and looked down, avoiding looking at him. "Well, not right now apparently."

"Like I said, piece of shit." He kicked a pebble at my foot, earning a glare from me. "Are you in love with me yet?" he asked.

"Not even close."

Chapter 8

I didn't realize we were walking to my apartment until we reached the parking lot. "Um," I said, gesturing at my building. "This is where I live."

"Let's go up," Everett said, walking towards the stairs to the apartment.

"Um," I said again. I was nervous about letting him see where I lived, but then I realized it didn't matter. We'd be on the road soon anyways.

"Come on," he said, gesturing with his fingers for me to follow him. "I'll help you pack."

I followed him into the building. "How long will we be gone?"

"I don't have a time limit. Unless you fall in love with me, then your ass is on a plane."

I rolled my eyes. "Not going to happen. And I start classes in two months, so I can't be gone longer than that." Was I really agreeing to a long road trip with this man, this man I barely knew? Apparently I was. I was throwing caution to the wind for the sake of convincing him to fight. But I couldn't figure out why I cared or why I was putting so much effort into it.

I opened the door and looked around cautiously. When the big room appeared clear, I walked in, letting Everett follow behind.

"Are you thirsty?" I asked.

"Yeah."

"Hmm," I hummed, grabbing a soda and a lime from the fridge. Instead of handing the soda to him, I opened it and grabbed a glass from the cupboard next to the fridge, filling the glass with soda.

I topped off the glass with a handful of sliced limes and walked out of the kitchen, sipping my drink. I purposefully didn't get him a soda.

A minute later, he followed me into my room. I noted his hands were empty. And then I noticed how large he seemed in my bedroom, a man clad in black taking up more space than I did. I averted my eyes and swallowed, moving to closet.

I tossed a suitcase on the bed before grabbing some underwear. I held it tightly between both hands as I walked towards the bed. Everett was sitting, no – reclining – on my bed. He'd settled back against the pillows and had his hands behind his head.

"Make yourself at home," I muttered sarcastically.

"Oh, I did. Don't worry."

I bit my cheek and walked to the suitcase, pulling it towards the end of the bed. Everett, though relaxed against my pillows, was staring at me, watching my every movement. I suddenly felt embarrassed about my underwear. Which was stupid. I tossed it in the bag, trying to be nonchalant about it, as I moved about my room grabbing additional things. When I turned around, Everett was playing with my underwear.

"Put that down." I stalked over to him and yanked it from his hand.

"You're a pretty basic girl, aren't you?" he asked. Something about the way he said it irked me. My best friend, annoyance, came through loud and clear.

"I don't need to impress anyone," I said, raising my chin in defiance.

"I didn't say you did." His hand snaked back into the suitcase before I slapped it away. "But I'm surprised you don't have even one lacy underthing."

"Why does it matter to you? It's not like you'll be seeing them anyway."

Everett raised one eyebrow and my knees went weak with the look he gave me. "I've already seen your underwear, Parker." I licked my lips. "I'd rather see them off of you, as in on the floor."

I coughed. I didn't know what else to do. I turned around and blew out a breath, trying to stay busy and focus on the task at hand. But with Everett sitting on my bed, he was a massive distraction. "Why don't you get yourself a soda or something?" I gestured towards the door with a hand-floppy wave.

"Oh, that's okay? I wasn't sure, since you didn't offer me one a few minutes ago, after asking if I was thirsty." His tone was dry, mildly annoyed. *Good*, I thought.

"You're a big boy, Everett. And I'm not your waitress." I bent over to grab a box under my bed. When I stood up, my back was against his body. I nearly dropped the box. My fingers tightened, white-knuckled, on the box, while he pressed against me from behind. I felt his lips at my ear, his breath warming the skin right behind it.

"If you're going to call me rude, especially like it's a dirty word, you better expect me to treat you the same when you are blatantly rude back." His voice crawled across my skin, igniting the goose bumps on my neck. "It was rude not to offer me a drink, Parker." His voice lowered when he said my name. It took everything in me to keep from shivering.

"I never claimed to be anything else," I said, once again using his line. My heart beat was beating like I had just finished a race.

His lips pressed to the skin behind my ear and my lips opened in a silent gasp. I felt my heart beat all the way down in my belly. The kiss was light. And then his arm wrapped around my waist from behind me. He was unknowingly holding me up at this point.

He squeezed his arm, squeezing my ribs slightly.

His other hand came up to my neck and pulled the hair to the side, pulling until I tilted my neck to give him better access. His lips and teeth grazed my neck then and my knees buckled. His lips were an electric shock; I absorbed it all. My eyes closed and Everett nipped my skin again. The arm he'd wrapped around me moved then, and before I could get a handle on what was happening, he'd spun me around to face him. I was breathing hard, keeping my eyes closed. My hands had involuntarily clasped his upper arms and I squeezed. Opening my eyes seemed an impossible task.

His lips descended, peppering kisses along my jawline. His hands moved to my hair, pulling it all back away from my face, pulling it hard enough to cause tension on my sensitive skin. I was drowning, sinking, into Everett.

His lips kissed my entire face, except for my lips and scar. I didn't think too much about that, because the places he was delivering kisses to were cramping all other thought. I'd never been kissed like this, without my lips actually meeting another's. He kissed to taste, not to deliver affection. He'd said he was self-serving and I knew this was another example of that. But this time, I was benefitting from it as well.

He finally pulled away from me. Breathless and aching, I opened my eyes, desire clouding my vision. When he finally came into view, he was smirking. His lips were red, swollen, and my skin felt raw.

His hands slid slowly from my hair. "How do you feel?"

His smug smile pissed me off. "How do you think I feel?"

He shrugged, that damn smirk staying in place. "Probably frustrated."

I blew out a breath. "That's one word for it."

He nodded. "Good." And then he walked out of my room.

I sank down onto my bed, hoping the blood would recirculate to all my limbs. I heard the fridge open and I sighed. I took a sip from my own drink before resuming packing. Before I could talk myself out of packing, I heard laughter from the kitchen. More specifically, feminine laughter. I bolted out of my room and slowed my pace as I stopped just outside the kitchen, peeking from behind the wall that separated it from the hallway.

Everett was pouring a drink into a glass. Jasmine was sitting on the counter a few feet from him, swinging her long tanned legs back and forth. She laughed again at something Everett said.

A second later, I was in the kitchen, interrupting their cozy chat.

Jasmine eyed me with humored malice. I braced myself.

"Is this the guy?" she asked, not bothering to lower her voice. She was closer to Everett than she was to me, so she might as well have yelled the question.

"What do you mean?"

"That date you went on?"

Everett turned to look at me. "Was that a date?"

"No." My answer came quickly.

Everett leaned against the counter, so now both Everett and Jasmine were facing me.

"Well, the first time wasn't a date. But what about the second time? Or the third time? Or the fourth time?" he asked each question between sips, as if giving each one contemplation.

Jasmine's eyes were so big, they looked like they'd fall right out of her face. "Four dates? How long have you known him, Parker?"

"Not even a week yet," Everett said, glancing at Jasmine. "And tomorrow, she's coming with me on a road trip."

I closed my eyes and clenched my fists. Damn, Everett. When I opened them, Jasmine was looking at me questioningly. "Is this a joke?"

"No." All I could manage was one-word answers, apparently.

Jasmine looked at me for a minute. I could practically see the gears in her head rotating. She pursed her lips and turned to

Everett. "Really? You're taking her?"

Everett had been sipping his drink until she asked that. He pulled the drink from his lips and his eyebrows drew together. "I am," he confirmed.

Jasmine narrowed her eyes. "You don't know her all that well. She's kind of a wet blanket."

Rage burned in my fists. What was wrong with me? I never let Jasmine get to me, ever. I usually brushed her shenanigans off. But what she said to Everett bothered me more than I cared to admit.

Everett set his glass on the counter and pushed away, putting distance from Jasmine, closing the distance to me. He was facing me now, on the opposite side of the kitchen, with his back to Jasmine. I watched his eyes roam over me. "She's not."

"What?" Jasmine asked, already forgetting what she'd just said.

"Parker isn't a wet blanket." Everett said, staring at me. "She's much more than that." He stepped closer. I gripped the counter behind me. "She's got a bunch of layers," he continued, advancing. I doubted Jasmine was even listening anymore, probably succumbing to her inebriation judging by the way she swayed on the counter.

"So, in fact, you're the wet blanket. For only seeing the superficial. " The words were said to her, but they were meant for me to hear. Everett was so close now that I couldn't see beyond him. And I didn't care to. He had a small smile on his face. He took the final step that pushed his hips against mine, pinning me to the counter at my back. And then he cupped my jaw in his hands and covered my mouth with his.

This time, he kissed me with affection. I felt it in the way his lips brushed my lips first, getting me used to the feel, to the pressure. And then he pushed softly against my top lip with his tongue. My mouth opened and my eyes closed and then his arms wrapped tightly around me, crushing me to him. I gasped in his mouth and gripped tightly to his waist through his shirt. His lips and tongue were moving a devastatingly slow pace against my lips, savoring me. Kissing me with emotion. My heart beat a passionate beat, echoing the beat I felt from his own.

"Parker?"

Everett slowly stopped kissing me. He didn't pull back immediately at the intrusion. Instead, he took his time leveling off the kiss, ending it with one chaste lips-to-lips kiss.

When he backed away, I couldn't move my eyes from him. He looked at me sadly before looking away, grabbing his drink and taking a large pull.

"Parker?" the voice asked again. Dazed, I turned my head to the right, finding Carly standing at the threshold to the kitchen, a bottle of wine in hand. And then I looked at Jasmine again.

"Are you drinking this early?" I asked.

Carly frowned. "Jasmine ran into an ex. She's self-medicating." Jasmine had one hundred exes. I tried not to roll my eyes. Carly shook her head.

"Who's that?" she asked as if Everett wasn't even in the same room still.

Everett rubbed his lips together. "I'm Everett." He nodded at Carly, but turned his brooding eyes back to me.

"Uh, hi," Carly replied. She walked into the kitchen, a look of confusion clearly evident on her face. She reached into the drawer next to me and grabbed the bottle opener. She placed it on top of the bottle and began screwing into the cork. Awkward silence hung in the air amongst us before I finally said, "Goodnight Carly," and walked out of the kitchen.

Thankfully Everett was close behind me. I opened the door to my bedroom and after Everett had followed me in, I closed it and leaned against it.

"Your roommates are nosey," Everett commented, sitting back on the bed. He reached into the suitcase again.

"You would know," I said, snatching a bra from his hands.

Everett shrugged. "It's underwear. More specifically, it's your underwear. I'm intrigued."

"Yeah, well don't get any ideas."

Everett leaned back into the pillows, resting his hands behind his head again. "Oh, but I have a lot of ideas." He winked at me.

I stalked away towards my dresser and began pulling things from drawers. When I turned back around, Everett was holding another bra.

"You don't wear padding," he commented, his fingers feeling along the lined cup.

"No."

"I like that."

My hands stilled. And then I moved them again. "Why?" I didn't care. Really, I didn't.

"Lies."

I turned around. "Lies?"

"I like the truth. In every way." He seemed lost in thought so I turned back around and packed my things.

"Am I really doing this?" I asked myself.

"Yes, you are."

I turned around again. "Why?"

It wasn't a question he should know the answer to. But he did. "Because you hate and you love the way I make you feel."

I was naked under his gaze. Skin was just that: skin. But to see your soul stripped, laid bare for the eyes of someone you barely knew – that was terrifying. I'd walk down the street naked a hundred times before I would let someone see what lay underneath.

I'd spent my life alone. Bounced from foster home to foster home. When my tastes outgrew my age as a teenager, I traded boys for men and found myself still alone. I reveled in the loneliness. No one could hurt me but me, and did I really care if I hurt me? Did I care? If I found pleasure in anything, it was my lack of feeling.

And that's how I knew, when Everett told me not to fall in love with him, that I wouldn't. I didn't love myself. And wasn't loving someone also loving yourself, the parts that saw the beauty in other people? I didn't have that part. And I didn't want it.

"I don't love anything," I said.

"I know." His eyes were unsmiling.

Chapter 9

Everett picked me up the following morning at seven. And then we were on the road without any fanfare, logging the miles to our first destination, a destination that Everett was silent on.

Silence existed in the space between the driver's seat and mine and it didn't bother me. Small talk was useless. There was enough talk in my head.

Everett turned on the music at some point. I didn't know who was singing, not that that was surprising. I didn't keep up on bands, ever. My world was a quiet place.

A few hours into the drive, Everett steered the Jeep off the freeway. Up ahead, there was a large monument and that's where the vehicle ended up, parked right off the road in a small parking lot directly in front of it.

I climbed out and stared up at it against the sun. And then I looked at Everett.

"World's Tallest Thermometer," he said, answering my question. I looked back at the monument. "It won't register your temperature."

I looked at him again. "What are you talking about?"

"Ten below zero," he said, hands tucked in the pocket of his black jeans.

I gritted my teeth. And then I gestured wildly at him. "It will probably register yours. Aren't you hot, wearing all black all the time, in California of all places?"

Everett walked up next to me. "I don't know, am I?"

I rolled my eyes. Nine in the morning and I was already annoyed. "We came all the way here to look at this?"

"Well, it's on the way, and I need to fuel up." Everett turned around and walked back to the car. I stared at the monument again before climbing into the vehicle.

"If this is how the rest of the trip is going to be, you can bring me back home now."

"There's only one World's Tallest Thermometer, Parker," he said blandly, driving down the street to the nearby gas station.

"What's next, World's Tallest Toothpick?"

"I don't know where that is," he replied, putting the car in park.

I sat back in the seat, fuming. "One thing's for sure: I don't need to travel to meet the world's biggest asshole."

"I knew you were obsessively practical in your thinking. That saves us a stop!" Everett grinned, climbing out of the car. He slung an arm over my shoulder when I left the car. "Thanks for looking out for this trip, Parker."

I shrugged him off with a grunt and looked over my shoulder. Just down the road stood the thermometer, still in sight. It made me think of Everett's words to me again. I knew I was cold. But no one had ever cared enough to point it out.

Not that Everett cared. He didn't. He couldn't. I was a shell. Hard on the outside, empty on the inside.

We ate at a small diner further down the road before continuing on. I was still angry, so angry from what Everett had said. But I didn't eat my hate this time, not like I had eaten the pizza. I ate calmly. Slowly. Just to annoy him. I ordered three waters with limes and ate the flesh from each lime leisurely. But Everett saw through it, saw through my attempts to annoy him. And he just ignored me, writing in his notebook the entire time, before I gave up and we got back on the road.

An hour later, our stop for the day came into view. "Las Vegas?" I asked, unimpressed.

"For someone who doesn't care about anything, you sure hate a lot of things."

"I never said I hated anything."

"Okay, supreme dislike."

"I think you see what you want to believe, Everett."

"Why do you think that?"

I unbuckled my seat belt. "I don't hate anything. I don't love anything. I do not care."

Everett pulled off the road into a gas station. "Buckle up, Parker."

I bristled. "No."

His eyes cut to me. "We are in Vegas. Do you know how many people drive drunk in this city? Don't be stupid. Wear your seatbelt."

"No," I said again, lifting my chin up.

"Fine," he said before opening his door. I watched as he walked to my side of the car. My heart jumped and I reached frantically for the lock. I was too late.

He swung open the door. "Buckle up, Parker," he said again.

We were staring at each other, fire in our eyes, anger in his voice and defiance in mine. "No."

"You're a shitty actress."

"I'm not acting," I protested.

Everett climbed up the step into the Jeep, so he was leaning right into me, his hands braced on the car and on my seat.

"You may not care about yourself, but you're not an idiot. You don't gamble with your life. That's the smartest thing about you, to be honest."

If his words could have color, they'd be red. He was mad. The maddest I'd ever seen him. "You don't know me." My words sounded weak in comparison. I was a mouse, like Mira said.

"You ran from me the night we met. Don't you remember? You run away from situations you feel threatened in. You're cautious. But you're not even sure why, because you don't care about yourself. Nothing about you makes sense. But I still know you."

"You know nothing." My jaw was clenched. I was mad. Mad at him, mad at myself for letting him get to me. Mad because he called to me on a deeper level, a level I didn't understand.

"Shut up, Parker. Just shut. Up. Stop talking. You sound like a petulant child." He leaned further in, so close I felt the brush of his hair on my face. "Grow up. Unbuckling your seat belt was a stupid idea. Against the rules."

"Whose rules?" I asked, anger making my cheeks warm and my voice loud.

Everett shook his head, exasperated. "Well let's see, besides the law," he said, his voice stating the obvious. "My rules. Wear your damn seatbelt."

"If you get to make rules, I want to make some of my own too."

Everett leaned back, leaving room for me to breathe. He laughed without humor. "Yeah, sure Parker. What are your rules?" He didn't sound like he cared.

"Stop invading my space, first of all."

Everett stepped of the step, and was now standing on the ground outside the car, arm braced on the door. "Sorry, can't promise that." But he wasn't really sorry.

I crossed my arms across my chest, annoyed. I let my eyes drift over the Las Vegas strip ahead of us and a thought occurred to me. "Okay, one rule. No drinking of any alcohol."

I could tell Everett wasn't expecting that. His eyes grew wide. "You can't tell me not to drink, Parker." His voice had lowered.

"You can't force me to use a seatbelt."

"Yes, I can."

"No, you can't!"

Everett leaned back in the car. "You could die, Parker." His voice was just above a whisper.

"Alcohol can be deadly too."

He shook his head. "Do I need to say it again?" he asked. "I am dying, Parker. Every second could be my last."

"Yeah, so let's speed it up by drinking until you're obliterated. You want to say I'm stupid? Well you're stupid too!" I put a hand on his chest and pushed. I couldn't breathe. Not with him in my space, his scent invading my nostrils.

Everett stood outside the car and watched me for a minute, seemingly in thought. "Okay, rules. Let's make some. Each rule I make, you get one too."

I sat back in the seat, relaxing. "What if one of us breaks the rules?"

"We'll come up with a punishment." His eyes glittered, and the side of his mouth lifted. It sent a jolt of desire through my body. I repressed the shudder I felt and nodded, swallowing.

"Okay."

"Let's get to the hotel and make the rules. Then we'll go out."

The hotel turned out to be a room at one of the nicer hotels right on the strip. It was a suite, thankfully, with two separate bedrooms. I needed to be alone, to have the space to think away from him, away from everything he brought out in me.

Everett had refused my offer to help pay and it bothered me deeply. Something to add to the rules, I supposed.

I was sitting on the deck just off the living area of the suite, eating limes that I'd brought along in the cooler. The sliding glass door opened and Everett stepped out, wearing his usual all black.

In his hands were his notebook and a pen. He took the seat across from me before flipping open the notebook. He flipped past the first several pages until he reached a blank page. I tried to keep my eyes disinterested, but Everett was right; I was a terrible actress. Everett looked up at me from beneath dark brows, catching me eyeing the pages filled with his scribble. He closed the notebook and put his hand on the cover, pulling it towards him.

He put down the single piece of paper before uncapping the pen.

"Rules," he said as he wrote the word at the top of the page. "Ladies first?" he asked, arching an eyebrow.

"No drinking."

"Do the rules we make apply to both or just one of us?"

"Both."

"Okay," he said before writing, "No drinking" on the first line. "Seatbelts," he said, adding it next.

"We split the costs for this trip," I started before Everett held up a hand.

"No." It was one word, but it was said firmly with no room for argument.

But I was all about arguing, especially today. "Yes," I replied. "I'm not your girlfriend, not even your friend. I don't want you paying for me on this trip." I shifted in my seat. "It makes me uncomfortable."

"Maybe I want you to be uncomfortable," he said, his voice low.

I set my mouth in a line. "Well you're an asshole. I want that added to the list, Everett."

"Everett is an asshole," he repeated, writing the words underneath "Seatbelts."

I huffed, annoyed. "You know that's not what I meant," I said, yanking the pen from his hand and grabbing the paper. I crossed off the last line and wrote, "We both pay."

Everett sat back in the chair and pulled out a gold lighter. It was the same lighter I'd seen him fiddling with the first night we met. I was momentarily distracted, watching him flick the lighter over and over.

"What next?" I asked, when I'd snapped out of my daze.

Everett closed the lighter and put it in his front pocket. "No falling in love."

I rolled my eyes, something I was beginning to realize was second nature in response to much of what he said. But I added it. "That goes for both parties," I said, reminding him of our agreement.

"I'll be dead before I could ever fall in love," he said, nonchalantly.

"That's my next rule. No talking about dying, Everett. It's obvious. You're not letting it be the white elephant in the room. It's the main attraction. So, just stop. I don't need to hear it every five minutes."

"Fine, then no lying. Add that next," he insisted. He leaned forward on the table, bringing himself closer to me. "That'll be easy for me, hard for you."

I eyed him, annoyed. I watched him look at me, as if this conversation didn't bother him in the least. He wasn't nearly uncomfortable yet.

"No black clothes."

His eyebrows shot up. "What?"

"No black clothing."

He shook his head. "No way in hell," he growled. There it was: the anger. Finally.

"Yes."

"All my clothing is black."

"What you wore to breakfast with Charlotte wasn't."

The question I'd had on the back of my mind since meeting Charlotte, seeing him wearing a color other than black.

"Because Charlotte is a work colleague. Or was. If I wore all black to work, people would assume I was depressed."

"Are you?" I asked pointedly.

He narrowed his eyes. "No. I wear black because it's comfortable. It's me. I work with depressed middle school kids. I try to project happiness when I'm at work, hence the color."

"You're essentially saying that black is unhappiness then."

Everett stood up then, signaling he was done talking about it. "That rule isn't going to happen, Parker. What do you know about happiness, anyway?"

He walked back into the suite through the sliding glass door. A second later I was on my feet, following him.

"Hey!" I shouted. He turned around, weary-eyed.

"I told you, that rule is not going to happen."

"Then talk to me like a normal, rational human being. Tell me why."

He shook his head, his anger still simmering. "Because I like black."

"That's not all it is. You said you always tell the truth," I protested.

Everett stalked toward me. The power in his stride, the fire in his eyes, caused me to step back. "I haven't lied. We said no lies. Not full disclosure. Unless you want me to add that as one of my rules? Because then I can push you, push you until you break." He was inches from me, yet again invading my personal space. "Until you're a hundred little pieces. Do you want that, Parker?" he breathed, the warmth from his lips fluttering over my face. And then he kissed me.

It took just a second for my brain to catch up. And then I was clutching him by the front of his shirt, grabbing fistfuls of his tee as I tried to pull him as close as possible.

Everett was devouring me. Absolutely devouring me. His lips were bruising, crushing against me. His tongue whipped in and out of my mouth, a gesture that mimicked what I wanted to happen between us.

Be brave, Parker, I thought to myself.

My hands found his shoulders and I lifted myself up. His arms moved to wrap tightly around my waist, bringing us so close that I could feel every ridge of muscle from his body to mine. His hands slid down, over my backside, cupping my bottom. My entire body ached to be closer. The next thing I knew, he was lifting me up, and so I wrapped my legs around his waist.

He carried me through the living room into his room. My heart picked up, thrumming hard in my chest. His hand slid down one leg, stopping at the skin behind my knee. I was wearing shorts, which allowed for his hand to travel up and down the back of my thigh, his fingers pressing into skin. I wanted to feel his hands everywhere, all at once. I wanted the pressure of his hands all over me. I wanted to be buried in his touch.

His hands snaked back up to my back, where the waistband of my shorts met my skin. He hooked his fingers into the waist band and yanked, muttering a curse in my mouth. I reached between us, unsnapped the button there and a second later, he set me on the ground, yanking my shorts down to my ankles. I shook them off, kicking them away. When I looked back up, he was whipping his shirt off his head. My eyes greedily took in the side of his torso, all lines and ridges and ink. My eyes caught on the words on his ribs, under his heart.

"This world has only one sweet moment set aside for us," I whispered. The words were vaguely familiar, and though the words weren't extraordinary by themselves, when strung together in a sentence, they resonated with me. I looked up at Everett and saw him staring intensely at me. He brought his hands up to frame my face.

"No talking," he whispered back.

"Okay."

He grinned, the skin around his eyes crinkling. It was then that I noticed how bright the room was. It was the middle of the day, and the sun streamed through the curtains, lighting up the entire room. My eyes darted to the window, but Everett grabbed my chin firmly in his hand and turned his face to me. "Just you and me, Parker." His voice brought me back to the moment. I nodded, swallowing hard.

He moved his hands to my waist and bunched up the fabric of my top. "Off," he said, slipping his hands underneath the bottom hem of the shirt. The moment the pads of his fingertips grazed over my torso, my stomach muscles clenched. He grinned, moving his hands up over my ribcage, pulling the tank with him. When he was up over my bra, I lifted my arms and allowed him to pull the tank top off. When I was free of the shirt, his hands came down to my shoulders, rubbing the tension from them. I closed my eyes and let out a breath through my mouth. And then his hands moved, down my arms. When his hand reached the scar along my left arm, I opened my eyes and held my breath.

His thumb ran along the raised skin, but his eyes were locked to mine. When he reached my wrist, he pulled up my hand and placed a kiss in the center of my palm, all the while keeping his eyes on me, with me. I suppressed a shudder, scared. I wanted to get back to the heat of the moment before. This more than sex. All I wanted was sex, not intimacy.

I slipped my fingers in the top of his jeans and pulled him close. With my thumb and forefinger, I unsnapped the top of his jeans. I moved my hand to the top of my zipper before I felt Everett picking me up and tossing me onto his bed. A second later he covered my body with his. "I'm in control."

"No talking," I replied, repeating his earlier demand. He smiled softly again before sitting up, straddling me.

He looked down at me, seemingly taking me all in. I wasn't uncomfortable with my body. I was ambivalent about it. The way Everett was looking at me was anything but ambivalent. He placed a hand on the center of my chest and pulled it down, tugging on the center of my bra before moving on. I heard him hum in his throat and I reached up to touch him.

He caught my hand on its ascent and held it still. He shook his head and trapped my wrist between his middle finger and thumb. I narrowed my eyes and lifted my other hand, only to have it trapped the same way. He shook his head again, before leaning forward and holding both of my hands in one of his, bringing our hands to rest above my head. I squirmed, my body's instinct to fight him taking over. I bucked my hips, but he pulled back to eye me. He held me still in his stare. But it only lasted a moment before I twisted my hands, releasing them from his grasp.

Before he could try to trap them again, I grabbed the back of his head and yanked, pulling his mouth to me, kissing him and then pulling back. I breathed against his lips for a moment, more to catch my breath than anything. And then his teeth tugged my lip and I moaned. I couldn't even be embarrassed.

One of his arms came to wrap around my back, supporting me as we kissed partially inclined on the bed. His hand slid open the snaps of my bra. Everett leaned back on his legs, pulling me up with him until we were sitting up straight, facing each other. My bra hung loose on my shoulders. His hands glided up my arms to the shoulder straps. He teased me then, his fingers playing with the straps, tugging them nearly free and then running his fingers under them.

Impatient, I shrugged forward so the straps slid off. The cups stayed on my breasts. Everett looked me in the eyes while he brought both hands up to cradle the bra.

He paused. We stared at each other, breathing heavily. I felt nearly drunk on desire and anticipation. The room was clear of sound, but full of sound too. Deep breaths, raging heartbeats. And then everything happened at once.

Everett pushed me back down, flat on my back on the bed. In a flash, he whipped off my bra and tugged my underwear down my legs and off, onto the floor. And then he stood at the side of the bed and stripped himself of his clothing. I stared, brazenly. His body was beautiful, but not because it was perfect. It wasn't. He had scars down his ribcage, biting into the ink he had there. His stomach was sculpted, tanned like the rest of his body, but there was another scar cut into one side of his belly. Imperfections were what thrilled me, not the shape, color or size of his body. My eyes traveled further down; his desire was evident. I looked up at his face, watching him watch me.

He climbed back over me, slowly. And then he laid on me, covering my body with his. I felt every inch of his body against mine. His eyes were on mine, his face so close it was all I could see. His lips touched my cheek, the side that wasn't marred by the scar. His lips moved up my temple and down again before settling on my own lips.

"Mmmm," he moaned against my mouth. He kissed like I was a meal to savor. I squirmed again, desperate.

"Everett." I bucked my hips slowly, indicating what I needed.

He sighed, blowing warm air into my mouth. He moved his lips to my chin, to my neck, over my shoulder, and around my breast. His lips moved down my torso as he reached for something next to my hip. I heard the wrapper being opened.

"Thank God," I whispered.

I felt his returning smile against my stomach before he stood back, slipping the condom over himself. He climbed back onto the bed and in a flash he was inside of me. I couldn't help it, I gasped. And then he moved. Again, and again, until my head was thrown back, my eyes closed, my breathing ragged. I felt pressure on my clit and opened my eyes, staring into his ice blue ones. Before I could close my eyes again, he spoke, his voice deep, gravelly. "Look at me, Parker." I couldn't help it; I did exactly as he asked. And when he saw me slip over the edge, spiral into my bliss, his own eyes closed and he hammered his final strokes, falling onto me afterwards.

We were silent for several moments then, Everett's face next to my right cheek, his breath in my ear. I stared up at the ceiling while my heart beat leveled out. I tried to make my mind blank, but it rebelled, unable to think about anything but Everett.

It was the first time I'd had sex since before Morris Jensen had cut into my life. Three years. There'd been a reason I'd avoided this sort of thing. I knew it would be hard to have such a physically intimate connection with someone and keep emotions from the situation.

I didn't want to feel. I wanted to roll out from under Everett and walk away casually. And the fact that I knew I couldn't do that was terrifying.

Everett turned his head and kissed my ear. "Stop," he said, before delivering another kiss to my cheek this time.

"Stop what?" I asked, a tiny bit breathlessly.

"You know what. Stop the turning in your head. You spent too much time in there." He turned his face so I could feel him staring at my profile. "It was fun. That's all."

Ouch. For some reason, that hurt more to hear than a messy confession of emotions.

I must have frowned slightly because Everett leaned over me. "You know what I meant, Parker." But I didn't. Did he just make me another Charlotte? I refused to meet his eyes, confused by my feelings.

His hands framed my face, forcing me to look at him. "It was fun. I want to do it again. Soon. Let's add it to the rules."

I frowned again. "Add what, exactly?"

"Sex. Lots of sex. No feigning me off with an excuse of a headache or some other bullshit, because that would mean breaking the no lying rule. And breaking the rules equals punishment." He cocked his head to the side, a smile lifting the side of his lips. "On second thought, please break a rule. I've love to punish you."

I squirmed, uncomfortable with his weight and his words. I tried pushing him off.

"No, Parker. We're going to lay here next to each other for a little bit. No running. Add that to the rules as well." His cheek was pressed to mine again. Each word he spoke grazed his facial hair on my cheek. I found it soothing, the bite of his stubble against my flesh. So soothing, my eyes closed, relaxing.

"Right underneath 'no black clothing'?" I asked, sweetly.

He huffed and laid down, wrapping his arms around me and pulling me so we were facing each other on our sides. "Can we change that one, slightly?" he asked.

"Depends."

"How about I can't wear all black clothing? Like say, black shorts and a color tee. Or vice versa."

"Hmm. Okay." I felt sleepy all of a sudden, probably thanks to the warmth of being wrapped up in his arms. I turned my face to his and inhaled, the smell of cool rainwater filling my nostrils. "You smell good," I murmured, slipping into sleep.

Chapter 10

I awoke cold and alone. A sheet had been pulled up over me, but the room was empty. I sat up, holding the sheet to my chest as I looked around. Bright sunlight still lit the room, so I safely assumed it was early afternoon.

I slid out of the bed, looking for my clothes. They were missing. All of them. In fact, the room looked like it had been picked up and straightened. I spied Everett's bag in the closet and strode to it, yanking out the first black shirt I found and slipping it over my head.

It hung off me like a sack, but it was my only option. I walked out into the living area that separated the two bedrooms, looking for Everett. I finally found him on the patio, holding his blue notebook with the cover closed, looking out over the view.

He turned his head to me, his eyes lighting up at the sight of me. I was sure I looked funny wearing a tee that was several sizes too large for my frame, my hair a mess. He patted his knee, indicating that I sit there.

Instead, I sat in the adjoining chair. Then he grabbed me, picking me up like I weighed nothing, and put me on his lap. "I like your choice of clothing," he commented, setting his journal onto the glass patio table.

"'Choice' is not exactly the word I would use. Where are my clothes?"

"Hiding." His arms were wrapped around my waist, my back to his chest, as we shared the view of the Las Vegas strip.

"Well then, I guess this is one less article of black clothing you'll be able to wear." I didn't know what to do with my hands. This position felt like cuddling, and I was more than slightly uncomfortable with it.

Everett squeezed his arms gently, pulling me even closer to him. His nose found my neck and I heard him inhale. "You smell great," he said after a moment.

"What do I smell like?"

"Me. It's a great smell."

I rolled my eyes. I squirmed again, uncomfortable being so close to him, with his face nuzzling my neck.

"We need to finish the rules before tonight," he said, his lips on my neck, his fingers on my thighs.

"Okay," I said, shrugging away from his touch and standing up. I saw Everett already had the paper out. He amended the "no black clothing" to say "no wearing all-black outfits."

"Outfits?" I asked, sitting in the chair next to him once again. I scrunched up my nose. "That sounds like something you'd dress a baby in."

Everett looked over at me with his eyebrow raised. "Do you have a better way to word it?" I shook my head. "Okay then, moving on." He wrote down his next rule. When his hand moved, I read it aloud.

"Sex all the time?" I looked at him dubiously. "How about just 'sex'? I don't want to add quantity to it."

Everett sighed dramatically, but crossed off the "all the time" part. "Okay, what's your next rule?"

I tapped my finger on my chin, in thought. "I need space," I finally said. "And I know you don't have a healthy understanding of personal space, at least in regards to me. But I need time to myself."

"You're by yourself all the time, Parker. You live and breathe more inside that skull of yours than you do outside of it."

"Why do you argue with all my rules?"

"You argue about mine too."

I shook my head. "I need space, Everett. I need space to breathe, without you around polluting my air."

"Polluting your air? I don't think I've ever been described so fondly before."

"You know what I mean. You're always there. Pinning me to a wall, getting up in my face, forcing me to stay in your arms when I wasn't comfortable." My mind drifted to his bed. "Sex or not, I want to fall asleep in my bed."

"I'm not opposed to sleeping in your bed."

I wanted to throw the pen at him. "I meant alone. Let me breathe. The more you push me, the more likely I'm going to run."

"Are you saying you don't want to run? You want to stay here for a bit?"

I shrugged. "I don't know what I want. You confuse me. I don't particularly like you, but I'm drawn to you. A moth to a flame."

"The feeling's mutual. I don't particularly like you either." He grinned.

"Can you live with my rule or not?" I asked impatiently.

"Sure." He didn't sound convincing. I added it to the list.

"Your turn."

"I want you to be open to new experiences," Everett said without hesitation. One of my eyebrows lifted up in question. "If there's something that I want you to try, but you're uncomfortable, I want you to be open to it. To try it," he elaborated.

"That could mean a lot of things," I protested. "Dangerous things."

"I would never put you in danger, Parker. Remember the seatbelt? Anything I want to introduce you to, it won't be dangerous. I can promise that."

No he couldn't. But it would be futile arguing. I nodded. "Fine."

I wrote my next rule on the list for Everett to read aloud. "Be nice?" he asked.

"You like to tease me a lot. I just want you to be nice to me once in a while."

"Your hair is pretty," he said, grinning.

I eyed him. "No lying, Everett. Or did you already forget your rule?"

"Okay fine. Your hair looks awful. Your laugh is maniacal. And you're a terrible driver."

"Clearly the concept of being nice completely escapes you. And how do you know I'm a terrible driver?" I racked my brain for the moment he experienced my driving. It was when I drove him home from the restaurant, when he was drunk.

"When you drove me home. I wasn't as drunk as you thought. Unlike you, I'm a good actor."

I focused my eyes on his. "Wow. You really are an asshole, aren't you?"

"Hey," he said, holding his hand up, stopping me. "These rules apply to us both right? Sounds like the concept of being nice escapes you too."

"Be nice," I repeated firmly, rewriting over the word to make it bold. "Next rule?"

"I'm done with rules for now. Let's get ready."

"Ready?"

Everett smiled slyly. "We've got plans, you and I. Nice plans." He put emphasis on "nice."

"Do these nice plans include clothing, or not?"

"Well, I had nice plans for both. You game?"

"I guess."

Two hours later, I was standing in front of the mirror in my en-suite bathroom. Everett had picked out a dress for me. It was a column of gold, starting above my breasts and ending halfway to my knee. It was modest in cut, but the color screamed flash. I wore my hair over my left shoulder, feeling the inexplicable need to conceal my scar as much as possible. I went heavy with makeup on eyes and slipped into the gold heels Everett had picked out for me as well.

"It'll be harder for you to run away in these," he'd said as he handed me the box. I'd shoved him away and then spent the next several minutes running my fingers over the heels, being reminded of a time when I'd have killed for heels like these.

I emerged from the bathroom and found Everett sitting in one of the sitting chairs, wearing a crisp white button up shirt, tucked into gray slacks. He had one leg bent over the other and was writing in his notebook as I approached. His eyes lifted up and lit up.

"Hi," he said, keeping his eyes on me as he set his journal down and stood up. "You look...*nice*."

I laughed at his use of the word. "Okay, you've given me a compliment. You can revert to being the asshole you truly are for the rest of the night."

"Phew, thanks," he said, blowing out an exaggerated breath of relief. "Ready?" He put a hand out, taking mine and leading me out of the hotel room. On the elevator ride, he squeezed my hand, sending shivers up my spine. "Hungry?"

I nodded, not trusting my voice. Why did he affect me so much? Only our hands were touching and yet it was as intimate as when he'd been inside of me, just hours before. The thought burned bright, low in my belly.

"How are you at poker?" he asked.

"Shit at it."

"Good. Let's lose some of your money."

Hours later and with a wallet short two hundred dollars, Everett took me to dinner. "I'll pay," he offered. "Since I helped you fail spectacularly in there."

My eyes were pointed. "How gracious of you." I opened the menu and scanned the items, noticing each of the prices. I tried to keep my eyes from popping out of my head when I saw the prices listed under each entrée.

After the waiter took our orders, I sipped the water he'd poured. "What does your tattoo mean?" I asked after the waiter had removed the wine glasses at Everett's request. I'd wondered if it was a way to avoid temptation or if he simply thought they were in the way.

"You're just as straight forward as I am, Parker," he said, swallowing a gulp of water. "Which tattoo?"

"This world has only one sweet moment set aside for us," I said. I couldn't forget the words.

"What do you think it means?"

I shook my head. "It sounds slightly morbid," I admitted.

"It could be interpreted that way," he agreed, playing with the rim of his ice water. "That's partially why I chose it. Because it was open to interpretation. Right now, I'm taking it in a very literal sense." He drank some of his water before setting his glass down and clasping his hands on the table. "Why do you think I'm taking this trip?"

"Bucket list?" I asked.

He pursed his lips. "Sure, in some ways. But I've yet to find my one sweet moment. I couldn't find it in California. Too much heat, sand. Too many people."

"So you thought you'd find it somewhere along the way?"

He nodded. "Yes. I want a moment to live for."

"But you're dying." He cocked his head to the side at my

response.

"I thought that topic was off-limits," he said.

"We haven't signed the rules yet. But what do you mean, live for?"

"I want one sweet moment, one moment in my memory to hold on to when my soul leaves this earth." It was the answer he'd wanted to say before, I could tell. But it was also an answer that made me feel a little sick to my stomach.

I looked down at the white tablecloth and smoothed it with my fingers. "I hope you find it." The words barreled from my mouth and I couldn't stop them. I recovered quickly. "I like your other tattoos."

"I've got a lot of them," he said.

"And scars. You have lots of scars too."

"I do." He drank his water and then set it down, his fingers making shapes in the condensation that had formed on the glass. "You do too."

"I don't have lots," I disagreed.

"You do," he insisted. "I'm not talking about the scars that separate your skin, Parker. I'm not blind, I can see those. I'm talking about the scars much deeper than that. The scars that exist within you. The ones you actually try to hide."

"You don't know me."

"I didn't think I did." He held my eyes. "Turns out I do. Why are you so scarred, Parker?"

"I've told you-Morris Jen-"

"I'm not talking about the surface scars, and you know I'm not," he interrupted. He was right. I'd tried to avoid this question. "Anyone can see those. I'm more interested in the scars unearth the skin. Tell me, Parker. Tell me your story."

"I don't have a story," I protested.

"Tell me who you were twenty years ago."

"Uh, a baby." I said it like it was the most obvious answer in the world.

"Who did you love?"

"I don't remember."

"Do you remember loving anyone?"

I thought for a minute. "No." It sounded more tragic than it actually was.

"You were a foster kid from the moment you were born," he added. He'd done his research.

"Yes. Until I was eighteen."

"And then you were attacked and became who you are now."

"Are these even questions?" I asked.

Everett shrugged. The suit he was wearing was a beautiful blue-gray, fitted well. He wore a white collared shirt and no tie, with the top of the shirt unbuttoned just a bit. I watched his hands hold his glass, watched the way his knuckles bent, the way his finger tapped on the glass. I could watch his hands forever. I swallowed more water, emptying my glass.

"Dance with me."

My head lifted up suddenly. "What?" my voice was small, weak.

He stood up and reached a hand down to me. "Dance," he repeated. "With me."

I shook my head furiously. "No. I can't dance." The music that was playing was slow and barely heard over the din of conversation. There was no one on the dance floor.

"Parker." His voice was patient, as if he knew I would bend to his will. "Did you forget the rules already?"

I shook my head. "There was nothing about dancing."

"I asked you to try new things. That was a rule. I'm not drinking. I want you to try."

I shook my head. "Dancing isn't new. It's just foreign." It was another language, another body language my body was uncomfortable with.

"Everyone's staring at us, Parker," he whispered, leaning down to my ear. "You dance with me now or I drop to one knee and make you really uncomfortable."

With that I stood up abruptly, not bothering to take his hand, and walked out to the dance floor. "You are such an asshole," I said between my teeth as he placed a hand on my hip and held onto my hand with his other. I placed a hand on his shoulder and looked up at him from beneath my lashes. I was uncomfortable. Not just because we were dancing, but because we were the *only* ones out here on the wood floor, the click of my heels calling attention to our presence. We swayed together, back and forth for several minutes before I started losing my cool.

"Everett," I started, nerves penetrating my voice.

"Shhh," he murmured.

"Everett," I said again, looking into his eyes. "Everyone is watching me."

The hand on my waist slid to my back, pulling me closer. Only inches separated us. "I'm watching you, Parker."

I tried to look around, but he was all I saw.

"Just me and you, Parker. You see me, I see you. Who cares about anyone else?"

It was hard to care about anything other than his body against mine, his lips inches from mine. He pulled the hand holding mine closer to our bodies, making the dance more intimate. He brought his cheek to lay against mine, to lay next to the scar, and I breathed relief. His lips were at my ear.

"Your hair smells good."

I couldn't help it, I rubbed my face against his a little, relishing in the bite of his facial hair. "Soap."

I felt his answering smile against my cheek. We swayed through one, two, three songs. I wasn't sure. My eyes had closed somewhere halfway into the first song and I forgot about being insecure. I forgot about everything, but the way Everett's legs moved against mine, the way his finger rubbed against my lower back. I was feeling the most delicious ache. Enjoying the way we existed on this tiny dance floor, but knowing I wanted to continue exploring our sexual attraction to one another.

I heard Everett whisper something against my ear, but didn't quite catch the words. "Hmm?" I asked, lost in the feel of his arms around me.

"Food's ready."

"Oh." I pulled back, breaking the spell I'd been under. Everett looked at me with an eyebrow raised but I ducked around him and walked back to the table. I slid into my chair and immediately started eating, not bothering to look up at Everett.

After a few minutes he asked, "Are you even chewing?"

I stopped mid-chew and looked up at him. I slowly chewed the rest of the bite and swallowed. "Yes. But I'm hungry." I was defensive. Embarrassed.

"Nothing wrong with that, but you're shoveling food in so fast that I think you're trying to avoid conversation."

It was true. The more food I shoved in my mouth, the less chance I had to engage in any conversation with Everett. He made me feel so many things, uncomfortable things. But at the same time, I was oddly drawn to feeling how he made me feel. It was confusing and scary and exhilarating.

So I didn't acknowledge what he said. Instead, I took another bite and slowly chewed, sipping my water and keeping my eyes trained to my plate.

"Red or blue?" he asked. I looked at him, confusion in my eyes. "If you had to choose a color, red or blue?"

"Choose a color for what?"

"Don't make this complicated. Just say the first thing you think."

"Red."

Everett nodded, as if he expected that answer. "Cats or dogs."

I wrinkled my nose. "Cats."

Everett sighed and sat back in his chair. "Well now I know for sure I won't fall in love with you."

"Dogs are needy. Cats aren't."

"Dogs are good companions. Cats are self-centered," he argued.

"I would have thought you'd have identified better with cats then," I said before sipping my water.

He narrowed his eyes but seemed to enjoy the verbal sparring match we were engaged in. "Okay, moving on. Cold or hot."

"Hot."

Everett shook his head. "That can't be true. You're ten below. Cold as ice."

I eyed him with annoyance. It was on the tip of my tongue to call him my favorite word for him, but he beat me to it.

"Let me guess, you want to call me an asshole, don't you?" He cut into his steak and studied the slice before looking at me again. "I'm surprised you don't just call me that all the time. Forget calling me Everett."

"Maybe we should add it to the rules," I replied thoughtfully, as if mulling it over.

"Technically, I did write it down, but you crossed it out."

I set my jaw in a firm line. "Why do you like riling me up so much?"

Everett finished the last bite of steak and chewed it for a minute, his fingers playing on the tablecloth. When he swallowed, he lifted his eyes to mine again. "Because."

If my jaw could have fallen from my face, it would have right then. "Really?" I asked, incredulous. "All that suspense for that answer?"

"Do you want to add full disclosure to the rules, Parker?"

That shut me up. I shook my head and finished my meal, just as Everett handed his credit card to the waiter passing by.

Everett pulled out his phone and tapped something on the screen. I watched him for several minutes, even after the waiter returned with the check. And then I stood up and walked out.

"Ass," I muttered under my breath as I stood on the sidewalk. Throngs of people passed me, some of them bumping into me in their inattentiveness. I crossed my arms over my chest as I looked around for a cab.

A moment later, I felt his chest against my back. Involuntarily, I sank back into his chest. I couldn't help it, I was relieved he'd come out after me. But a moment later, I remembered why I'd walked away. I turned around and stared daggers at him. "You," I said, lifting a finger to push into his chest, "are so...rude. I don't care if I've said it one hundred times. If anything, that should show you just how rude you are."

"I'm not sorry."

I gritted my teeth. "It's disrespectful to ignore my company while you concentrate on your phone."

"It's disrespectful to stuff your face nearly to the point of choking just to avoid speaking with me," he countered. "And yet," he brushed a hand over my shoulder, down my arm. "You still did."

I watched his arm progress down to my wrist. I became oblivious to the sights and smells around us. It was just Everett. He had a way of making the rest of the world fall off, as if he was the only thing I saw clearly.

"Where's your phone?" he asked.

"I left it back at the hotel."

He frowned. "Why?"

I shifted in my heels, growing uncomfortable standing in them on the concrete. "Only a couple people contact me regularly. And two of them only contact me for a favor. The other happens to be an asshole and is currently crowding my space. Which, if you remember, is against the rules."

Everett moved closer. Our legs, our hips, our chests-all touching. "I'm not giving you space when we're in a public. If you want space once we get back to the hotel, fine. But if I gave you space here, that would be violating my rule."

"Which one?"

"The seatbelt rule is more or less a blanket rule. In any situation that I feel could potentially be dangerous, we will both exercise safety." He looked up the sidewalk, noting the inebriated patrons making fools of themselves. "This is not a situation in which I'll give you space."

I could live with that. I'd been so focused on Everett, I hadn't paid attention to my surroundings. That was unusual for me. Come to think of it, I had even left my knife behind at the hotel room. I shuddered involuntarily.

I ran my hands over my utter arms. "You're a bad influence," I muttered.

"I hope so." His grin was wide, as if he was very pleased with himself. "Hotel or club?"

"Hotel." I said it quickly. I didn't need to give any thought to it. And then I had a gut punch of guilt. "But if you want to go out, I can go back by myself."

"Yeah right," Everett said, grabbing my upper arm gently, steering me down the sidewalk.

"Did you come all the way to Vegas to not experience the nightlife?"

"All the way to Vegas?" he asked, dubiously. "Vegas was more or less a pit stop. And besides, I came here for the steak."

"Did you find your one sweet moment with the steak?"

Everett looked at me impatiently. "What do you think?"

I shut my mouth as we walked back to the hotel.

When we walked back into the suite, I immediately walked into my bedroom and closed the door, locking it for good measure. I needed my space. I didn't want to fall into Everett's bed and let it become a habit. Habits were hard to break. And I didn't want to rely on anyone for a fix.

I slid out of the dress and heels, tugging on Everett's shirt from before. Out of the corner of my eye, I saw the flash of my phone's notification.

I picked it up and turned it on, noticing six text messages in a row, all from the same sender.

Everett: You're right, I do enjoy riling you up. But if I tell you why, you'll run. And I'm enjoying my dinner too much to abandon it.

My breath caught. He'd been sending these at the table when he picked up his phone and ignored me.

Everett: So I'll tell you via text instead.
Everett: I like seeing color flush your cheeks. When you're angry, your cheeks burn bright.
Everett: I like seeing you feel something, even if it's animosity.
Everett: It humanizes you. You're so cold, I didn't think you had any warmth in you.
Everett: But with your pink cheeks, I'd say you're closer to five below zero now.

The last text did just what he'd set out to do-it made me angry. Angry enough that I stood up and walked towards the door, intending to give him a piece of my mind. But then I realized that would be just what he wanted. So I stopped, my footsteps stalling on the carpet in front of my door. I looked back at the bed, where I'd tossed the phone in anger. And I strode back to it with purpose in my stride.

Me: I'm changing your name in my phone to read "Asshole."

A minute later my phone chirped.

Asshole: At least you're keeping me in your phone.

And I was pissed off all over again.

Chapter 11

We were on the road early the next morning. This time, Everett told me where we were headed.

"The Grand Canyon," he'd said, turning up the music and drumming his fingers on the steering wheel.

"Good," I'd replied, still clinging to the remnants of annoyance from the night before. "I can throw you off a cliff."

He'd just grinned and slid his sunglasses on, happily singing along to the song on the radio.

Three hours into the drive, Everett pulled off at a gas station. While pumping gas, with my credit card this time, he received a phone call and walked away from the pump.

I took over the pump and tried discreetly watching him walk away. He had the phone pushed against one ear and a finger plugging up the other. We were at a large truck stop, so there was enough noise to make it hard to hear what he was saying.

At one point he unplugged his ear to wave it in the air. Whomever he was speaking with was frustrating him, it was clear by how he ran his hand through his hair, how he kicked at the dirt at his feet, and how he hung his head near the end of the call. People-watching had never bothered me, even when I'd been witnessing the most personal moments of someone's life. But watching Everett struggling with whoever was on the other end felt like a major invasion of privacy.

I tore my eyes away and finished pumping. Noticing he was still on the phone, I went into the gas station and grabbed a fountain soda, intending to fill it with limes as soon as I returned to the vehicle. As I was ringing up my drink, I saw Everett get back into the vehicle and rest his forehead on the steering wheel. Something tugged within me then. So I grabbed a large coffee with just cream and returned to the car.

I opened up the passenger door, set the drinks in the center console, and then went to the backseat and grabbed a handful of limes from the cooler. When I returned to the front seat, Everett had collected himself. He was eyeing the coffee. I slid cautiously into the seat and opened up my soda, dropping in the limes.

"Is this for me?" he asked, confusion on his face.

"I hate coffee," I said without really answering him.

He picked it up and looked at it with suspicion.

"I didn't poison it." I rolled my eyes. "You are, after all, driving us. I'm not an idiot."

"You put creamer in it," he said, peering into the cup from the mouthpiece.

I buckled my seatbelt. "Yes."

"Thanks," he said and leaned towards me.

Instinctively, I backed up. It was so quick that my head bumped the window and I winced. Had he been leaning in to kiss me? And that was my first instinct? To move away?

Everett looked confused. "Sorry," he said shaking his head. "I don't know why I did that."

The words stung. They shouldn't have, given my reaction, but they did. Tiny little pinpricks in my chest. I nodded and grabbed my soda like it was a lifeline, sipping from it and keeping my eyes trained ahead.

I saw Everett take a sip of his coffee out of my peripheral

vision. "Thanks, Parker."

I didn't like this Everett. This polite, thankful, impersonal Everett. It felt unnatural, like I was traveling with a stranger.

I shrugged. "No big deal. You paid for dinner last night," I reminded him. Though a steak dinner at a fancy restaurant wasn't exactly on the same playing field as a gas station coffee.

"Right," he said, distractedly. My skin itched. Where did this weird Everett come from?

A few moments later, he pulled back on the road. This time he kept the sunglasses on, but turned the music off. I didn't realize how much I missed the music until we were starting to see signs indicating we were closer to the Grand Canyon.

"Have you been here before?" I asked. It was unusual, no-it was an anomaly-that I would initiate small talk. But Everett had been brooding, distracted, the entire three hours since we'd left the gas station. It was making me incredibly uncomfortable. I needed to do something.

"No," he said. Usually, Everett said one-word sentences like they were packed with desire, or venom. This one word was short. Indifferent.

"So...does that mean this visit is popping your cherry?"

There was silence for a second. And then the side of his mouth lifted up subtly. So subtly, I nearly missed it. And then he turned his eyes to me for a moment. "You want to pop my cherry, Parker?"

I bit my lip. The way he'd spoken it was normal Everett. His voice was rich, a little gravelly. Sexy. I nodded. A smile tugged at my lips. Apart from the laugh I'd had earlier, the one Everett had likened to the sound of an animal dying, I hadn't smiled. But I wanted to.

Everett sighed, as if releasing the tension that had held onto his muscles for the last three hours. He followed the signs to the entrance of the Grand Canyon and pulled into the parking area.

"Ready to pop my cherry, Parker?"

I slid out of the car and walked around, following him to an overlook.

It was my first time at the Grand Canyon. Growing up a foster kid didn't usually mean any sort of vacation. This road trip with Everett was me reliving a missed childhood.

The Grand Canyon was, in a word, spectacular. It was filled with color and ridges and edges. There were colors painted in the rock, reds and browns and yellows. The park was mostly empty aside from a few tourists, so we were able to enjoy the view without a crowd. Everett turned and looked to me. "Beautiful, isn't it?" he asked, his eyes lit up. Whatever had haunted him before all but disappeared, leaving his face relaxed.

I watched his face. His eyes were closed, the lines around his eyes had settled. The sun washed over his face, warming it. I watched him for another minute before turning to look back at the view.

"It's okay, I guess. A big hole in the ground." It wasn't how I really felt, but it was what I said. The words tasted sour to me, but to Everett they were hilarious. He couldn't stop laughing. I turned and looked at him again.

"Just 'a big hole in the ground'?" he asked. "You're hard to impress."

"What do you want me to say? Oh look, rocks and stuff."

Before I knew it, Everett was walking towards me. "Ready?" he asked.

I looked at him with a question on my face. "What?"

Everett moved behind me and placed his hands on either side of mine on the railing. "Want to visit our next attraction?" he asked, his voice at my ear.

"What is it?" I asked, holding my breath. The warmth of his chest to my back was soothing in the cool morning air.

"A ghost town. Four hours away."

"More driving?" I asked.

"Last stop of the day."

I nodded. "Okay. You don't want to see more of the Canyon?"

Everett shook his head. "It's just a big hole in the ground, isn't it?" His words were teasing.

I shrugged. "Yeah, basically. I just figured you'd have wanted to see more of it."

"I want to make it to the east coast." He stopped, didn't finish saying what was on the tip of his tongue. He was a time bomb, prepared to go off at any time. And he wanted to get as much in as possible before the east coast.

"Anything in particular you want to see on the east coast?"

"Yes." He knew I was intrigued and teased me by not continuing his sentence.

"Okay, let's go."

His arms moved from the railing to wrap around my waist. I stood still, a statue in his arms. He brought his face to my neck and nuzzled. "Mmm," he murmured, the vibration against my skin tickling my skin. "You smell good."

"I don't smell like you."

"No," he said on a sigh. "You smell like you."

I wriggled out of his arms, uncomfortable with the affection. Sex was one thing. It was explosive. This was intimacy and I was not ready for it.

"Let's go," I said again, walking towards the car.

"Hey, Parker?" he asked. I turned my head to look at him. "Do you love me yet?"

It was very hard to not roll my eyes. "Definitely not."

On the drive south, Everett was his normal happy self. It relieved and annoyed me. He bounced along to the music on the steering wheel, singing loudly along with the lyrics. That part was immensely annoying.

I kept looking over at him, watching him bounce his head back and forth to the music. He was wearing black shorts and a navy blue tee. It was the closest to black he could get, and a shirt he'd had to pick up at a department store before we left Las Vegas. I'd helped him grab a bunch of colored tees and a few plaid cargo shorts. He'd eyed with me annoyance then, so this was likely my payback now. I cleared my throat and he finally looked over at me.

"Do you mind?"

"No, I don't." He grinned at me. There was something about the way he looked, with his scruff and his sunglasses concealing his icy eyes. His hair was sticking up and actually seemed styled. He looked so at ease with himself, and I couldn't help but let my eyes travel down his chest, taking in the short sleeves of his tee and the muscles they exposed. I let my eyes travel back up to his face again, which was facing the road again. I'd made fun of him for his hair before, but the truth was it suited him. It wasn't floppy nor was it perfectly styled. It was thick, inky black, and did its own thing.

Everett was handsome. I hadn't known before if he was society's idea of handsome, but that didn't matter. He was mine. With his wide smile, his scruff, tanned skin, he lit a fire within me that I thought had been dormant.

"What are you thinking?" His voice interrupted my thoughts.

"That you are very attractive." I couldn't lie. Not just because of the rules, but because Everett made it hard to tell a believable lie.

Everett turned to look at me. My left side was facing him, and I'd put my hair up in a pony. There was no concealment of my scar. But it was as if Everett didn't notice it when he looked at me. His eyes never dwelled on it. He only ever acknowledged it when he was kissing and touching me. I crossed my legs then, thoughts of Everett touching me flooding my memory.

"You're beautiful, Parker."

I shook my head. Compliments were uncomfortable to listen to.

"I don't need compliments."

"I know," he said, pulling in a gas station. "But I won't lie to you. And I'm compelled to say what's on my mind. So get used to it."

"I'm trying."

"Good." He parked the car and leaned across the console, coming close to me. "I want you to try."

His words brought me back to the rules. And then I noticed our surroundings. "We're not getting gas?"

"We're eating. Lunch. There's a small diner inside. All I've seen you consume today are soda and limes, so I want to put something with a little more sustenance in your belly."

I followed him into the diner, one long row of brown booths. It looked like it was straight from the seventies. There were a handful of older patrons at the counter, sipping coffee and eating pie. It reminded me of the first breakfast I'd shared with Everett, in a restaurant similar to this one.

Our waitress, an older woman with a wild mane of red hair, led us to our table. Everett ordered a coffee and I ordered water with limes. My mouth puckered in anticipation.

While we perused the menus, I kept sneaking glances at Everett. He'd slid the sunglasses to the top of his head, effectively moving back the hair on his forehead and exposing his scar. My eyes followed, morbidly fascinated by the idea of having a head cut open. His eyes lifted and he caught me staring.

"You're staring," he said.

I didn't apologize. Instead, I shrugged and turned my attention back to the menu, my eyes gliding over the many laminated choices, but I was distracted by Everett setting his sunglasses on the table and running his hand through his hair.

"Do you know what you want?" The way he said it, I knew he had a double meaning.

"I do," I said. His eyes glittered at my answer.

The waitress returned with our drinks and took our orders. Everett deferred to me.

"A cheeseburger with fries. I'm not picky."

"She wants extra cheese," Everett interjected. "And I'll have the same thing." The waitress took our menus and walked away, leaving Everett leaning on the table on his elbows, staring at me.

"I still want your story, Parker."

"I don't have a story. I'm a foster kid. At eighteen, I was attacked. And here I am three years later, sitting in this diner with you."

"I know there's more to you than that."

"What is it you want to know, exactly?" I sipped my water through the straw and then stirred with the straw as I swallowed.

"Do you know who your parents are?"

I shook my head. "I don't remember them. Just vague little things."

"Did you have any good foster parents?"

"Sure." My hands played with the napkin my drink was on. It was a nervous habit of mine, to straighten the corners of papers and napkins. "They were all basically good people. But I was a foster kid, you know?"

"Meaning they didn't form any emotional attachments to you?"

"I didn't form attachments to them. After the third family, I started rebelling a bit. I was twelve. There wasn't anyone to disappoint. My foster parents were annoyed with my shenanigans, but that's all." Once the words left my mouth, I squeezed my lips tightly together. I hadn't meant to say so much.

"Do you have anyone in your life?"

"I have Mira." Why was I saying so much? I sucked my lip into my teeth and bit.

"Who's Mira?"

I didn't think I could lie and evading the question would only encourage him. "She's the one who found me. She saved me."

"When Morris Jensen attacked you?"

I nodded and sipped my water. "I don't remember the attack. That's why I won't testify. There's no point if I can't remember. All I remember is the asphalt, warm under my body. I was covered in blood. And then I smelled smoke and there she was, Mira."

"And you stayed in touch?"

"Yes. We don't talk a lot. She's busy with her jobs. But she helped me. She helped me a lot."

Everett nodded and sipped his coffee. "Anyone else?"

"I have my roommates."

"No, you don't. They don't care about you, not really."

It was a harsh truth. "Okay, they don't. But it doesn't bother me. I don't care about them either."

"What do you care about?"

I looked up at him, feeling cut open. "I care about school," I started. I racked my brain. "I care about being financially stable." Boring answers. "I care about staying in shape." These said very little about me. Which was true, at the core. There wasn't much to me.

"You like limes and you like extra cheese on your burgers," he offered.

"I do. And space. I really like space."

"I'm sitting across from you at the table, Parker. I'm not in your lap. I'm not encroaching on your space."

"But you are," I insisted. "Your presence surrounds me. I breathe your air. My eyes find yours. Even when you're not physically next to me, I'm thinking about you. It's really, really annoying."

"I'd say I'm sorry, but then I'd be breaking the no lying rule."

"I've never felt more annoyed by any one person in my life."

"Good. I like that I make you feel annoyance. Really, I do." He drank his coffee and then set it down. I watched every movement. "I'd rather you feel anything than indifference. Indifference is the absence of feeling. And you've been indifferent far too long."

I stared at him, unable to form words.

"I know the Grand Canyon wasn't just a big hole in the ground to you. You keep trying to hide from me, but you're not succeeding."

"I'm not hiding."

Everett raised an eyebrow. "No?" he asked. He had a look in his eye, a look that made me nervous.

"No."

"Then I'm just going to come sit beside you."

Before I could tell him no, he was sliding onto my side of the booth.

"Scoot over, won't you?" he asked, bumping my hip. I had no choice. I moved over, shoving my purse to the wall. He was now sitting directly to my left. I pulled my arm from the table top to under the table, resting my left hand on my thigh. His cool water scent was stronger when he was this close. I turned my head to face forward, but he was too close for me to ignore him.

I felt his arm go around the back of the seat while his other hand held his coffee. "Do you like coffee?" he asked.

I made a face. "No."

"Let me guess, you don't like tea either?"

"I don't like warm beverages in general."

"Oh," he said, taking a sip of his coffee. "We wouldn't want to thaw you out, would we?"

I bit on my cheek. "I'm not ten below zero."

"No, you're not. You're five below zero now."

"I am not."

"Well you're definitely heating up at this conversation. Okay, you're closer to two below zero."

"And you're an ass!"

"Um." The waitress was at our table with our plates. I refused to be embarrassed for yelling. Instead, I crossed my arms over my chest as the waitress set out plates down in front of us. Even after she moved away, I was still sitting there, like a child in time out.

Everett dug into his food, making annoying little moaning sounds with every couple bites. I hoped he choked.

Chapter 12

We were on the road again. I hadn't spoken a word to Everett since calling him an asshole, for the twentieth time. He was stupidly singing along to music again. I knew he was trying to get under my skin, but he'd succeeded long ago. He lived under my skin. And he made it go wild whenever he was near.

I stared at the window at the surrounding landscapes. "Where are we going?" I couldn't keep my mouth shut any longer.

"Vulture Mine," he answered, tapping on the GPS. "We're about an hour away."

"It's a ghost town?"

"Yes. I was going to go to another one on the other side of Phoenix, but it was more of a tourist trap. I wanted a real place. Not with shows and entertainers."

I frowned. "Is it a ghost town if there are people working on it, even for tourism?"

"Don't be so judgy, Parker. It's still a ghost town, but it's not what I want."

"Why do you enjoy lecturing me so much?"

"I don't enjoy it necessarily, Parker."

"And why do you use my name so often?"

"Would you prefer me call you ten below zero?"

I glared daggers. "Why do you think I'm so cold?"

Everett turned down the music. "Because you are." His looked at me briefly. "You resist touch, as if the warmth of another human touching your skin will thaw you out too much. You harden yourself to experiences. You don't say nice things. You inflict pain with your words. You do these things to push people away. You're cold."

I let that percolate a bit in my brain. "I'm on this trip with you. I had sex with you. Therefore, I'm experiencing new things and allowing another human to touch my skin."

"Well don't romanticize this situation, please, that would be too much." He was angry. I could hear it in the bite of his words.

Confused and annoyed, I threw up my hands. "What do you want me to say?"

"After we had sex, did you willingly come into my arms, or did I have to pull you to me?"

I rewound my mind back to that moment, when he tugged me close. It'd been nice. But I would have never initiated it. "You tugged me."

"Is that how you live your life? By people forcing you out of your comfort zone? Why not willingly put yourself in situations that make you uncomfortable?"

"Why would anyone do that?" Our voices were getting louder, taking up space in the Jeep.

"How do you expect to understand anything if you don't take a step out of your comfort zone, if you don't embrace the scary?"

"I don't need to understand anything."

"Then you're not alive. You don't want to feel, you don't want to connect, you don't want to exist outside of that big head of yours. I should have told you that you were six feet under instead."

"We don't all have to live the way you think we should live."

"Of course not. But what is living, really? Are you going to spend the next sixty years of your life alone? You'll die in your sleep and no one will know, no one will care."

I held up a hand. "Now wait a minute, Everett. You have no right to tell me how I should be living. You're choosing to die."

Everett swerved the car so quickly off the road that I had to grab onto the door and the center console. He unbuckled and was out of the car a minute later. I waited for him to round the car to my door like the last time, but instead he stalked away, out in the middle of nowhere, Arizona.

I watched him for twenty seconds before I unbuckled and followed him. When I was ten feet from him, he spun around. The look in his eyes stopped me in my tracks. I expected anger, rage. Instead I found grief. I opened my mouth to say something but clamped it shut a second later as he walked towards me.

"I'm not telling you how to live, Parker. I just want you to live. To enjoy however many years you have left to roam the earth. Do you think it's easy for me? To tell my family I'm done? Do you think they don't think I'm giving up?"

We were three feet from each other, dust swirling up around us from the wind and our movements to this spot in the middle of brush and sand.

"Why aren't you fighting it, Everett? I still don't understand."

"Why aren't you fighting, Parker? Fighting whatever it is that keeps you from connecting with someone, anyone. Keeps you from feeling, healing? When you can answer that, I'll answer your question."

"I don't remember it, Everett." Frustration filled my voice. "I don't remember what happened to me. I don't want to remember it. I've been in therapy. Every single doctor thinks my mind is protecting itself from the memory of that night. So why should I fight to remember something like that?"

"Because it's holding you back. You're so immersed in your indifference that you are missing out on everything out there in the world for you."

"Why do you even care? Why bring me along on this trip?"

"Because," he said, stepping closer to me. "That's what I do. It's second nature for me to care for people. It's my job."

"I thought you worked at a school."

"I do. I'm a guidance counselor."

Whoa. I stood completely still. A million things went through my brain. "You work with depressed middle school kids," I said, remembering. I turned away, needing space to think. "You're a counselor."

"Well technically I'm not anything now. I was a counselor though, yes."

I tried to sort through the mess of emotions I was experiencing. "You asked me along on this trip to cure me or something?"

"No."

"Don't lie to me, Everett," I said, eyes wide with anger.

He shook his head. "I. Don't. Lie," he said through his teeth. "Don't be an idiot. Do you think I ask every person I'm counseling to come on a road trip with me?"

"Then why? Why me?"

He walked towards me again, as if he didn't think I could process what he told me unless he was in my face. "I don't know, okay? That's the truth of it. Sure, I'm stuck on you. But I don't know why!" He ran his hands through his hair and yanked them out, doing this over and over. "You're annoyingly observant, you like to argue about every single thing, and you go out of your way to push my buttons. But I'm still drawn to you. I don't get it. You're not my type, not at all."

"What does that mean?" I asked, a little stung by that statement. My mind went back to pretty, perfect Charlotte and her perfect skin and hair.

Everett groaned. "I know what you're trying to do. But it's not what you think. I don't go for women who challenge me on everything, much less challenge me at all. I've had a hard life, so I'm not naturally inclined to work on a hard woman."

"I didn't ask you to pursue me." My defensive instincts kicked in and I took a step back.

Everett reached forward and wrapped an arm around my waist, bringing me back to him. "I know. You don't play games. Well, not the usual games women play." He wrapped his other arm around my waist pulling me tighter. I put my hands flat on his chest, ready to push him away. "You're a bad actress anyway, so you'd suck at most of those games." I rolled my eyes and pushed slightly. It was futile. The arms around my waist wouldn't budge. "I like you, Parker. In spite of yourself and all your bad habits, I like you."

"Ugh," I said, pushing against him. "What happened to being nice? One of my rules?"

"I'm getting there. But you keep interrupting. One of your bad habits." One of his hands slid up to my neck. I felt his fingers press into my skin there and I stopped breathing. "I like that you challenge me. That's new. I like that you don't go easy on me. I like that you question everything. I want you to keep questioning everything." He brought his cheek to mine, so he was holding me closely. Not quite a hug; he made sure there was enough distance to make me comfortable. "I like how you smell." He nuzzled into my neck and my knees went a little weak at the contact of his facial hair on my skin. "I like seeing the fight in your eyes. I like seeing anger color your cheeks. I like hearing your breathing stop when I'm close to you, and I like feeling your heart pick up its speed in your chest when we're close like this. I like that a lot, actually, the sound of your heart beating. So alive, a frantic mess of beats." He kissed the skin behind my ear. "I like the feeling of you in my arms, the way our bodies align." He moved his lips across my cheek. "I like watching your eyes close and knowing I'm the reason, the reason you're feeling this." He pushed his lips to mine and pulled back slightly. I felt his hands cradle my cheeks. One thumb brushed against my scar, but I kept my eyes closed. I was afraid to open them. "So those so-called bad qualities? I actually like them. It's why I'm stuck on you. I want you to make me explain myself. I want you to get a rise out of me." He kissed me again, longer this time. I wanted to drown in this moment, with Everett.

When he pulled back, he was still holding my face in his hands. I slowly opened my eyes. "I booked our hotel tonight while you used the restroom at the last gas station."

"Okay?"

"No suite this time." He searched my eyes before the side of his mouth lifted. "One bed. We're going to have to share a bed tonight."

I was surprised to find that I didn't mind. Probably because I was itching to spend more one-one-one sans clothing time with Everett, especially after that kiss. So for once, I made it easy on Everett. "Sounds good to me."

His eyes widened. It had to be shock registering on his face. "You're not going to argue?"

I shook my head and brought my hands up his chest to link around his neck. "That actually sounds like a good idea."

"Wow, you're just full of high praise for me." He laughed and pressed one more kiss to my lips. "Let's go, explore the ghost town, and hurry to the hotel then. I'm feeling impatient."

Chapter 13

Vulture Mine was a legitimate ghost town. There were dozens of structures still standing, some brick, some stone. All of the buildings were neglected, but they looked like someone had picked up and left, leaving things behind. There was mining equipment left on the side of the road, rusted and brittle from exposure. There were clusters of buildings along a slight slope, with cacti growing in between each of them. The gas station was primitive and clearly from another era. There were still tires resting against the building, and a bunch of random objects scattered around the building itself. It was spooky, seeing that whoever had left hadn't bothered bringing these things with them.

There was barbed wire up over some of the buildings, preventing us from doing a lot of exploring. And as the sign we'd seen on the way in had informed us, we'd missed the mine tour. Instead, we walked along the property in silence, the only sound came from the natural sounds of the desert around us and our shoes crunching into rock and branches.

We passed an outhouse that was falling apart. It was a walk through the past.

"It's kind of sad, isn't it?" I asked Everett.

He nodded, looking around at all the abandoned buildings. "It is. Let's get out of here."

I followed him to the car. Instead of feeling intrigued, I felt like an intruder. It was uncomfortable, seeing the ruins of lives all around us. We climbed into the car and Everett backed out.

"Sorry," he said as we drove off.

"I didn't think I'd feel that way seeing it all."

"Me neither." He frowned. "I'm ready to get off the road, are you?"

"Yes."

I was still trying to shake off the discomfort I felt at seeing Vulture Mine when we checked into the hotel room. Both of us were in weird moods. We didn't speak as we settled in, eating our drive-thru dinner we'd picked up on the way.

When I slid into the sheets, I turned on my side to face Everett. He was wearing glasses and writing in his notebook, careful to keep what he was writing from my view. His lips were pursed, his eyebrows drawn together.

"What are you writing?" I asked, while yawning.

"Words."

I sighed and rolled onto my back. "You're really good at telling the truth through evasion."

"I thank you for the compliment."

"It wasn't one." I pulled the sheet up higher, to my neck. "For someone who is so forthcoming, so brutally honest, I'm surprised you keep little things to yourself."

"Who said what I'm writing is a little thing?"

"Is it the next Pulitzer?"

"Probably not."

"So why can't you tell me then?"

"Tell me why you stopped fighting."

It was really hard to not roll my eyes. "Is that going to be your requirement for every question I ask you to answer? For me to open up and tell you the things I don't even know the answer to?"

Everett closed his notebook and set it down on his nightstand. "Some things are personal. What I'm writing is personal. And we're not there yet. We're not at that level." He slid down into the sheet and turned to face me, propping up his head. "Let's try something. You ask me any question. I ask you any question. And we decide how much we're willing to reveal with our answers."

I thought about it for a minute. "Keeping the earlier questions off the table, I'm assuming?"

"Yes. I won't ask you why you aren't fighting and you won't ask me why I'm choosing to not treat this cancer. Or my notebook."

"I want you to ask first."

"Okay," he answered. He fluffed up his pillow and considered. "Tell me about Mira."

"What do you want to know?"

"She's the only person in your life. I think learning about her will enable me to learn about you."

I thought for a minute and then stared at the ceiling as I spoke. "I remember her voice. It was warm and smooth, like red wine. It was the sound that woke me up. When I'd managed to open my right eye, I saw her. She had this fire engine red hair and eyes caked in black liner. My first thought was that she was a hooker." I almost laughed, saying that aloud. Instead, the side of my lips tipped up just slightly. It was a compromise. "She smelled like smoke and coffee and she kept clapping her hands in front of my face, to keep me awake. Her voice was impatient, as if finding me on the side of the road in the middle of the night was a massive inconvenience for her. I blacked out then and didn't see her again until I signed myself out of the hospital early that morning. She didn't baby me. I remember being grateful for that. She didn't hold me or console me. Instead, she had me move in with her for a little bit. It was an odd pairing.

"She trained with me, every day, for months. She's a firefighter and on the side she teaches self-defense, so she'd be gone at random hours of the day. I spent a lot of time alone then. And the time I spent with her didn't involve any boy talk or hair braiding or chick-flick watching. She helped me a lot."

"Do you still stay in touch?"

"We do, though not in a traditional sense. Mira has, or had, a boyfriend. He was a scary-looking dude, but nice enough. He didn't exactly approve of her taking me on, but he didn't make me feel like a burden. Mira wouldn't have it. Mira and Six have always been on and off, but he's the center of her world. She doesn't like to admit that, but he is." My mind flashed to memories of him sitting in Mira's living room, watching her train me. "She's it for him too, but they haven't been able to get their shit together and make it work. I don't know a lot about him, because of how private Mira is, but I know he is often gone." When I was done speaking, I turned my head to look at Everett. He was watching me, thoroughly invested in what I was saying. I hadn't meant to say as much as I did, but telling Everett about Mira didn't bother me. He had been correct when he'd said she was the only person in my life. She was.

"My turn?" I asked. Everett nodded solemnly. I had wanted to ask this question for days, so it was out of my mouth a second later. "Tell me what it was like, fighting cancer as a teenager."

Everett frowned, but sighed, and seemed committed to answering my question. "When I was first diagnosed, no one thought it would be a years-long ordeal. But it was. I eventually missed enough school that my mom started home schooling me from my bed, at home or in the hospital. I watched my mom suffer through a lot of grief, and my dad lost his job from so many absences. My sister is a couple years older than I am, but she was still in high school when things were the worst for me, health-wise. My parents' marriage crumbled and my sister was largely ignored as I laid in a hospital bed, unable to do anything useful or productive. No one blamed me, of course, but I still felt responsible. I still do. When surgery was a viable option, we proceeded with it. It was successful, obviously, but I wasn't prepared for the side effects."

"What do you mean?"

"When I awoke from surgery, my parents were divorced and my sister was pregnant by a guy ten years her senior. She hadn't yet graduated high school. And the guy was married."

I rolled on my side to face him. "Your parents got divorced during your surgery?"

"No," he shook his head. His hand moved to his head, and he pushed his hair back. "This," he said, indicating his scar, "took my cancer. But it also took my memory. Or, at least six months of my memory." He dropped his hand. "I came out of surgery another person. I was angry. I still have a short fuse, as you might remember with my blowup over the seatbelt, but it was worse back then. I was angry with my parents, for not fighting harder for each other. I was angry with my sister for wrecking a marriage while our own parents had let go of theirs so easily. Before the surgery, I was happy. I played sports every season, I had a handful of really close friends and dozens of other friends I spent time with regularly. After surgery, I pushed those friends away with my temper. I got headaches all the time, and by the time I could legally purchase alcohol, I was already a functioning alcoholic."

I tried to wrap my brain around it. I understood memory loss to some extent, though I'd only lost minutes, not months. I finally understood why Everett had first made me feel sadness. There was sadness tinged in his smiles. The grief I initially read on his face went deeper than his skin.

"I got my GED and went away to college. My parents aren't the same people they were before. My mom used to be social, she used to have book club and she organized activities for the youth members of her church. Now she works a job that makes her miserable, but she can't afford to not work, not as a single woman living on her own. My father is mostly absent from my life. He's still in love with my mom, and he can't move on from her. My sister is raising my nephew on her own, working odd shifts. They say tragedy brings families together, but all it did was split mine apart. None of us are the same. We smile when we're together, but we don't mean it, not really. Being together for holidays is only a reminder of how good we used to be. It's painful, Parker. To continually know, year after year, that it will never be as good as it was. That by the next year, we'll have grown further apart."

I understood then, why he wasn't fighting the cancer. I didn't agree with it, but I did understand why. It made me uncomfortable, to hear of Everett's tragedies. Which was confusing itself, as I usually lived for that kind of entertainment. It was all I lived for really: people watching. But with the visit to the ghost town and hearing of Everett's life with and after cancer, I felt like I'd more than just observed someone else's life.

"Nothing to say to that? Have I depressed you?"

My eyes turned back to Everett. I didn't know what to say, so instead I leaned in and gave him a kiss. It was tentative, as I was unsure if it was the right reaction to what he said. Just when I was about to pull away, he cupped a hand behind my head and pulled me closer.

His hand fisted in my hair as we kissed. Despite the grip on my hair, he kissed me leisurely. As one might savor a rare treat. But I was hungry, desperate. A fire had been smoldering all day long, sparking with each look he gave me. I didn't have the patience to savor. I wanted to devour.

I climbed on top of him and whipped my shirt off, tossing it off the bed. Everett's hands went to my hips, squeezing, before moving up my torso to my chest, tugging on the center of my bra. "Get this off." He all but growled it.

I leaned forward, capturing his mouth with a kiss. I tasted impatience and heady desire on his lips. I was drunk with it.

His hands scaled my spine until the met the clasp of bra. A

second later, he was ripping it off of me. His fingers moved around to my breasts and squeezed before he flicked my nipples with his thumbs. My back arched in response and Everett took the opportunity to flip me onto my back, so he was on top of me. His lips met mine again and again while he took care of the rest of our clothing. My nails grazed down his chest when he was over me again. His hair was hanging over his face, his lips were swollen and he was breathing heavily.

"Are you okay?" I asked, seeing a trickle of sweat on his brow.

"I will be. Now, no more talking."

He slid a waiting condom on and was inside of me before I could say anything.

When we were both spent, Everett collapsed on top of me. I felt his arms wrap around my back and then I was pulled, lying on top of him. He was asleep in seconds.

I, however, was wide awake. Sex with Everett was energizing, both in body and in mind. I slipped out of his arms and cleaned up in the bathroom. When I came out, he was still asleep, completely naked on the bed. I admired him for a minute, my eyes traveling over his entire body. It was my first chance to really see him without just a few glimpses in between driving me crazy.

I climbed back onto the bed, sitting up right next to him. My eyes slid over the tattoo on his ribcage, about the sweet moment. My eyes stayed there a beat before moving on. Below that tattoo, near his hip, was a tree. It started at his pelvic bone and moved up, with gnarled branches gliding around the front of his body and his back. The tree had no leaves, just twisted branches and straight roots. It was something I wanted to ask him about.

Along the right side of his ribs were a group of four, colored swallows, all flying in different directions. Along his upper right arm were three straight lines wrapping his bicep. I wondered about them. They weren't just art; there was something more significant about them.

I heard my phone vibrate from inside my purse and slid off the bed to check it.

Mira: Hey, mouse. Where are you?
Me: Arizona.
Mira: I went by your apartment yesterday. The blonde one said you were gone. She's a real piece of work.

My lip twitched. But why had Mira gone by the apartment?

Me: I'm on a road trip.

I hesitated, fingers over the keys, trying to decide what else to say. Before I could elaborate, the phone vibrated long pulses, signaling an incoming call.

"Hey Mira."

"Mouse. Why are you in Arizona?"

"Because I'm on a road trip." Talking to Mira sometimes felt like talking to a parent. Except Mira wasn't keen on telling me what to do, which is what I would imagine a parent *would* do.

"No shit, you said that. But why?" I heard her exhale and the sound brought back memories of her cigarette smoke.

"I..." I looked over at Everett. "Hold on," I whispered.

I looked at the time. It was only ten, so I threw Everett's tee on over my head and ducked outside of the hotel room onto the small balcony.

"We should meet up," she said before I could explain further.

I wrapped my arm around my upper body, shivering against the slight chill in the air. "I don't know when I'll be back in California."

"I'm not in California."

"But you said you went by the apart-"

"Yesterday, mouse. Yesterday I went by the apartment. I'm in Colorado."

"Why?"

She blew out a breath, loud and short. "Long story that I'm not going to get into, but you should come up this way. We'll have a drink."

Shit. I paused long enough that she spoke again.

"The blonde one already told me about him." The sounds of her inhaling on her cigarette came through the phone. "Bring him along."

I bit my lip. Everett was very much a secret still. Even for me. But in a weird way, I'd missed Mira. "Okay," I agreed quietly.

"Great." I heard her exhale and imagined the curl of smoke around her phone. "Text me when you get to Denver."

"Denver?"

"That's what I said, right?"

I hesitated. "Okay. I'll have to see if-"

"Just come. Bye."

And then the line was dead. Mira didn't bother with goodbye, not with me at least.

I sighed and looked out at the desert around us. There were weird noises in the desert, different than the city I was used to. The air smelled different, the heat felt different. I felt different. I turned back to the sliding glass door and slid back into the room. The only light in the room was the lamp on Everett's side of the bed, the light he'd left on.

Everett hadn't moved from the spot he'd fallen asleep in. I climbed in beside him and laid on my side, watching him. In sleep, his face was relaxed, free from the lines that furrowed his brow when he was annoyed with me, free from the lines around his eyes when he was flirting with me. He looked so peaceful, and a part of me, a small part, felt a tinge of sadness. He was dying. Soon, he'd always have this look on his face.

Despite it being against my self-imposed rules, I curled up

close to Everett, laying my head on his bicep. I wasn't sure if it was instinctual or not, but his arm curled around me, wrapping me closer to him. I hoped it was instinctual. And I hoped it wasn't.

Chapter 14

When I opened my eyes the following morning, I had the distinct feeling that I was being watched. I was warm, from being in Everett's tee and under the covers. The fact that I was lying on a warm body was definitely part of that. I lifted my eyes up and met his chest, my eyes moving over the words on his ribcage before meeting his.

"Hi," he said, his voice raspy from sleep. The room was still dark, so I safely assumed it was early in the day.

"Hi," I returned. He was facing me on the bed, my head still on his bicep and his arm still wrapped around me.

"Why are you wearing my shirt?"

"Because I couldn't find mine."

"Did you go somewhere?"

I couldn't help it. I rolled my eyes. "Yes, I went for a stroll down the road in just a tee, no pants or panties."

"Why'd you bother with a shirt on then?"

I remembered my conversation with Mira. "I got a phone call," I answered. "From Mira."

Everett sat up a bit straighter in the bed. "What's up?"

Was my face that transparent? I thought I had done well to

keep my emotions, my thoughts, in check. But Everett seemed to see right through it all.

"Can we go to Colorado?"

"I'd planned on it. To hit the Four Corners."

"Okay." I rolled away from him and grabbed my phone from the nightstand. I pulled up the text Mira sent after she'd hung up, with a location in Denver, a place for us to meet. "Can we go here too?" I put my phone up to his face.

He blinked and took the phone from my hand, studying the phone. He reached for his phone next and typed something in. A second later he looked at me. "That's about twelve hours from here." He looked at his phone again. "It's 5:30 a.m. We'll have to get on the road in a few minutes if you want to make it there at a decent hour."

I climbed off the bed and searched for my underwear. "Let's go then."

I kept my eyes averted from Everett's as I searched for my underwear, hoping he wouldn't question me about the trip. To his credit, he just started searching for his clothes too. I took his tee off and tossed it at him. "Here."

I watched him hold the tee up to his nose. "It smells good."

"Because it smells like you."

"No, because it smells like you."

I looked over at him, and saw him watching me get dressed, his eyes warm despite their cool color. Desire flicked low in my belly. "We don't have time."

He pulled the shirt over his head. "I know," he sighed dramatically.

I turned away as my lips tilted up slightly. I wasn't ready to fully smile just yet.

The drive was a long one, the longest we'd done in a single day so far, which wasn't saying much since it was only the third day of the road trip. Part of me couldn't believe it was only the third day. It felt like it'd been longer. At the same time, I was reminded of how little I knew about Everett.

"What's your last name?"

Everett turned over to me, sunglasses shielding his eyes. "Seriously? You're asking that now?"

I shrugged. "Probably should have asked it sooner, but I'm asking now. Mira is going to grill you tonight. I should know the basics."

He turned eyes back to the road. "O'Callaghan."

"Irish?"

He looked at me with that look I was growing to loathe, that "duh" look.

When he didn't say anything else, I asked, "Aren't you going to ask my name?"

"I already know it, Parker Sloane. And before you accuse me of something stupid, remember I had your credit card that first night we met. And then you told me about Morris Jensen. I would have figured it out that way, too."

I felt it, that rumble of annoyance. We'd had a relatively easy-going morning too. "How old are you?"

"Twenty-six. I already know you're twenty-one, before you get your panties in a twist over me not asking you your age."

The annoyance was simmering, threatening to boil over. "My panties aren't in a twist."

"Not yet," he said. He slid his eyes over to me and pulled down his sunglasses. "But tonight? They will be."

"You're pretty sure of yourself," I commented. I sat back in the seat and forced my eyes to face forward.

"I am," he agreed. "I'm also pretty sure about you. Some of the time."

I wanted to roll my eyes. Why did Everett inspire the most childish behavior out of me? Before I could say anything, he was pulling off the road, into the entrance of the Four Corners. He paid the fee and parked the car.

"Hey Parker?" he asked, turning to look at me.

"Yeah?"

"Let's go stand in four states at once." He exited the car before my hand was even on the seatbelt release.

I scrambled after him, nearly falling onto the pavement as I exited the car. I laughed. It was short, loud, but I actually laughed. It stretched my cheeks and lasted for just a few seconds, but I laughed. When I looked up, Everett was staring at me.

"That's a scary sound," he said. "What is it you're doing with your mouth that causes that sound?"

I stalked towards him, wanting to feel annoyance but all I felt was…light. "It was my laugh. You're supposed to say nice things to me."

He grabbed my hand and pulled me along with him towards the monument. "It didn't sound as awful as the first time I heard it."

I yanked my hand away. "That's still not nice."

He turned to me and pushed his sunglasses up on his head. With a sly grin, he leaned in. "You look incredible when you come."

My eyes popped open wider than they ever had. "That's…" I started. "That's…not appropriate."

"But it's still nice. Really, really nice."

And then he was off, jogging towards the monument, leaving me standing there slack-jawed.

When I finally caught up, Everett was sitting on a bench on the Arizona side. He held a hand out to me. "Stand with me."

Reluctantly, I slipped my hand in his. He led me to the circle in the center of the monument. He turned so we were facing each other, with our feet directly on the lines that intersected. And then he pulled me in for a hug. I stopped breathing for a second. Had he hugged me before? I couldn't remember. I closed my eyes for a moment. I was in his arms, breathing in that scent that belonged only to him. If he had hugged me, I would have realized it.

It was my first hug in years. So long, I couldn't recall my last one. His arms were safe. I couldn't help it: I snuggled closer. We stood in four states at once, together, holding each other for real for the very first time. My heart skipped several beats and my breathing returned to normal as I settled in. It was the nicest thing I'd felt in years. Who knew that two arms wrapped around you could feel so completely right?

I wasn't sure how long we stood there, hugging each other. But it was the most connected I'd felt with another human in my life. Realizing that, I pushed away when the feelings got to be too much.

I backed up and tucked my hair behind my ear, looking everywhere by Everett.

"Come on, we're on a deadline." He grabbed my hand again and walked with me back to the car.

I was quiet on the walk back to the car because my mind was such a mess. I couldn't decide how I felt about the hug. It was just a hug, but it was also the first human contact I'd had in years that wasn't violent, sexual, or educational.

When we neared the car, I pulled my hand away from Everett's and walked to my side, jumping in before he could say anything. I needed emotional and physical distance from him.

It was just a hug, I tried telling myself. But some other part of me didn't listen.

Just after eight that evening, we walked into the lounge of Mira's hotel. I pulled my phone out and shot her a quick text, letting her know we were downstairs.

My hands shook a little as we had a seat in a dark booth and I wiped my hands on my cocktail dress, hoping to rid the sweat that made them slick. My dress was a last-minute purchase just outside of Denver, at a mall. Cringing at the price, I'd slapped Everett's hand away when he'd offered to purchase it.

"Absolutely not. I'm the one dragging you along." The idea of Everett meeting Mira made me a little sick to my stomach and had affected my mood.

And it hadn't improved once we'd arrived to the hotel and Everett had booked a room. It wasn't exactly a motel. In fact, it was fancier than I'd have pegged for Mira. Instead of carpet, my heels clicked on pristine marble floors. Instead of smelling moth balls, the scents of roses and lilacs infused my senses.

So when Mira sauntered in with blue hair and an electric green dress, carrying the weight of stress on her shoulders, I felt relief. This was the Mira I knew, the Mira I remembered.

Everett scooted out of the booth and reached a hand for her. I didn't bother standing, didn't reach for a hug as was probably expected. Mira and I didn't have that kind of friendship.

"The blonde one said you were pretty," Mira muttered, shaking Everett's hand. "I guess you are."

Everett looked back at me in question and I shrugged, just as Mira turned her eyes to me. "Mouse."

"Hi, Mira."

She slid onto the seat opposite us and flipped open a menu. I watched her hands a moment, watched the jitters she was trying to hide as she flipped through the pages over and over.

I tried to ignore Everett and the way he observed Mira, but it was becoming painfully aware that Mira was not speaking.

"Why are you in Colorado?"

Mira closed the menu with more force than necessary and looked up. "Order whatever you want, it's on me." She tapped her fingers on the table as if she thought it would mask the trembling. "Or," she said on a laugh, "it's on Six."

Six. Mira's boyfriend, a man of no words. I looked around, half-expecting him to show up.

"Oh, he's not here." Mira waved it off and sat back against her seat. "But he's the reason I'm here and he owes me, big time."

I didn't know what to say to that and knew Everett was looking at me for an explanation. "Okay."

When the waiter took our drink orders, Mira finally spoke to Everett. "What are you doing?"

"I'm presently waiting for a drink."

Biting on my lip, I gently nudged Everett under the table with my foot. I tried not to smile at the way he handled Mira's question.

Mira learned forward on the table. "What are you doing with Parker?" she asked, eyes twinkling.

"Right now, we're sitting down."

I bit my lip harder. Laughter threatened, so I focused on the wood grain pattern in the table.

"You're funny. The blonde one didn't mention that."

"Jasmine," I clarified. Mira's eyes slid to me and I stumbled over my words. "The blonde one. That's her name. Jasmine."

"Jasmine," Mira spoke, trying the word on her tongue. "It fits." She nodded. "She's a bitch, right?"

Nodding, I swallowed. "She's not my biggest fan."

Mira hooked a thumb towards Everett. "And is he?" I blanched a little, at how she referred to him in the third person.

"I…" my voice trailed off, not sure how to answer this.

"I'm warming up to her. Or, rather," I felt Everett's hand land on my bare knee, "she's warming up to me." His hand squeezed.

The waiter dropped off our drinks before Mira shooed him off. "Why'd you bring her along?"

"Mira-" I interrupted.

She held up a hand, halting me from continuing. "Parker, I know damn well that you aren't the ringleader of this-" she gestured a hand to the two of us, "-trip." She enunciated the word enough that I could tell she was concerned. Cocking my head to the side, I studied her. Mira rarely showed interest in my activities-not that there were many-nor did she ever inquire about my relationships-not that there were any-so this behavior from her was puzzling.

"This trip is my bucket list. Everything. I met Parker and thought she might like to do something different." The hand on my knee squeezed again. "She agreed. We're figuring it out together."

I scrunched up my nose. Figuring what out? What was Everett talking about?

Mira seemed less confused than I, however, and nodded, her blue hair swinging around her face. She picked up her whiskey and sipped it delicately. "Where's your drink?"

It was only then that I realized we were at a bar. Eyes wide, I looked to Everett's hands, which were holding a glass of ice water. Lifting my gaze, I met Everett's. He nodded once at me before turning back to Mira. "I'm abstaining at the moment."

"I already told you not to worry about paying for this," Mira said. Her eyes switched to mine. "Still on the limes, eh?"

I glanced down at my gin and tonic. The glass was full to the brim with limes. "Yes," I answered softly.

"It's not a matter of paying for it," Everett continued. "But I don't want to use it as a crutch."

Mira's eyes narrowed in contemplation before she picked up her glass and tossed it back.

"I need a smoke," she murmured. "Come on, Parker." Mira was already out of the booth and making her way to the hotel lobby before I'd managed to get out of the booth to follow.

I walked through the revolving doors onto the street and into Mira's cigarette smoke. It was like walking back in time. The ER visit flashed through my memory in an instant.

"So," Mira said after inhaling her cigarette. "What's the deal?"

As much as I knew Mira needed to smoke, I knew the smoke break was also Mira's way to grill me a little. While some girls would use the bathroom together as an attempt to get details, Mira didn't waste time. She wanted a smoke and wanted to talk to me privately, and this was a way for her to get both.

I shrugged, a little self-conscious on the busy sidewalk with pedestrians moving about. "I met him at a bar," I began, moving closer to Mira and away from the entrance to the hotel. My heels felt foreign on my feet, causing me to teeter as I avoiding walking into a stranger. "He's…" my mind searched for an appropriate word, "nice." Nice? What kind of word was that to describe Everett?

"Mhmm," she said after exhaling. "He's easy on the eyes, I suppose." I watched her suck on the cigarette, highlighting the way her cheekbones cut into her face.

"Are you okay, Mira?" Instantly, Mira's eyes shot to mine. Shock dissipated and gave way to suspicion.

"I'm fine," she answered, her words as sharp as the line of her chin.

"Why are you in Colorado?"

She waved off my question with the hand holding the cigarette. "It's a mess, and not something I want to get into with you," she insisted.

The sting hurt more than I'd expected, but I shut it down as quickly as it came. "Okay. Well." I looked back towards the hotel. "Everett has been kind." Another word for "nice." I tried again. "He's not a bad guy."

"Well," Mira laughed short and loud. "That makes me feel better. 'He's not a bad guy.'" She laughed again.

Defensive, I spoke again, "He's not holding a gun to my head. I went along on this trip to see a few places. New places." I wrapped my arms around my upper body. "I quit my job."

"Can't say I'm sorry to hear that," Mira answered, stabbing out her cigarette and lighting another one. "But you seem well enough." She held the new cigarette at her lips as she peered at me. "He puts color in your face." Her eyes settled. "Color is good on you. You look more alive."

Alive. Everett had told me before, how little I was really living. Maybe he was having more of an effect on met than I knew.

Before I could analyze that thought any more, Mir and I were interrupted by someone stumbling into Mira.

"Hey!" she barked, losing grip on her cigarette. The cigarette fell from her mouth onto her cleavage, and she jumped back to keep the lit end from burning her skin. Brushing it aside, she immediately pushed the person who'd fell onto her. "Back off, asshole!"

The man meandered down the sidewalk, away from us, and then I heard Mira's phone ring. "Shit." She fumbled to pull it out her clutch and looked at me. "One sec, Mouse." I nodded as she answered the phone. "What, Six?"

Mira walked down the sidewalk a few feet. I was so focused on her that I didn't hear someone come up behind me until I felt breath, hot on my neck.

Whirling around, I came face to face with the man who'd fallen against Mira. And, judging by the smell on his breath, he was drunk. He didn't say anything, just stepped closer to me.

Alarm set in then, a thousand dings in my head to run. Instead, I stood, immobilized, on the square of concrete. My mind was racing, but my limbs would not move. There was a definite disconnect between what my brain was telling me to do and what my legs were actually doing.

Before I knew what was happening, the man had fallen on me, knocking me on the ground.

I froze. His breath was hot on my neck, his hands groping. Wide-eyed, I could do nothing but stare up into the stars. I heard my name being called by a voice that soothed me and then all outside sound stopped with a whoosh; the only sound I could register was the thudding of my heart as he breathed all over my chest and my neck. My mind went to another place. A safe place. I didn't feel fear anymore.

But the voice that had soothed me called my name again, this time it was closer. "Parker!"

Snapping back to reality, I registered the weight of the man being removed from on top of my body. My eyes searched the dark and found Everett's bright eyes right before he threw a punch into the drunk man.

I was still in shock, still paralyzed on the cool concrete. I stared at Everett throwing punches left and right into the other man, watched him hit Everett back. My mind was screaming at me to get up, but I couldn't.

A flash of blue filled my vision as Mira leaned over me. "Parker." Hands touched my shoulders before I felt my upper body being lifted. "Are you okay?"

I could only look at her, stunned. I felt as if I'd been underwater and needed to clear my ears.

"Can you stand up?"

I didn't answer, instead I held her hands as she pulled me up to my feet and then backed me up against the building. "Wait here for a second."

She pulled Everett off the drunk man and roughly pushed him in one direction and the drunk man in another. "Get the fuck out of here," she growled to the drunk man before whirling around and putting a fist on Everett's chest. "Calm the hell down."

Everett turned to face me, chest heaving up and down.

Stalking towards me with a hand around Everett's upper arm, Mira thrust him towards me. "Get him out of here." She grabbed my hand and wrapped it around Everett's. "Now."

Walking down the sidewalk, Everett squeezed my hand. Something about the way he squeezed my hand grounded me. Looking down, I saw wetness on my chest. It only took a moment for me to register what it was: saliva. Not mine. Hastily, I wiped it away. Everett stopped walking for a minute and turned to me.

"Here," he said, his voice gruff. He reached out and used his sleeve to wipe away the rest of the saliva. When I met his eyes, I saw he was battling hard to keep cool. "Parker. You..." he hesitated. "You didn't fight."

I blinked. "What?"

He turned back to the direction of the hotel, the movement illuminating the blood on his face. "Back there. You didn't fight. You didn't push him off. You just laid there."

I closed my eyes a moment, remembering how I'd felt when the man had fallen on me. When I'd heard Everett's voice calling my name. Swallowing, I opened my eyes. "I know."

He opened his mouth to say something, anger and frustration swirling in his eyes.

"Let's go," I whispered.

He squeezed my hand again.

Chapter 15

"Sit here," I said, dragging a chair from the table to the bathroom in our hotel room.

Everett looked at me warily from by the window. We'd walked to a convenience store to get some bandages for his knuckles. Everett had received just one blow to the face, a cut on his eyebrow, before he got the rest of the hits in. His knuckles were red and swollen, and I worried he'd broken more than one of his fingers.

We hadn't spoken since leaning the drugstore and returning to the hotel. All I'd managed from Everett were affirmative grunts.

When Everett still hadn't moved from the window, I walked over to him and gripped his arm in my hand. "Don't be a baby."

Everett yanked his arm from my hand but still followed me to the chair. I held a hand out for his and looked up to his face. Blood from the cut on his eyebrow was slowly trickling down his face. I knew head wounds often bled more than wounds on other parts of the body, but it still unnerved me a bit to see blood trickling down with some dried blood plastered on the side of his face. That could wait, I'd decided. His hands needed to be looked at.

I crouched in front of him and looked over his hands. All the self-defense training I'd done with Mira had given me a lot of bloody, bruised knuckles, so I knew a little bit about how to treat them. I looked closely at the knuckles on his middle fingers especially, as they'd taken the brunt of the beating.

"Bend your fingers."

Everett didn't. I looked up at him from my position crouched on the floor in front of him. "Bend them," I said again, one eyebrow raised. I felt him bend them, though I could tell it was uncomfortable. "Good." I flipped his hands over and set them, palms up, on the tops of his thighs. I ran my fingers over them, from tip to base, making sure they felt fine. Nothing seemed to be dislocated or broken. "I think you're going to be okay, but you'll need to ice them and take something for the swelling."

Holding his hands, I pulled him to standing and led him to the sink. "Let's wash the dried blood off so I can bandage them." He remained silent. I looked up in the mirror over the sink as I washed his hands, and met his eyes. He was looking at me with such intensity in his eyes that his silence spoke volumes. I swallowed and looked down at his hands again, carefully washing them.

I gestured for him to sit in the chair again and then carefully patted his hands dry with a washcloth. "You probably don't need this, but I don't want to hear you whining because your hands hurt and are infected," I said, opening up the package of bacitracin.

His silence was getting to me. For someone who spent so much time in the silence, I was baffled why it bothered me so much now. But it did. So I kept making little comments, trying to get a rise out of him.

He didn't flinch as I applied the cream to his knuckles. Some of the knuckles had their skin ripped off from the repeated blows Everett had delivered to the other man. I applied band-aids to the knuckles that were especially torn up and then wet a washcloth. "Your knuckles don't look too bad, but your face looks pretty rough."

Still silence. I gritted my teeth and warmed the washcloth with the water. As I wrung out the excess water, I looked at him in the mirror. He was still watching me, his eyes on mine. I couldn't read what his body language was saying, but his eyes were smoldering. With anger, with lust? I wasn't sure. I turned back to face him and applied the wash cloth to the dried blood on his cheek first. With one hand, I pushed back his hair to clean the blood along the blood along his hairline. My hand gripped a bit in his hair, my fingers feeling the silkiness of his strands.

The room got smaller and the walls moved in while I cleaned his face. I tried to focus my thoughts away from my attraction to him. But I couldn't. Lust was beginning to suffocate me as my fingers played with his hair and my other hand rubbed the washcloth on his skin. I purposefully avoided looking into his eyes and concentrated on cleaning the blood away.

I was close enough that his breath was on my neck, blowing warmth right down to my chest. I swallowed and knew his eyes tracked the movement of my throat. My legs tingled and my blood rushed to the surface of my skin.

I moved the washcloth up his face, slowly rubbing circles into his skin to remove the dried blood. There shouldn't have been anything erotic about that moment, but with his warm breath on my neck and my hand in his hair while I was inches from his face, I could feel desire all the way in my bones. I blew out a breath on his skin, right over the wetness left on his skin from the washcloth. That seemed to be his undoing, because before I knew it his arms wrapped around me and yanked me onto his lap so I was straddling him. We were face to face, his arms crushing me to him, our breathing mingling in the small space.

But he didn't kiss me. He didn't do anything more than hold me tightly to him. So, after blowing out a shaky breath, I continued rubbing the wash cloth, up his temple and into his eyebrow. I was tender when I reached the actual cut and found it had stopped bleeding entirely.

One of my hands went up into his hair that fell on his forehead and I pushed it out of the way, to give me better access to his skin. My eyes immediately found the scar on his forehead.

With the thumb of the hand holding back his hair, I rubbed over his scar. Everett's arms tightened around me and his breathing picked up.

My heart rate was climbing, blood was pounding in my veins. I wasn't even concentrated on cleaning his wounds anymore, I was trying not to combust, just from his arms around my waist and his breath on my neck. I braved a glance at his eyes and finally, I was able to name what it was I saw there.

Hunger.

We stared at one another for a few moments. Me on his lap, one hand in his hair. His arms wrapped tightly around my waist so that I was straddling him. And then his hands slid from my waist to my neck and pulled my lips down to meet his.

I closed my eyes upon impact. This kiss was different than every other kiss. It was like gulping that last breath of air before diving deep, as if it would be the last time you'd ever breathe again. I certainly felt like I was drowning.

His lips were hard on mine, almost punishing, before his hands tugged the ponytail out of my hair, sending my hair falling around us. He wrapped his hand around my hair and pulled, forcing me to raise my chin and expose my neck.

And then he was kissing down the column of my neck, from my jaw to my collarbone. Slowly, but torturously. My chest heaved with exertion and my eyes refused to open. While he kept one hand in my hair, the other moved around my waist to my ribcage, squeezing. My breathing was so ragged at this point that I wanted him to reach in and spread my ribcage apart, to free my lungs from their confines.

"Stand up," he said against my neck. I did, albeit on shaky legs. And then Everett lunged for me again, pushing me against the counter at my back as his lips met mine over and over.

Clothes were being pulled off of us like the unwanted obstacles they were, thrown on the floor in a heap. Everett whipped me around so I was facing myself in the mirror as he yanked me free of my underwear. I could do nothing but stare at our reflection, see him staring at my back. He made a sound deep in his throat as I felt his hand touch the top of my shoulder blade. "Exquisite," he said while running his hand down the center of my back, right over my spine. When he reached my tailbone, his hands grasped my hips and a second later he was inside of me.

It happened so fast that I threw my head back in a moan. Everett stilled. "Look," he said. "Look in the mirror."

I couldn't. It was too much. But Everett was bossy.

"Look. Look at yourself in the mirror, Parker."

With great struggle, I pulled my head down and opened one eye, my entire body overcome with the lust he brought out in me. The first thing I saw was our skin – moreover the difference in color. I was pale, he was deeply tanned. I ran my eyes up my body, which took center stage in the mirror, until I saw his face reflected back at me. His eyes were narrow, the ice blue of them lit up. Blue was suddenly the warmest color I'd ever known.

"Keep looking," he said as he thrust again. I had to fight my body's instinct to close my eyes. "Look," he said again, thrusting again. He kept up a rhythm, slowly increasing his speed, until my eyes involuntarily closed.

"Open them, Parker. I want you to see this." I moaned but did as he said. He started again, slower this time. Excruciatingly slow. "If you close them again, I'll start over."

"Arrrgh," I moaned from my throat, totally overcome with so many feelings. I couldn't process them. The resounding one was desire-that was obvious. But there was more. It was in the way he was staring back at me, his eyes completely on my face in the mirror. It was how his hands were holding me, lifting me. He wasn't just touching me. He was holding me. That was more. And most of all, it was the way I was looking at him, something I couldn't, wouldn't define. It was too much, frighteningly so.

His pace picked up and I gripped onto the counter as my knuckles turned white, my shoulders hunched as my body started rapidly ascending.

"Look, Parker. Look," his voice demanded.

I didn't realize I'd closed my eyes again, so I forced them open and watched, watched the moment we were both overtaken.

I fell onto the counter then, completely, utterly spent. I felt Everett pick me up and then carry me to the bed. As I fell asleep, I heard him whisper something along my neck, but I was too far gone to know what he said.

I awoke in the dark to the sound of moaning. It wasn't a moan of desire, but rather of fear. I flipped over in the bed, seeing Everett writhing and soaked in sweat.

"Wake up," I said. When he didn't, I tentatively put my hand on his chest and pushed. "Wake up, Everett," I said louder this time.

Everett thrashed harder, tangling the sheets all over the bed. I sat up.

"Everett!" I yelled. "Wake up!" I grabbed him by the shoulders and shook him until his eyes opened and he was staring at me.

"Everett," I said, softer than before. "It was just a bad dream."

Everett coughed and rolled away, sitting on the side of the bed with his back to me. I watched him put his face in his hands and rub away the sweat. "Sorry," he said gruffly before standing up and walking into the bathroom. He closed the door behind him, leaving me in the darkness alone.

I looked at the door, heard the shower turn on, and then looked at the clock beside the bed.

3:00 a.m.

3:00 a.m. was a terrible time of day. It was too late to go to sleep if you had to be awake at a reasonable hour and too early to stay awake for the rest of the day. Even then, I wasn't sure that I could go to sleep.

I lay back in the pillows. My hand reached over and felt the wetness of Everett's pillowcase, so I grabbed it, intending to replace it with one of the spare pillows. Instead, I uncovered Everett's journal.

I looked at it for a minute, lit only barely by the light from the moon outside our window. And then I looked at the bathroom door.

I told myself it was none of my business, to let Everett have his privacy. I told myself I'd be pissed if he invaded mine any more than he already had.

But my hands ignored the reasoning in my brain and reached for it anyway.

I kept my hand on the cover, running my fingers over the cloth-like material. And then I flipped it open to the first page.

I knew right away it was a drawing of me. My head was thrown back, my neck was exposed and my arms were wrapped around myself. My lips were partially open but my eyes were closed. It was sensual, and very intimate.

What stood out the most was the scar he'd drawn along my cheekbone. It was drawn exactly the same as my own scar. My fingers touched the drawing. Was this how he saw me? The girl he'd drawn looked sad. I wasn't sad. I wasn't anything, except annoyed. But, I wasn't annoyed at this photo. This photo made me feel the way the artist himself made me feel: confused. He'd written words around the drawing, but I was far too uncomfortable with the drawing to focus on them.

Deciding not to continue looking at the journal, I closed the lid and pushed it back to its spot, replacing his pillow with a fresh one from the closet.

The water turned off in the bathroom, so I rolled onto my side, my back to the bathroom door. I heard Everett come out and cough again. I made no move to acknowledge him, still processing my feelings.

The bed dipped and I heard him slide in. And then there was silence. I wasn't sure if I wanted him to come to me, to cuddle me from behind, but I couldn't deny the small ache I felt now that he'd put separation between us.

Chapter 16

When I woke again, the room was dark except for the slight illumination of the light on the table. Everett was tying his shoelaces in the chair across from the bed. I noticed his hands were free of the bandages, the knuckles looking even worse than they had the night before.

He looked up from tying his shoes, his freshly-washed hair falling over his forehead. "Are you going to be ready soon?" His voice was lacking its usual warm quality. Gone was his playfulness. Something had changed him in sleep.

"Yeah," I croaked, climbing out of bed. I was completely naked. Everett stood up and walked into the bathroom. "What time is it?"

"Here," he said as he tossed a pile of clothes at me. I caught them clumsily and then stared at the bundle in my arms. "It's four," he said, moving out of the bathroom and gesturing for me to go in. I was cold, but not because of the lack of clothing. Everett was a totally different person.

"Four?" So early. Self-consciously, I grabbed my suitcase and wheeled it in the bathroom, shutting the door to change. I looked at my reflection. My hair was a wild mess, my eyes wide. Probably with shock. Everett had never treated me so coolly.

I washed myself quickly in the shower, drying hastily with the too-small towel.

As I was dressing, I noticed the small bag of cosmetics I'd brought with me. I bit my lip while I decided what to do.

When I emerged from the bathroom, I was wearing shorts and a tank, both more revealing than I usually wore. I was wearing makeup, not a lot, but enough that it should be noticeable. I wore my hair down, shivering each time a wet strand made contact with my skin.

Everett barely glanced at me. "Ready?" he asked, his gaze focused on his phone.

"Um. Yes."

"Great," he said without feeling, and grabbed both of our bags on his way out the door, without giving me his usual grin or sarcastic comment.

Something small cracked from within my chest. That was how I was introduced to a new emotion, one I hadn't felt before.

It was unrequited longing. And it was the loneliest emotion I'd ever felt.

I was going crazy. Everett had turned the music off, his fingers stayed still on the steering wheel. All of the things that annoyed me about him were absent and, inexplicably, that annoyed me even more than before.

He still wore his sunglasses, though they seemed more to shield his eyes from mine than to protect himself from the sun. He hadn't said a word since we'd arrived at the car. I'd gone from relishing in loneliness, from preferring silence to conversation to my current situation: feeling a gamut of emotions from sadness to anger. The sadness, the longing, was most predominate. I tried to imagine what I'd done wrong, but I couldn't come up with anything.

It was as if I'd imagined funny, out-going, asshole Everett. In his place was something I recognized all too well: indifference. Indifferent Everett was frightening. Suddenly, I was wishing for something, for anything. For Everett to call me ten below zero, or five below zero, or whatever it was he'd decided on. For him to say something inappropriate. I'd take my Everett, the Everett I knew, over this Everett any day.

And that was an epiphany in itself, but something I chose to set aside, in the corner, until I was more able to analyze why I preferred the Everett that made me feel good things to the Everett who ignored me.

"Where are we going?" I finally asked.

"Picketwire Canyonlands." He didn't turn his head in my direction.

"Where's that?"

"South."

Well, this was going well. "What are we doing there?"

"We're going on a guided tour through the canyon."

"What's in the canyon?"

"Stuff."

I clenched my jaw. "You're an asshole today."

"I'll be one tomorrow too."

"What is your problem?"

Everett turned into a gas station. "What makes you think I have only one?" he asked as he got out and slammed the door.

Well, angry Everett was better than indifferent Everett.

Everett poured out the ice that had melted in the cooler and dumped in more, along with a bunch of water bottles, fruit, and some deli sandwiches he'd picked up from inside the store. I filled the tank as I watched him. He'd grabbed sun screen and I saw him pull some towels out of his suitcase.

"Did you steal those from the hotel?" I asked, a bit incredulously.

I saw the slightest lift of his lips as he looked at me and held the towels. "Yes."

"They're going to charge you, you know."

"Let them. We need towels for today's trip."

"Are you going to tell me anything else? Or am I going to have suffer through your silence for the trip?"

"It's eight hours long, so I'm sure there will be some conversation." He put the cooler in the backseat and shut the door, bracing one hand on the door while he rubbed his forehead.

My frustration was growing. "Why the cold shoulder? You were fine until your nightmare." As I said the last word, his eyes shot up to mine.

"I don't want to talk about it." Everell opened the driver's door.

"You don't seem to want to talk about anything."

I watched him close the door without getting in. He turned towards me. "You're one to talk."

"Is that a pun?"

"No."

I put the nozzle back and closed the door on the Jeep's fill spout. "Who are you? Do you regret what happened last night? Because you're the one who initiated that." I chewed on my cheek, wishing I could take back the words.

"I don't regret that." He finally let some emotion show on his face. "How could I regret that, Parker?"

I leaned against the Jeep, just a handful of feet from him. "Why don't you tell me what's wrong?"

"I just don't feel great. My knuckles hurt and my head is pounding and you keep looking at me like a wounded animal."

I straightened my back. "No I don't," I insisted. "You're just being exceptionally assholery today."

"Assholery? Is that a word?" A little bit of playful Everett was coming through his voice.

"Yeah, it is. I can't lie, remember? It's against the rules."
Everett's lips lifted a bit.

"Let me drive," I said, holding out my hands for the keys.

Everett looked at me like I was insane. "Not going to happen."

"Come on," I said, putting my hand closer to him. "Your knuckles are swollen. Let them rest. I can handle it."

Everett looked at me and then at my hand. A second later, he'd pulled me up against him. "I like my car."

"I'll be careful," I said, my voice soft. "Please."

Everett eyed me warily. "On one condition."

"Okay," I immediately agreed.

"Kiss me." I leaned in to give him a kiss, but he put his hands on my shoulders, stopping me. "Wait. Kiss me like you mean it."

"Like I mean what?"

"Like you mean it. I shouldn't have to explain." His voice was patient and he stared blandly at me, waiting to see what I would do.

I placed a hand on his chest, feeling his heart beat through the shirt to my palm. I was struck how beautiful its rhythm was, and then instantly saddened to think of its beat stopping one day. *Too much, Parker*, I scolded myself. *He's dying. Don't romanticize this.*

My hand on his chest moved up to his neck, wrapping around the back to the nape of his neck. I scratched just the tips of my nails into his scalp and then he hummed a sound of pleasure. I felt the vibrations in my fingers and was spurred on by them. With my other hand, I brought it up to cup his chin and brushed my thumb over his lower lip. His mouth opened slightly, releasing a breath, and I took the opportunity to steal the breath he was about to inhale by closing my lips on his.

One of his hands went to my hip while the other dove into my hair. His lips opened and he took from me, kissing me deeply, passionately.

I knew I wouldn't forget this kiss. In the middle of a parking lot with dust swirling around us, his fingers dug into my hip bone while his other hand cupped the back of my head, holding me tightly, so tightly that I never wanted to let go. All other sound disappeared, and all I could feel and hear was Everett's body against mine.

Over and over, he pulled away from my lips only to return to them again, as if my lips were his lifeline, his oxygen.

I pulled back and nearly stumbled away. Where had that come from? I held a hand to my lips and avoided looking at Everett. I couldn't think. I closed my eyes and willed myself to turn off, to close off from Everett.

I walked away, towards the restroom of the gas station. I nearly fell into the door, falling onto the cold, dirty concrete floor. I shut the door with both hands and shakily secured the lock. And then I walked to the sink below the mirror.

My reflection revealed what I feared. The feelings Everett inspired in me were becoming something more.

"Shit!" I yelled, alone in the bathroom. I slammed my hand onto the sink. I turned on the water and washed my arms up to my elbows before cupping it in my hands and splashing my face over and over.

With my face dripping wet, I looked back at the mirror again. "What am I supposed to do?" I said aloud. I didn't want this. Didn't want these feelings. But I wasn't ready to go home. If anything, I was only more determined to stay on this road trip with Everett. I wanted him to change his mind. Despite my personal feelings – that I wasn't ready to explore – I wanted him to want to live as much as he wanted me to live.

When I returned to the car, Everett was sitting in the passenger seat and had turned on the music. He'd grabbed a cold water bottle from the cooler and placed it on his knuckles.

When I had climbed in and was settling into my seat, he looked at me funny for a second. "What happened to your face?"

I flipped the visor down and slid open the mirror. Makeup was smeared around my eyes and down my cheeks. I looked like a total mess.

Using my thumbs, I rubbed away the worst of it and then pulled up the bottom of my tank top to wipe the rest away. "It's your fault," I said, my head buried in the tank top.

"Why is it my fault?"

"I only wore this makeup for you."

"Why would you do that?"

"Because," I said, pulling my face away from the tank top and checking my reflection for any missed spots. "You were so cold this morning. I wanted to get your attention." It sounded pitiful to me and once again I regretted the words.

"You'd have to be dead to not grab my attention, Parker. And you were barely living when you first grabbed it, so that's saying something. So imagine how I feel now."

"How do you feel?"

"I don't know, Parker." I looked up at those words. "I honestly don't."

"Me neither," I admitted.

Chapter 17

We were in the middle of a fifteen vehicle convoy on a rugged road, a guided tour through Picketwire Canyonlands. The road was rocky, steep, and at some parts a bit scary, but having the Jeep made it easier. We descended down into the canyon and soon the convoy stopped and the tour guides pointed out a set of petroglyphs. Everett stood beside me and pointed out a few drawings on the walls, from many years before.

There was something moving, seeing drawings in rock that were hundreds, possibly thousands of years old. Standing in the same spot as someone else once did, leaving their mark on the world. I turned to look at Everett and saw him studying me, studying the images.

"Now, you can find petroglyphs in many national parks around the country. Take the Grand Canyon for instance, has anyone been there?"

Everett spoke up. "We were there a couple days ago."

The tour guide nodded animatedly. "Did you explore it?"

Everett looked at me. "No. Parker," he aimed a thumb at me, "called it just a big hole in the ground, so we didn't stick around."

My eyes flew to Everett. He was grinning at me. I glanced

around the group and saw everyone looking at me with shock.

"You're an asshole, Everett," I said through gritted teeth, keeping my back at group and narrowing my eyes at Everett.

Everett slung an arm over my shoulder and pulled me close. "Do you love me yet?" he whispered.

I shoved him away. "Definitely not."

After the awkward silence from the tour guides and other members of the tour group, we continued on the road to a rock formed in an arch. Everett grabbed something from the backseat and then followed behind me while everyone climbed up to the arch to check it out.

"Wait a second, Parker." Everett put a hand on my shoulder. "Turn around."

I turned around while everyone took photos up on the arch. He stood behind me. "That's the Purgatoire River."

I scrunched up my brow. "Picketwire. Purgatoire."

"Yes. Spanish explorers called it their translation of "The River of Lost Souls in Purgatory" after having a tough go of it. French trappers later called it the Purgatoire River. The pronunciation was bastardized when American Explorers came through, and so this canyon was called Picketwire." He leaned down, putting his mouth over my shoulder, next to my ear. "Everyone comes here to see the arch, but I think the arch is the fortunate one, to have this view, a view that was named for purgatory."

His voice tickled my ear but I tried to focus on the view of the canyon and the river that cut into it. "But isn't purgatory a place of suffering, a place you have to atone for your sins before being admitted to Heaven?"

Everett's arms wrapped around my waist from behind and he pulled me closer to him. "How very Parker of you to think of purgatory so negatively." I felt his lips at my temple as he said his next words. "I prefer to think of it as a place to cleanse, to purify your soul before heaven." He left a brief kiss on my temple. "And is there a better place to see while you're waiting for your forever in the afterlife?"

I closed my eyes, let the heat of his arms around me and the sun beating down on us wash me with comfort.

"Come," he said, grabbing my hand and pulling me up the small hill to the arch after everyone else had started walking away. He handed the thing he'd grabbed from the car to someone walking by. "Would you mind taking a photo of us at the arch?" he asked politely. Why he never spoke to me so kindly, I didn't know.

Everett pulled me up to the arch and sat right beneath it, pulling me next to him, our legs dangling over the little cave that was carved out directly underneath us.

"Look, Parker." He pointed at the view we'd been looking at before. "Look at this view as this man takes this photo of us." He turned to me, putting an arm around me and pulling me closer. I felt his lips at my ear. "Everyone who sees this photo will see us under the arch. But when you see this photo, you'll see the canyon and the water and all the beauty in front of us." I was vaguely aware of the man setting the camera down on a rock after taking our photo. "Remember that, Parker. When you look at this photo, remember looking at purgatory with me. While everyone else was looking at the arch, we were looking at that."

My heart was in my throat, blocking words from coming. I turned to look at him. His blue eyes were brighter than usual. They searched my face for a second before his lips moved to meet mine. He held my face tightly in his hands, keeping me still. The entire world dropped away when he kissed me. I wanted nothing more than to exist forever in this purgatory with Everett, with his hands on my skin and his lips pressed against mine and the warmth of his skin on my fingertips. He'd made me feel. With only words and the touch of his skin, he'd made me feel.

When Everett pulled away, he was staring at me, unblinking. He swallowed hard and let out a breath. "Let's catch up to the group," he said before jumping down from the arch. He put his hands up, indicating for me to jump into his arms. So I did.

Further down the road all the cars pulled off and people exited their vehicles, grabbing food and water and removing their shoes or putting on water shoes.

"What are we doing?" I asked Everett as he tossed some things from the cooler into a backpack.

"We're crossing the river to eat lunch."

"Why?"

"Because," he said, throwing the backpack on his shoulder. "The longest set of dinosaur tracks in North America lie on the other side of that river."

"Are you serious?"

"Dead serious." His lips twitched.

"Hey! No dead talk. Against the rules."

"It's an expression, Parker. Chill out." He winked at me before closing the door. I knew he was teasing me, and I wasn't angry. Instead, my own lips twitched.

Everett looked at me with a bit of shock. "Don't tell me you're on the verge of smiling."

I shook my head, willing my lips to relax. "No. You're still rude."

"Like I said, I never claimed to be anything else." He winked at me and then reached a hand out for me. "The water is relatively low, but I want you to hold on to me while we cross it." His mood had taken such a drastic turn from earlier that I couldn't help but feel a little whiplash.

"Why were you so cold this morning, Everett?"

"I'm not allowed to talk about it, against the rules." He pulled me close as we took the first steps into the water.

"Okay, forget the rules for a minute. Or, abide by your own – no lying. Tell me."

He sighed. "Do you want to know how I first knew the cancer

had returned?"

"Sure," I said, eager for any information.

"I drove a student home from school. They didn't wear their seatbelt as I pulled out of the parking lot. And it was on the tip of my tongue to say something biting, to yell. Remember how angry I became when you removed your seatbelt?"

I nodded, grabbing on to his forearm when my bare foot slipped on one of the rocks. He wrapped an arm tighter around my waist. "The cancer, it makes me angry. It messes with my head. I get nightmares, headaches, and it changes how I feel about things. Or, rather, it exacerbates it. It's why I don't mind being an alcoholic."

I watched the others reach the other side of the river and wait for us. "But you haven't had alcohol on this trip." I almost regretted asking him to stop drinking as part of our rules. It was a weird feeling. You'd think helping an alcoholic refrain would be an obvious thing to do. But instead, it seemed like I'd only increased Everett's torment.

"I would be lying if I told you I didn't miss it. Especially when I woke up with that nightmare. But I don't mind being sober, not with you. You're not a work colleague or a concerned friend."

We reached the shore and Everett loosened his arm from around my waist, grabbing my hand instead. "I am concerned," I disagreed.

"But I don't have to put up a front with you. We both see each other for who we are. And you haven't run."

"Yet."

He smiled. "Right. But you're barefoot and clumsy, so if you try to run from me now, you're likely to fall on your face in the river."

I shook my head. "There you go, proving you can't say nice things to me like the rules stipulate."

"I thought I was supposed to forget the rules."

"Just for that question!" I was amazed at how quickly he could frustrate me. He knew he was being ornery. And he knew how rile me up.

"What about the friend who set you up with Sarah?" It was one of the questions I couldn't get out of my head.

Everett looked at me for a minute. "Oh. Jacob." He set the backpack down and crouched down, helping me put my shoes back on.

"Yeah. You thought you texted a Sarah and instead-"

"I got a Parker," he interrupted, tying my shoelaces. He stood back up. "Who did you think Sarah was?"

I shrugged. "A date?"

Everett smiled. "Sarah wasn't a date. Jacob was a concerned friend."

"Who was Sarah then?"

"A therapist. Jacob was concerned about my drinking. He arranged for me to meet his friend Sarah, who happens to be a therapist."

I thought about that for a minute. "And you thought that meeting her at a bar was a good idea?" Everett never failed to surprise me.

He laughed. "I thought it was an appropriate venue."

My lips lifted again. Everett put his hands on my face, his thumbs at the sides of my lips and then pulled. "So that's what you'd look like with a smile." He tilted his head, his thumbs still stretching my lips. "Looks weird." He dropped his hands.

"You're rude," I said, not really feeling the annoyance that usually accompanied that statement.

"Come, let's go look at these footprints so we can eat." He grabbed my hand again and tugged me along to the footprints. "I'm glad I texted the wrong number," he said quietly, when I was close enough to hear.

I swallowed. "Me too." He squeezed my hand once and tugged me to the end of the tracks, away from everyone else. The tour guide was explaining the species of dinosaurs that left the tracks, and how the tracks explained a lot about dinosaurs and their movements. But Everett was still leading me away, to the other side of the tracks. We were outsiders, Everett and I. We didn't travel in a pack, like the rest of the group. We were solitary creatures. Much like the dinosaurs that had once walked in this area, leaving their impressions in the earth long after their extinction.

Everett sat by one of the footprints and gestured for me to sit next to him. I did and he turned to face me. "Pretty unreal, right?"

I nodded, putting my hands on the ridges that formed the print.

"Apatosaurus," he said. "I grew up calling them Brontosaurus."

"Oh," I said.

He leaned back on his hands. "It's been millions of years since they roamed the earth. These prints have existed for millions of years." I saw him turn to look at me. "That's one hell of a legacy to leave."

I stewed on that for a minute, thinking about Everett's meaning. "Do you want to leave a legacy?"

"Who wouldn't?" he answered. I didn't think I would. I didn't think I cared. "But mine doesn't have to be a literal footprint. I'd like to leave something, somewhere. A small reminder to the world that Everett lived." He scooted closer to me and put his arm around my shoulders, pulling me close to him. "I don't want to merely exist, Parker. I want to live. I want to leave the world with that one sweet moment. I want to take. I want to dominate a memory. So when I'm gone, a part of me is left to live somewhere else."

My nose twitched. My eyes burned. I blinked quickly, clearing them.

He stood up, grabbed my hand. "Here," he said, leading me to a different set of prints. "These belong to the Allosaurus. A predator. It was the top of the food chain during its time. And now it's gone. But it lived here once, and thousands of people know, thousands of people travel here just to see its steps on this ground."

He tugged my hand as we followed the steps. "I don't need a thousand people to know I existed. I just want someone to know I lived."

I felt a tickle right between my eyes. I cleared my throat. "People will."

Chapter 18

We ate lunch by the bank of the river. Everett and I didn't talk much with each other, because I was still processing all that he'd said. And the things I was feeling as a result of them.

After cleaning up, we removed our shoes to start the trek across the water again. Everett put out trash in his backpack and put a hand out for me.

Placing my hand in his felt like more now. A gesture that seemed casual was actually heavy with meaning, for me. Each time he held my hand now, I thought about when I would have to let go. When the warmth of his hand in mine was no longer. It filled my stomach with dread.

I was so focused on my thoughts that I slipped, my left foot sliding out behind me. I was falling, face first, in to the water when I felt Everett's arms wrap around my torso, stopping my descent two inches from my face falling onto a rock. It had happened so fast that I hadn't had a chance to react during the fall, but the seconds after, I was frantic, my limbs shaking from shock.

"Hey," he hushed, pulling me up to standing. He calmed my trembling by wrapping his arms around me, holding me tight to him. "I've got you. You're okay." He rocked me back and forth slowly. No sound came from my mouth, but inside my head I was screaming.

He held me tightly, pressing his lips to my hair, over and over. We stood there, in ankle-deep water, for what felt like an hour. My heart rate was slowing, and my trembling was subsiding. And he continued to hold me. That's when I felt something throb painfully in my chest. In causing me to feel, Everett was healing me. He was showing me how to live. But the healing, the living hurt. They hurt with the knowledge that Everett was still dying.

He pulled back and put his hands on my face. "You ready to continue on?" he asked, his eyes searching mine.

My hands found his wrists and I closed my eyes, briefly. "Yes," I whispered, opening my eyes again. I took a step, but my left ankle was weak, sore from the fall. Everett wrapped an arm around my waist. And then he handed me his shoes.

"Here," he said before putting an arm behind my knees and lifting me up, carrying me through the water.

"I'm fine!" I protested.

"Stop wiggling," he said, eyeing me sternly.

"I can walk," I protested again.

"Shut up and let me carry you, Parker."

I did just that, grateful for a reprieve from the emotions I'd felt when he was hugging me.

Everett carried me all the way to the car and set me on the passenger seat so he could better examine my ankle. "It's a little swollen, but I don't think you sprained it or anything."

I huffed. "I didn't. I'm fine."

Everett opened up the backseat and put some ice in a plastic cup and then grabbed one of the stolen towels. He returned to me and started wiping away the water from my legs. "Everett," I said, trying to grab the towel from his hands. "I'm fine."

He looked up at me through the hair that had fallen over his forehead. "It's not a big deal. I'm just drying you off. And then I'm going to have you prop this leg up on the dash and ice your ankle."

I sat back in the seat. "It's not a big deal."

"It could've been," he returned. His eyes met mine. "Just let me do this, okay?" There was something about the way he said it, the way he looked at me to make sure I understood. He wasn't just doing this for my benefit, but also for his.

When he was done, he poured the ice from the cup into the towel and set it on my ankle on the dash.

"I'll drive the rest of the trip," he said, buckling me in and closing the door.

I watched him round the vehicle to the driver's seat. Everyone was already in their vehicles and I was a little embarrassed to know that the entire convoy was being held up by me. Everett climbed back in and buckled up. "We're going to go to the Dolores Mission and cemetery next," he said, putting the vehicle in drive and following the car in front of us. He reached behind and came back with a water bottle. "Here, it's getting hot out there."

I took the water bottle but stared at Everett. "Why are you being so nice to me?"

He kept his eyes forward, focused on the vehicle in front of us. He shrugged. "Everyone needs a little help sometimes, Parker. Don't be ashamed to ask for it."

"I didn't ask for it."

He looked at me with eyes that saw beneath it all. "Maybe not with your lips." He turned the radio down. "But you did, Parker."

I had a feeling he wasn't talking about the moment just then. My mind replayed the night I'd met him in the bar.

"What did you think, when you met me?"

Everett smiled slightly and turned his eyes to the road. "I thought you were as bitter as the limes you were eating."

"I wasn't bitter. I was indifferent."

His eyes whipped back to mine. "And now you're not."

The Dolores Mission was established in the late 1800s by a

group of eleven families from New Mexico. Most of the mission itself had long deteriorated, but there were several ruins standing, crumbling brick buildings, and beyond that, a cemetery. My ankle was still sore, so Everett and I waited in the car while the rest of the group toured the ruins. It reminded me of the ghost town we'd visited in Arizona, so I wasn't all that bothered to miss out on the tour.

"After this tour is over, I thought we'd head down to Texas. We'll have to stop somewhere overnight, but I want to visit Texas next."

"What's in Texas?"

"Lots of stuff. And some people I should probably see."

I scrunched up my brow. "Who?"

He ran his hands over the steering wheel. "My family." He was uncomfortable.

As much as I didn't relish the thought of meeting his family, I knew it was something he'd need to do before this trip was over. So I just said, "Okay."

The trip ended at a ranch, but Everett and I stayed in the car again, as my ankle had swelled up even further, rendering me unable to do much exploring. When we returned to the trailhead, it was already late in the afternoon. Everett immediately took to the road, heading south.

When we pulled over that night, we had made it to Amarillo, Texas, which was a few hours from our final destination in Texas.

As we walked through the lobby of our hotel for the night, Everett grabbed my hand again. Something had changed for us in Colorado. Everett reached for my hand as if it was the most natural thing in the world to do, but more surprisingly, I reached for his too. After checking in, we passed the bar to the bank of elevators. I looked at Everett after looking at the bar.

"I prefer being clear-headed with you," he said, answering the question I hadn't spoken. "Even if it means a little more pain." He looked down at me and gave me his little half smile. "I don't want to forget."

I squeezed his hand, gently, understanding that though the pain he referred to was due to the cancer in his head, I was feeling the same pain, but in my chest.

"Is your ankle better?" he asked, pressing the button for our floor. He didn't let go of my hand.

"Yes. Thank you, for what you did." It was uncomfortable for me to say what he did. How he'd helped me.

"I'd do it again," he said. And I knew he meant it. Not because Everett refused to lie, but because of how he said it. The way he looked at me. I couldn't explain where things had changed for us, where we had decided that holding hands and meaningful looks were now our "thing." But nothing felt more right than my hand in his, and his eyes on me.

We walked down the hall to our hotel room, stealing glances at each other. His hand shook a little when he put the key card in the door. It was subtle, but I noticed. And I knew, based on our conversation in the canyon, the trembling was caused by his cancer.

His cancer was always in the back of my mind, reminding me of my goal in going on this trip with Everett. It was the reminder that my time with Everett had an expiration date. That though we could live forever in a memory, we were all but mere mortals.

"What are you thinking about, Parker?"

I looked up, breathless, and saw he'd opened the door to the room and was waiting, his hand in mine, for me to join him. "Mortality," I said, tasting the word and the bitter aftertaste it left on my tongue.

His face softened. His smile left as quickly as it had come. "Come," he said, tugging my hand into the hotel room. He closed the door and we stood there, facing each other in the short hallway to the main bedroom area, the bathroom to my left.

"You're sad," he said. It wasn't a question.

I stared at the floor, my eyes tracing the patterns in the hotel carpet. "I don't want to be."

"At least that's honest."

I raised my head. "I don't want to feel, Everett."

"And I want you to," he said, grabbing my shoulders. "Even if it hurts, I want you to feel. And even more, I want you to tell me how you're feeling."

"Sad," I said, my voice flat.

"Why, though?"

"Because thinking about death is sad."

"And why are you thinking about death?"

"Because I'm staring it in the face, Everett!"

He grabbed my hand and placed it on his chest. "You're not. Feel that. I'm not dead. I'm alive. And so are you." He grabbed my other hand and placed it on my chest. "That muscle is keeping you alive, scientifically speaking. But you're not living, Parker. Your life was paused when you were attacked. You stopped living your life. You have no drive, no purpose, and no reason for breathing. What value is there in your life, Parker? Honestly?"

My lungs were tight, straining against my ribcage.

"I think," he said before swallowing. "No one has ever valued you before. How can you see the value in life if no one saw the value in you? I'm sad for *you*, Parker. And I'm sad for all the blind people who couldn't see you."

I tried backing up. Space. I needed space. I couldn't breathe. Everett stopped me, wrapping his arms around me and pulling me to him.

"I see you," he said. I shook my head back and forth, disbelieving. "I see you, Parker. You're broken. Not all broken things can be fixed. And that's okay, don't you know that? It was your brokenness that drew me to you, because I saw in you the same things I saw in me. It was our brokenness that connected us.

So I can't wish away those broken pieces in me, because without them I wouldn't have seen you."

I couldn't stop shaking my head. I didn't want this. I didn't want to draw people to me with my broken pieces. I wanted to be left alone among all those pieces, sitting in the middle of them so if people dared to come close, they'd cut themselves on all the pieces to get to me.

"Be broken, Parker." He grabbed my face in his hands, forcing me to look at him. "For fuck's sake. Be broken and be okay with it. Be okay that I know." His words, though rough with their meaning, were delivered gently. He kissed me then, pushing his lips hard against mine.

I tried to resist. Giving in would mean what he said was true. But kissing Everett was paramount.

He pushed me against the wall, looking down on me and breathing heavily. "Parker," he whispered against my lips before diving back in again. My hands found his hair and pulled hard. His words had hurt me. And the hurt made me feel out of control, violent. So I took, took whatever I could.

Everett lifted me up so my legs were around his waist and our lips were perfectly aligned on each other. He caught my hands as they slid down his chest and held them in his one hand, raising them to the spot just above my head.

My mind wanted to record this moment. To save it for another time. This is what I would remember: his hands on my wrists, keeping them from exploring. The way his lips pulled on mine, as if he wanted to pull away but couldn't. It reminded me of the pull of gravity. They way gravity held us to the earth to keep us from flying away. I so desperately wanted to be his gravity, to hold him on this earth and keep him from leaving me. Despite my confusion with everything else, I knew I wanted Everett to stay with me. I wanted a different future. And so I did what Everett pushed me to do, to try always. I took control of my life, of this moment, and I kissed him back with everything I felt. Confusion, longing, fear.

Everett set me down only long enough to remove the clothing from the lower halves of our bodies. I was shaking with need, fingers itching to touch him again. When I heard the familiar sound of foil ripping, I quivered. A second later, he'd picked me up again, encouraging me to wrap my legs around his waist once again. And then he stopped moving and put his hands on my face, pushing the hair away. "Parker." It was one word, but he timed it with the first thrust and my head fell back, rapping on the wall behind me.

"Ah!" I yelled out. He thrust again and again. He kissed my entire face with each thrust, moving down the column of my neck. His hands were on my thighs wrapped around his waist. He reached to the undersides of my thighs and dug his fingers in, lifting them up until the tops of my thighs were touching my shirt, completely pinning me to the wall with my knees at my chest. And then he thrust harder, faster.

"Let go, Parker," he said, leaning in with his lips on my neck. He nipped my neck softly, but it was just enough to drive me over the edge. I heard his grunts as he followed closing behind my climax, and then we both slid down the wall to the floor.

Everett had laid on his back, one hand over his eyes. His chest was rising and falling rapidly from exertion.

I was still leaning against the wall, my tank top slipping over my shoulder. I stared at Everett in a daze. My eyes found his tattoo again.

"This world has only one sweet moment set aside for us," I whispered.

Everett removed his arm from his eyes and looked at me with just one eye open. "That wasn't sweet," he said hoarsely. "That was passion." He sighed and sat up slowly, one hand on his head.

"Are you okay?"

He shook his head and stood up, holding on to the doorway to the bathroom as if he was dizzy. It hurt, to see him weakened. And I knew, by the look on his face, he didn't want to be seen that way.

"Fine," he said. He reached his hands down to me and I took

them, standing up with him. "Let's shower and go to bed. It's been a long day."

"Sit, I'll start the water and grab our toiletries." I led him to the toilet and put the lid down, helping him sit.

He looked up at me, his eyes a little lost. And the crack, the one that had started earlier that morning at his indifference towards me, broke a little more. I didn't think there was anything left to break.

I grabbed the toiletries and returned to the bathroom, seeing him look wearier. Minute by minute, he was fading. So I turned on the water and waited for it to get hot enough, and then I helped him into the shower with me.

The water seemed to rouse him a bit and we took turns shampooing each other's hair. I loaded a loofa up with his body wash and started first on his back. "Will you tell me about your tattoos?" I asked, rubbing the loofa over each of his muscles. My hand traced the tree with its twisted branches that wrapped around his lower torso.

"The tree was something I got shortly after I was in remission. The roots are straight, because that's how we all start out in life. All babies are innocent. Your roots are straight. And then once you first loose some of that innocence, when you emerge through the earth, you are changed. For a tree, nature changes how it forms as it grows. Are there things in the way, does it have to grow around obstacles? Does weather strip it of its leaves in the winter? Do outside factors, like birds and squirrels, destroy the bark? Humans are very similar. Once we lose our innocence, there's no way to predict the future, how your branches will grow. You have to go with the flow until you're cut down."

It hurt to swallow the lump in my throat. "Turn around," I said, standing under the spray. He turned so I was facing his chest. "These?" I asked, running the loofa and then my fingers over the four swallows on the other side of his ribs.

"The people who matter the most to me. My mom, dad, sister,

and nephew. I want them to be free." My eyes burned. He didn't have to say what he wanted them to be free of. I already knew.

I knew I shouldn't, but I continued. I ran the loofa up over his chest, up his bicep to the three straight lines that wrapped his right bicep. I didn't trust my voice so I looked up at him, trying to communicate my thoughts through my eyes.

"Those are how many times I've been told I have cancer. This line," he said, pointing to the line at the bottom of the stack, "was added a couple weeks ago."

"Three times."

"I had cancer twice in my teenage years. The first time, it was caught early and required little treatment. The second time," he said, touching the middle line, "was when my family fell apart." He let his hand drop and looked at me. "Three strikes," he said.

I was glad I was standing directly under the spray, because I didn't want him to witness the tear that slid quickly from my eye, mixing with the water from the showerhead. I couldn't explain it. It was more than sadness I felt. Something deeper, more poignant.

"If you want to wear all black, I won't mind. We can strike it from the rules."

Everett looked down at me. "Where did that come from?"

I shrugged. "You're the man in black. If you want to wear black, I want you to." My leg bounced nervously.

"The man in black?" he asked. "Like Johnny Cash?"

My leg stopped its movements. "Who's that?"

Everett shook his head. "You really have a lot of life to catch up on, sweetheart." Before I had time to process the ache I felt at that endearment, Everett tapped the quote on his chest. "Take this for example. It's from a song."

"'This world has only one sweet moment set aside for us' is from a song?"

He nodded. "It's by Queen. Who is probably another band you haven't been acquainted with, so before you open your mouth, I'll just tell you they are a rock band that formed in the 70's. This line," he said, running his fingers over the soapy skin of his tattoo, "is from a song called 'Who Wants to Live Forever'."

"Sounds like a really uplifting song," I replied drily.

Everett laughed, took the loofa from me and rinsed it, before trading places with me in the shower. After pouring some body wash onto the loofa, he started rubbing it on my chest.

"This still smells like your body wash," I said, understanding now why he always had the scent of cool water.

"Because it is. I want to smell this on your skin." He rubbed the loofa down the front of my body before having me turn around. After running the loofa over my back, I felt his hands replace it and his fingers pushed into my shoulder and down my back, massaging the muscles there. My head fell back.

"That feels good," I felt the words vibrate from my throat.

"Does it hurt?" he asked.

"Only a little, but it also feels good."

"There's pleasure in a little pain then."

I opened my eyes and straightened my head. "I guess so."

"There is, Parker." He wrapped his arms around my front and rubbed the body wash over me again. "You just have to be brave enough to endure it."

Chapter 19

After Everett fell asleep, I was left wide awake. Thoughts from our day wouldn't leave my brain. Our moment at the Purgatoire River and then again when I fell in it. And what Everett had said while admiring the dinosaur tracks, about leaving his mark on the earth somewhere.

Quickly, I pulled out my laptop and made a few calls, making an appointment for the following morning. Everett breathed heavily next to me the entire time, not stirring once, so I was able to make our plans without interruption.

After the excitement, I put my laptop away and crawled back into bed beside Everett. I watched him breathing deeply before I laid my head on his bicep. Like he had the first time I did it, he pulled his arm towards his body, pulling me in with him.

I let Everett sleep in the following morning. Though he was normally awake before I was, I knew he'd been exhausted the day before so I packed our things as quietly as possible, to keep him in his deep, peaceful sleep.

I brought food up from the continental breakfast in the lobby, and brewed a pot of coffee in the tiny hotel coffee maker.

It was the coffee that finally roused him. I watched him from the chair opposite the bed, watched his arms stretch above his head as he looked around. When his eyes found me, he settled back in the pillow, seemingly relieved. I got up from the chair and poured the milk I'd grabbed from the breakfast buffet in the cup before climbing on to the bed. "Here," I said, handing him the mug.

Everett sat up and took the mug from me, drinking. "Thank you," he said, his eyes never leaving mine.

"How do you feel?"

Everett set the coffee down. "I'm fine, Parker. Okay?" There was mild annoyance in his tone. I knew why. So I didn't push him.

"Okay. I have plans for us before we see your family."

"What's that?"

"I want to get a tattoo today."

Everett shook his head. "Are you serious?"

"Dead serious."

He laughed at my word choice. "If you're getting a tattoo, I'm getting a tattoo."

It was what I'd hoped he'd say. "So we'll both get tattoos," I said, biting my lip.

"Yeah." He sat up straighter in the bed. "And you'll be the last one to see mine."

I pushed him. Not hard, but enough for him to spill coffee all over the bed and himself. He looked down at the coffee-soaked sheets and then looked back at me.

Before I knew what was happening, he grabbed me and pulled me on top of him, smearing my clothes with his coffee mess.

"Kiss me, Parker." I pecked him on the lips. "You can do better than that." I pushed my lips to his again, trying to wriggle out of his arms. "Kiss me with feeling," his said, bringing a hand up to my cheek, cradling my face in his hand.

"But I don't know what I'm feeling," I breathed.

"You don't have to. Whatever it is, let it come from your lips to mine."

My heart pounded painfully in my chest. But I did as he asked. I let my lips hover over his for a moment before changing course and kissing up the side of his face. I kissed his ear first, letting out a breath after that kiss and then moved up his temple. My hands pushed the hair away from his forehead and I hesitated for only a beat before my lips pressed to the small dent in his forehead. And then I kissed along his scar. I felt his breath shudder against my throat. I kissed down the center of his forehead, slowly, until I reached his eyes. They were closed, so I kissed each eyelid gently before moving down his face, placing a kiss on his cheek, the tip of his nose, his chin and then down his chest.

I tasted coffee on his chest, but I didn't stop kissing the trail across his body. My lips pressed to the skin that concealed his heart, and I felt thankfulness at its steady beat to my lips. I kissed the tattoo that had words and then down the trunk of the tree. I kissed across his abdomen and then over the sparrows on the other side.

When I reached his bicep, my breath was coming in shattered. Partly because of the desire I felt whenever I was in his presence, but overwhelmingly because of the feeling of kissing all the broken and the perfect parts of Everett, with all the feeling that I held for him.

I kissed each one of the lines on his bicep before resting my forehead on his shoulder, overcome with whatever this feeling was that I had for him.

His hands were cupping my jaw and pulling me up. His clear blue eyes stared into mine for a minute, and then he pulled me down and kissed me, gently, softly. Each of his kisses so far had been different and this was no exception. It was a healing kiss. Healing the parts of me that hurt with how he made me feel.

I pulled away and let my head rest on his chest, mind-numbingly terrified of the kiss I'd just given to Everett. Terrified of what it meant, what he saw in that kiss. I felt his hand come down to my hair and he brushed it with his fingers.

We laid on the bed, my head on his coffee-covered chest and his fingers in my hair as I tried to wrap my head around what was happening with Everett.

"When did you make the appointments?" he asked, pulling into the tattoo shop just outside of Austin, where his family lived.

"While you were asleep, last night."

Everett looked happily surprised. And it planted a little seed of happiness in my chest, to know I'd put that on his face. Happiness was truly a weird emotion. It filled your chest with little flutters. It made me nauseated, but I chose to let it come. It wasn't painful like the other feelings.

Everett climbed out and walked around to grab my hand. "What are you getting tattooed?"

"It's a secret."

"Well then mine will be a secret too." He squeezed my hand not once, not twice, but three times. So I squeezed back three times.

Everett looked down at me and squeezed my hand three times again. Whatever it was, it was intentional. He furrowed his brow for a minute before clearing his features. "You ready?"

"Yes."

When my tattoo was finished, I walked outside and looked for Everett. When I didn't see him, I sat on the curb and waited. I decided to text Mira.

Me: Hi.

It was as articulate as I could manage. I tapped my feet on the asphalt as I waited for her reply.

Mira: Hi, mouse. How is Everett?
Me: Fine. His knuckles are just a little bruised.
Mira: He's good, mouse. He cares about you.
Me: I know.
Mira: I hope you do.

I stewed on that for a minute, a little annoyed. But the door to the tattoo shop opened and Everett stepped out. He'd decided to wear long sleeves and shorts, so I knew that I wouldn't be able to see where he'd gotten his tattoo. Luckily, mine was hidden as well.

He reached a hand down to me on the curb and pulled me to standing. "What'd you get?" he asked.

"What did you get?"

"Ah," he said, understanding coming into his eyes. "You're not going to tell me, until I tell you."

I nodded.

"You're going to have to wait then, because I plan on keeping this on lockdown until you get me naked again."

I chewed on my lip. "Same goes," I replied.

Everett grinned. "I can't wait." He winked and pulled me towards the car. I was struck by how our relationship was developing. Despite the emotional feelings I was collecting for Everett, he still had to pull me, pull them from me. And for some reason, I wanted to be the one pulling him.

"Are we off to meet your parents?"

He nodded. "We're going to go to a late lunch with my sister and nephew first."

I continued chewing on my lip. Everett opened the passenger door to the Jeep for me. "You okay?" he asked, stalling on helping me in.

"Yeah," I said nonchalantly.

"No lying."

I rolled my eyes.

"I wish I had added 'no eye rolling' to the rules right now," he laughed. "Come on, what's on your mind, my precious Parker?"

I raised an eyebrow at that. "Precious Parker? Really? That makes me sound like your pet."

He put an arm around my shoulders and brushed his hand down my hair. "My precious."

I pushed away from him. "That's so creepy." But part of me wanted to smile. A big part. I moved from chewing on my lip to chewing on the inside of my lip.

"Don't smile, Parker," Everett said, leaning in to me. "It would look weird on your face."

I resisted the urge to roll my eyes again. "Why are you being so playful this morning? Where's my dark, broody Everett?"

He cocked his head to the side. "When did I become yours?" he asked.

I stopped breathing for a second, not realizing until that moment that I'd referred to the Everett I was accustomed to as 'my Everett'.

"Relax, Parker. Breathe. I was just teasing you. Dark and broody Everett is on a high from getting new ink. Don't worry; I'm sure he'll return when we meet my parents for dinner tonight."

Whatever smile had been teasing my lips left quickly.

"Come on," he said, gesturing for me to climb into the Jeep. "We have pizza calling our name." He patted my butt as I climbed into the car so I gave him a sharp look over my shoulder.

He just laughed and climbed into the driver's seat.

Chapter 20

Everett's sister was pretty. Not the kind of pretty that you'd see on a beauty queen, dolled up with makeup and spray tan. She was tan like her brother, natural, or boosted by the sun. Her black hair was styled simply, long and straight. She had the same eyes as Everett, that unnerving ice blue. But her face looked softer than Everett's even though she was a few years older.

"Bridget," she said, her face split open with her bright white smile. She was the kind of person that was so pretty, she was intimidating until she smiled. Her smile was warm, friendly. And there was hope in her eyes. I instantly looked away, uncomfortable by that. I didn't want to responsible for whatever hope she saw in my presence.

"Parker," I said, shaking her offered hand and looking at Everett.

"Sit," she gestured to the opposite side of the booth. I climbed in and Everett slid in next to me. Almost immediately, he grabbed my hand under the table and squeezed. It was reassuring, so I relaxed a little bit.

"So," Bridget said, her eyes sparkling with excitement. "Everett says you've been on a road trip for the last several days?"

"Yeah," I answered and looked to Everett. "Almost a week?"
Everett shrugged. "Almost."

"And he's taken you to some of his favorite places?"

I drew my eyebrows together. "Well, he said he hadn't been to the Grand Canyon before."

"He hasn't." She took a sip of her soda. "But he said he took you to the Four Corners?"

I looked at Everett. "You'd already been there before?" Something about that bothered me.

Bridget interrupted, "Only with family. And he took you to see the dinosaur tracks?"

I looked away from Everett to the table. Part of me was angry. Part of me felt betrayed. I had no right to feel either, but I did. "Yes, we saw the dinosaur tracks and the river." Bridget nodded, completely oblivious to the unwanted pain I was feeling, knowing he'd lied to me.

Everett squeezed my hand under the table but I needed distance. Not much distance could be achieved when we were so close to one another, but I still wriggled my fingers free from his.

"I didn't know he'd seen those places before," I said, still staring down at the table. There was silence between Everett and Bridget and I felt even more uncomfortable. So I shrugged and blurted, "Not that it's a big deal or anything." I didn't dare look at Everett. Something had shifted between us with Bridget's admission about Everett having been to those places before. And I didn't want to think about it.

When the waiter brought our drinks and took our orders, nothing else had been said. It was the most uncomfortably awkward silence. And then a boy, about eight or nine years old, bounded up to the table. "Mom, do you have more quarters I can have?"

"Hey bud," I heard Everett's voice, but my attention was on the boy.

"Uncle Everett!" he exclaimed, wrapping his arms around

Everett's neck. I couldn't avoid looking at Everett. His eyes were closed and his arms wrapped around the boy, the boy who looked so much like him that it was uncanny. My chest felt tight with emotion as I watched their reunion.

Everett pulled a handful of quarters from his pocket and poured them in the hand of the little boy. That was when the little boy noticed me, staring at me with his guileless blue eyes. "Hi," he said, cocking his head to the side, the way Everett did when he was studying me. I ached then.

"Hi," I croaked. I swallowed. "I'm Parker. What's your name?"

"Clark," he answered. "How'd you get your scar?"

I heard Bridget suck in a breath. This was why I liked kids, they said things that made other people uncomfortable. Adults made me uncomfortable, but not kids.

So I said what I told all the little kids who ever asked. "Shark attack."

There was silence from Everett and Bridget, but Clark's entire face lit up. "Cool!" he exclaimed. He turned to Bridget. "Mom, isn't that cool?"

Bridget nodded slowly. "Sure is. Why don't you go play some more in the arcade and check back here in a few minutes?"

Clark didn't need to be told twice. He was gone from the table, leaving us adults in our awkward silence.

"Thanks," Bridget finally said. I looked up at her. "You're going to be his hero now."

"It's a nicer story than being attacked with a knife," I said, sipping my drink. I watched Bridget exchange glances with Everett. This was becoming unbearable.

Bridget sighed. "Everett, can you go check on Clark?"

Everett climbed out the booth. I could feel him looking at me, but I aggressively avoided looking at him. I knew Bridget had asked him to leave for a reason. After he left, I looked at her. As someone who enjoyed studying people, I was able to pick up on a lot of body language cues. And Bridget's body language was telling me to be prepared. I sat up straight.

"Everett's told you about his cancer." It wasn't a question.

I nodded. "And his decision going forward from his diagnosis."

Bridget nodded. "What do you think about it?"

This was going to be a heavy conversation. "When he first told me, I didn't understand." I took a sip from my straw, formulating my response. "And then he told me," I started. Ugh. This was going to be even more uncomfortable. "He told me about when he had this cancer as a teenager. And how he felt like his family fell apart because of it."

Bridget pursed her lips, nodding slowly, absorbing all that I was saying. "Well, our family did fall apart. But Everett likes to blame it on himself. He's got a touch of dark on his soul, just a touch, but you'd think his soul was black with how he won't forgive himself for something he had no control over in the first place."

"Everett likes control."

"He does," Bridget agreed. "That's why he's choosing this. Choosing not to have the surgery, choosing not to fight. He wants the choice. But it's the wrong one."

Whoa. I didn't know how to respond to that.

Bridget sighed and sat back in the booth. "How much has Everett told you about his tumor? The one he has right now?"

"Not much. Just that it's decently sized and in his forehead, where I'm assuming his last one was, based on the scar."

"Everett hasn't had the tumor evaluated. Not extensively. His doctors are here in Texas, the doctors that treated his cancer the first time. He saw an oncologist in California a month ago. Had a CT scan. The doctor recommended a biopsy, but Everett said no. He said he was done. But," Bridget put her hand on the table, "he doesn't even know what kind of tumor it is. He has no clue! It could be something so treatable, and he's choosing not to do anything about it."

This was all new information. I had assumed Everett had checked it out thoroughly before deciding not to deal with it. "Then why was he so quick to decide not to operate?"

"You didn't see him go through cancer when he was a teenager. It was, well, devastating. He lost so much weight. He lost a lot of himself. He lost friends and his family fell apart. Physically, the cancer weakened him. Emotionally, in his mind, the cancer destroyed his life itself. And treating his cancer took away his memory." I watched her fingers trace the wood grain on the table top. "Everett had an exceptional memory growing up. He remembered people he'd met only briefly, years later. He always did well in school. After the surgery, he had trouble with his short term memory. He forgot everything that had happened in the months prior to the surgery."

I nodded, letting this all sink in.

"Everett," she continued, looking to the arcade that was adjacent to the restaurant. "Everett is a good man. A very good man, Parker. He's kind, he's giving, and he's selfless. But he doesn't see those things in himself. He sees a man who tore apart a family. I wouldn't say he is depressed, but like all of us, he does have his demons. But his demons are robbing him of a future that may very well exist."

This conversation was causing me pain. I felt betrayed by Everett. For not telling me about having visited all those locations we visited. For not telling me his real, more meaningful reasons, for not having the surgery. But again, I didn't feel like I had the right to be upset, to feel betrayed. I sat back in the seat.

Bridget leaned across the table. "I haven't told you anything in confidence. You're free to discuss this with Everett if you'd like." She looked to the arcade before looking back at me again. "I've never met any of Everett's girlfriends before."

My eyes widened. "I'm not his girlfriend."

"I know." She licked her lips. "But you're the closest thing he's ever had to one."

Before I could reply, Everett had joined us at the booth again. Bridget and I lapsed into silence while Everett looked between us both. "Did you have a nice chat?" he asked, seeming unconcerned. He had to have known we talked about him.

"Sure did," Bridget said, winking at me. "We talked about what an idiot you are."

"Parker doesn't think I'm an idiot," he said, pointing a thumb at me.

"No. You're just an asshole."

"A rude asshole," Everett clarified, angling his head towards his sister.

"Well you are that," she agreed with a straight face and a wink to me.

The waiter delivered our food, but Clark was still in the arcade. "His dad fed him lunch before we came, so he'll likely spend the entire lunch in the arcade," Bridget apologized.

"He's a kid," I said, shrugging. "He's got his priorities."

"He does." Bridget smiled softly. "Where are you two headed next?" She seemed genuinely interested.

I was still conflicted in my feelings towards Everett, so I stayed quiet while he spoke up. "We're headed to New Orleans next."

My head popped up at that. New Orleans was like a gold mine for people like me, people who loved to watch other people. But I kept my eyes away from looking at Everett.

"What are you going to do there?" Bridget asked between bites.

I felt Everett's shoulders shrug next to me. "Stuff," he replied, before taking a bite of his slice of pizza.

"Stuff?" Bridget asked, an eyebrow raised. "That's it? That's all I get?"

"I'll take pictures. I'll send them to you," he said, waving his hand to brush the conversation aside. That reminded me of the photo we took in the Picketwire Canyon.

"We've already taken one photo," I said, staring at my plate, "of us under an arch." Everett stiffened, halting in taking another bite. He knew what I thought of, what I would think of, every time I looked at that photo. But it felt personal, too personal to say aloud.

"Oh?" Bridget asked, apparently unaware of the thoughts that were sucking up space in mine and Everett's memory. "I want to see." She leaned over the table. "The arch in the canyon?"

"Here," Everett said, handing her the camera from under the table. I didn't know he'd brought it with him.

Bridget set her fork down and wiped her hands on her napkin before grabbing the camera greedily. I watched her start to scroll through the photos. She stopped and looked up at Everett for a second before focusing again on the camera. I hadn't realized Everett had taken more than one photo.

"Ah," she said. She looked up at us both. She seemed to want to say something, but stubbornly set her lips in a line before handing the camera back to Everett.

"I want to see," I said, reaching an arm out to intercept the camera. Everett tried to take it from me but I yanked it away. I stared down at the screen on the back of the camera. I saw the arch, and I saw Everett leaning towards me, an arm wrapped around me. His face was facing mine, his lips at my ear. The expression on my face could have been described as serene. I couldn't help but close my eyes, remembering.

"Everyone who sees this photo will see us under the arch. But when you see this photo, you'll see the canyon and the water and all the beauty in front of us. Remember that, Parker. When you look at this photo, remember looking at purgatory with me. While everyone else was looking at the arch, we were looking at that."

I opened my eyes and looked at Everett for the first time since he'd left the table. He was staring at me with feeling. I wasn't sure what the feeling was, but I knew it was likely the same thing I felt. I licked my lips, unable to look away.

"I already took care of the check. Clark has soccer practice, so

I have to get going." Bridget's voice interrupted the haze I was in while staring at Everett.

"We'll walk you out," Everett said, reaching a hand to pull me out. There he was again, tugging me. I followed.

When we got to the parking lot, I let go of Everett's hand, lagging back so he could visit with his sister a bit. Clark ran ahead to the car while Everett and his sister talked.

"I wish you'd come to dinner with us tonight," Everett said, putting an arm around her shoulders. I watched her look at him wistfully. "It's my shift tonight, and I can't get anyone to cover. And besides, you know how dad is. I'd rather not watch him embarrass himself or attempt to embarrass me."

Everett nodded, sighed, and then ran a hand through his hair. They both turned to look back at me and I turned away, trying to pretend I hadn't heard.

"She's good, you know?" Bridget said, still looking at me.

My skin itched.

"Yeah, I know she is," Everett replied.

My stomach burned. Everett reached down, hugged her. I turned my body completely away from them, looking at the other people milling about the parking lot.

"What's this?" Bridget said. I kept my back to them, feeling uncomfortable witnessing their exchange. There was silence, and then I heard her say. "They say that's bad luck."

Curiosity was whispering in my head to look, to see what they were talking about. But I was stubborn, and kept my back to them.

"I'll take my chances," Everett replied, laughing. I turned around and Everett was hugging Bridget again. I watched her face go from happy to sad the moment she had her arms around him. Her arms were so tight that she shook. I turned my face away again, not wanting to see this moment between Everett and his sister. Too much.

"Parker," she said. I opened my eyes and looked at her. She had her arms out for me. Reluctantly, I walked the few feet towards her and let her wrap her arms around me. My own arms felt awkward, like sludge, so I lifted them up and self-consciously patted her back. I looked at Everett while she hugged me, curious by the way he was staring at us.

"I hope to see you again," she said, pulling away and looking me in the eyes. It was a loaded goodbye. I didn't know how to answer so I just watched her walk away towards her car.

"Have you been hugged often?"

I shook my head and looked at Everett. "What?"

"It's a simple question. Has anyone hugged you? Growing up, did your foster parents hug you? Did your teachers? Boyfriends?"

I didn't need to think about it. "No."

Everett nodded as if he expected that answer. "Not even your boyfriends?"

I thought of my boyfriends. I'd never had an emotional connection with any of them. It was never about that. So we didn't hold hands, hug, or be affectionate unless it was a prequel to the main event.

"No."

"That's a damn shame."

"No it's not."

He stepped closer to me. I took a step back. "Don't run," he whispered, his eyes engaged with mine.

"I'm not."

"You want to."

He wasn't wrong. He reached his hand for mine and I placed it in his with a little apprehension. "Let's go," he said, breaking the spell he'd had me under.

I let him lead me towards the Jeep. He walked me to the passenger door but before he opened the door, he pulled me to him and wrapped his arms around me.

My heart fell, landing in the pit of my stomach. I closed my eyes, felt his lips at my ear. "You haven't be hugged enough, my precious." His joking nickname for me didn't feel like a joke this time. He squeezed his arms tighter, so tight I couldn't move.

At first, I resisted. I tried to pull back. The feel of his arms around me, squeezing me was overwhelming. But then something changed within me and I found myself relaxing.

Even more shocking, I found my arms gliding up his back, holding on to him myself. It was comforting. And warm. I wanted to live, really live, in this moment. So with my eyes closed, I committed this moment to my memory. His cool water scent. The muscles of his back under my fingertips. His breath at my ear. When he pushed his lips to my hair, my heart was volleyed from my stomach to my throat.

Chapter 21

We checked into a hotel before dinner with Everett's parents. I thought it was a little odd to go to dinner with both of them, considering they were divorced, but Everett seemed like it wasn't a big deal. But it made me curious of Everett's father, about what Bridget had said.

I dressed in the pink dress I'd borrowed/stolen from Jasmine, the one I'd worn the night I met Everett. When I exited the bathroom, Everett was sitting in the chair by the bed, rubbing his head. I watched him from the doorway a minute, worrying about him. The range of emotions Everett brought out of me ranged from good things to things that hurt. The worrying hurt. I never wanted this, this pull of responsibility, to make another human happy.

His head lifted up and he stared at me, blinking. "You're not Sarah."

"No." A smile ached to spread my lips, remembering the night we met.

He stood up and walked towards me. "You're beautiful, you know. I've told you before, but you like to shake your head." He put a hand on the side of my neck. "Stop shaking your head. Let me give you a compliment."

His hand was warm around my neck and a second later, his other hand went to my waist. My eyes opened when his fingers rubbed there, right over the bandage.

"This is where your tattoo is," he said, a smile playing on his lips.

I nodded. "Where's yours?"

"You'll see it later."

I frowned, a little annoyed. His finger came to the space between my eyebrows and he rubbed. "Don't frown. I'd rather see you smile."

"You said I'd look weird with one," I reminded him.

"Doesn't mean I still don't want to see it. Or be the reason for it." He dropped a kiss on my lips. "Let's go."

When we arrived at the restaurant, Everett's parents were already waiting. I watched them with interest before the hostess led us to them. His father had his arm over the back of his mom's seat and was watching her as if she was the only thing in the world he could focus on. His hair was black, like Everett's, speckled with white. Everett's mom looked soft, youthful. She had pale blonde hair, curled softly around her face. Her eyes were the same blue as her children. When she saw Everett, it was as if something awakened in her. Her smile filled her face and she stood up to hug him. I watched her hold him tightly, as Bridget had, before I turned my attention to Everett's father.

Where Everett's mom was warm, Everett's father was cold unless he was looking at his ex-wife. He didn't glare daggers at me, but he seemed very impersonal, reaching a hand to me with a little reluctance. His eyes roamed my face without a smile. It was the first time in my life I was self-conscious about my scar.

Everett's mother hugged me next. The hugging was weird. A comforting kind of weird. While she hugged me, I watched Everett and his father exchange handshakes. It seemed odd again. But I remembered Everett saying his father was distant.

After introductions, I sat down with Everett to my left, putting me directly across from Everett's mom, Patricia.

Patricia propped her elbows on the table and set her chin on top of her hands while she gazed at her son. There was no doubt of her love for him. And by the way he'd hugged her, there was no doubt of his for her. It made me a little breathless, to be a part of this, to so closely witness a mother and a son who loved each other. Parental love was foreign to me. And this was my first experience, witnessing it so closely.

Everett's father, whom Everett had called by his first name, Robert, had yet to warm up. He drank whiskey in a short glass and when the waiter came by the table, I noticed he asked for another. "Everett will have one too, and-"

"No, actually water is fine," Everett interrupted.

Robert looked over at him. "I'm buying," he said, as if that would be the only reason Everett would turn down a drink.

"I'm not drinking," Everett said, his voice firm. He looked over at me. "Water? With limes?"

I licked my lips and nodded. Maybe the acid from the limes burning my throat would keep my mouth shut from the acid that would want to spill out during this dinner. Judging by the way Robert looked at Everett, it was going to be a long dinner.

When the waiter left, Patricia looked between us. "Everett tells me you've been to the Grand Canyon," she said, looking at me with excitement, her eyes sparkling.

Before I could open my mouth, Everett said, "Yeah, but it was just a big hole in the ground."

"Oh, that's too bad," Patricia answered, her forehead creasing in disappointment. I kicked Everett as discreetly as possible from under the table. "We never made it there on our trip. Everett got too sick."

"When you went to the Four Corners?" I asked, remembering

what Bridget had said about visiting there with Everett once before.

"Yes," she said, smiling wistfully. "It was his wish trip."

"Waste of a trip too," Robert butt in. I tried to suppress my shock, but Patricia merely tsked him.

"It was not a waste," she admonished him.

"It kind of was," Everett said. I turned to look at him. I wasn't following the conversation and knew I'd missed out on something.

Patricia sighed but before she could say anything, I blurted out, "Why was it a waste?"

"Because he can't remember it," Robert said, gesturing towards Everett with his whiskey. "We spent a week touring the southwestern states and after the surgery, poof!" He gestured an explosion with his hands. "It was wiped from his memory."

I let that sink in. And then I turned to Everett. "That six months you lost?"

He turned his head, nodded. Everything was starting to make sense. Everett had lost the memories from that trip. And he was experiencing it again, anew, with me. His eyes were concentrating on mine. My hand that was on my lap moved to his thigh and I squeezed and nodded my head once, indicating I understood.

Before I could move my hand from his lap, his hand laid on top of it. And then he squeezed, three times. Like he had outside the tattoo shop.

I turned my attention back to his parents. Robert was focused on his drink, but Patricia had clearly watched our exchange. "Tell me about yourself, Parker," she said kindly.

"There's not much," I answered. And I was bothered by that. Bothered by knowing there wasn't much. I'd seen more of living in the last week since meeting Everett than I had in the last three years. I cleared my throat. "I'm a waitress. Or," I frowned, "I was a waitress. I'm going to school for anthropology." And that was it. That was all that I was.

Everett squeezed my hand under the table again. "She's funny," he said to his mother, but looking at me. "She's really stubborn and smart." He lifted his free hand to brush my hair from my face. I couldn't breathe. His blue eyes penetrated mine. "She's clumsy, but she's strong." His hand on mine squeezed again. My chest was tight, aching. "She'll tell you she doesn't care, but she does. It's just deeper than the surface." The hand that had brushed away my hair was resting on my shoulder. "That's what's so great about her. She's not artificial. When she feels, it's real. She's real, down to the bone." His eyes were soft, warm, and it hurt to keep looking into them. He squeezed my hand a third time. "She's the warmest person I know." Under his gaze, I was transparent.

Everett smiled, but it was a sad smile. I blinked rapidly, trying to chase away the liquid that had formed in my tear glands. And I looked away, over my right shoulder, inhaling a deep breath. When I turned back to the table, Patricia was staring at me with what I could only describe as elation. It felt like another obligation to me, however. Once you made someone happy, you were obligated to keep them that way. It was a responsibility I didn't want. I didn't want to own a piece of anyone's happiness.

Nothing would come of me and Everett. He said I was stubborn, but he was more so. He'd rather die than live. And that realization caused me to excuse myself from the table.

I first went to the restroom, thrust my hand in the cool water from the sink, trying to cool any part of my body. But then I felt like I couldn't breathe. My chest hurt, my head hurt. The dress was too tight, the air was too recycled. I was breathing in air that had been inhaled and exhaled repeatedly. I needed real, honest air.

I stumbled outside, into the dark parking lot. My ankle was still a little swollen from the fall at the canyon the day before, and walking on gravel that badly needed repair while wearing heels was not exactly smooth sailing.

I walked all the way into the parking lot, out to Everett's Jeep. It was parked near the back, so I hobbled my way to it, intending to change into the flip flops I'd left in the backseat. I peered in the windows of the Jeep, unable to see my flip flops through the darkness.

It was at that moment that I felt something, something in my brain that warned me to pay attention. I turned around, looking over my shoulder. There was a man watching me from about twenty feet away. I couldn't make out his features because he was standing between two vehicles, shadowed, watching me. I braced a hand on the Jeep, feeling the warmth of it under my hand. And then a memory came through.

I was looking in my car windows while unlocking the door when he came up behind me. I couldn't see his face. Only the reflection of his hooded head facing the window I was looking into. I spun around, hitting him with my purse. He moved away for a second and my eyes scanned the parking lot, looking for help anywhere.

My eyes focused from the nightmare to real life. The man standing between the two vehicles was staring at me. His features blurred. All I could see what a hoodie. I screamed and the memory came back to me in stunning clarity.

"Get away from me!" I screamed. My voice sounded unnatural, animalistic. I felt the heat of my car at my back as I held my purse up, ready to hit him again. My hand trembled, the surge of fear and adrenaline mating in my veins rendering me unstable.

"You won't be doing that again." His voice. Oh god, his voice. It sounded like he swallowed sandpaper. It was deep, and there was no mistaking the threat it promised. That's when I saw the glint of what he had in his hand. He held it up, the one small light in the parking lot reflecting off of the knife. "Give me your keys. Get in the car. Shut up, or I will cut you open." The way he said that word, said "cut" was enough to make my blood run ice cold.

A sob tore from my throat and my knees shook so hard I fell onto the concrete. His arm grasped mine and he took the keys from my fingertips. The next thing I knew, he'd hauled me to my feet and shoved me from the driver's door to the passenger seat. It had to be a nightmare, I told myself. I willed myself to wake up. But this wasn't a nightmare. This was reality. My entire body was shaking. I couldn't process what was happening. Fear was prominent, it was keeping me from feeling anything else.

He pushed the knife to my neck. "Don't try anything stupid," he warned, pushing the tip of the knife into my flesh. I felt the prick from it slicing my skin. When he pulled the knife back, I saw my blood on its tip. "Just sit in that seat," he spat. His saliva hit my face in a spray and I closed my eyes, swallowing back the vomit that climbed up my throat.

He put the car into gear while I shuddered a breath. I felt the shock sliding from my shoulders, felt it leaving my brain, and then my synapses started firing off. When the shock completely left my body, several minutes had passed, and we were well on our way out of town. He had plans for me, I knew. My brain was now in fight mode.

I didn't think. I just grabbed the steering wheel and pulled it, swerving the car up onto a curb, jolting me against the door. My head slammed against the door window and I saw stars, but I forced myself to stay awake.

The man's eyes bugged out of his head. I couldn't make their color, but the whites of his eyes were so overwhelmingly dominant beneath the hoodie that fear choked my throat again, right before one of his hands clamped and squeezed that spot itself. He alternated his eyes from the road to me as he settled the car back onto the road and increased his speed. "Are you stupid?" he screamed. His eyes were bulging, like a cartoon nightmare.

I grinded my teeth. I would not die this way. I would not. Vomit threatened again and instead of swallowing it, I turned my head to him and let it go.

The next ten seconds were a blur. The knife cut my face first as he reached blindly for me, the car still speeding. I turned my head so he caught my cheek, felt the blood trickling down my face a second later. I reached for the handle of the door and heard the swish of the knife by my head. The sound it made as it cut the air, desperate to gain purchase on my skin, made my skin burn with shock.

I swung my arm to block a hit that was aimed for my face, felt the knife cut my arm. I could barely hear a word he yelled over my screaming. I reached blindly, touched skin that didn't belong to me and dug my nails in. I felt the flesh ripping under my fingertips and vomited again. And then I reached for the door handle behind my back with one hand and pushed it out. Another sob, a sob of relief, fell from my lips as I fell out of the car, hitting the pavement and rolling.

I heard the slam of his breaks. Heard him swearing. And then I heard another noise. A gun shot. Steps running. Tires squealing. A shout. I smelled rubber burning, but my eyes were throbbing, coated in blood and tears; I couldn't open them. I was in and out of consciousness when I smelled the smoke and coffee. "Fuck." It was a woman's voice. "Fuck fuck fuck." I felt her going through my pockets. I made a noise, but everything hurt. Every movement ached. Breathing was exhausting me. I heard her clapping and the sound made me open one eye.

"Mouse."

I came out of the memory screaming, my hands on my face.

"Shh," a voice said. I pushed against it, screaming, my hands punching anything they could reach. "Parker," the voice said.

Everett. I stopped fighting and clung to him. We were sitting on the ground, in the parking lot, so I climbed into his lap, my fingers searching for him. "Everett," I breathed.

"You're safe, Parker. You're safe." I clung to that while my breathing evened out. Terror still wracked my veins, but I knew what Everett said was true. I was with him. I was safe.

"Do you need us to call an ambulance?" I opened my eyes and

looked around. We weren't alone. There was a small crowd in the parking lot. The voice stepped forward and I recognized it as the hostess of the restaurant.

I buried my head into Everett's shoulder. "No, we're fine thank you," he said.

Embarrassed, I held tighter to Everett, pulling his dress shirt to its breaking point. He lifted my head, forcing me to look at him. "Everyone is watching us," I said, embarrassment overpowering the terror that was slowly leaving my veins.

"I'm watching you." He held my face, running his fingers over my cheekbones and my lips. "I'm watching you, always."

It reminded me of our first dance. He'd said the same thing then. So I concentrated completely on Everett, let the background drop off, out of my vision.

"Let's go back to the hotel," he said, dropping a kiss to my forehead. He walked me around to the passenger side of the car, out of view.

"Everett," I said, my voice slipping. I wrapped my arms around his neck, squeezing him. His arms immediately wrapped around my waist, his lips touched the side of my face. "I remember," I murmured against his neck.

"I know." He kissed my temple. "You're going to be okay." He held me a minute longer before pulling back. He touched his lips to mine briefly. "Now, it's time for you to heal," he whispered against my lips. And then he helped me into the car.

It wasn't until we were almost to the hotel that I realized I'd hugged him. I'd reached out, for comfort, from him.

Chapter 22

My knees were scuffed up from falling on the pavement. Everett sat me on the counter in our hotel bathroom and cleaned them. He kept looking at me from beneath his eyebrows, while he was bent over cleaning my knees.

"I'm sorry about dinner," I said, wincing with each touch to my knees.

Everett gave me his trademark, 'don't be stupid' look. It was a look filled with impatience. "Do you think I really care about dinner? My dad was so drunk that he was out of his mind anyway."

"I liked your mom."

"Who doesn't? She's the most self-sacrificing person in the world. She's given so much of herself and still has so much to give. There aren't many people like that. In fact, there are more people who abuse that, who take from those kinds of people." Everett tossed aside a dirty cotton ball. "My dad included."

I didn't know how to reply so I kept my mouth shut, chewing on my lip.

"What happened?" he asked.

I sucked in a breath when he dug a pebble out of my skin. "I couldn't breathe," I said. "I went outside for air and my ankle hurt, so I decided to change into flip flops before going back inside."

"Did you black out?"

"No," I frowned. "I had just reached the Jeep when I turned around and saw someone watching me from a shadowed area of the parking lot. I touched the door of the Jeep and then the memory came rushing to the surface."

"Did the man come any closer?"

I shook my head. "I honestly think he was harmless. But the memory was coming so fast that I panicked." I looked down at my knees. "I must have fallen."

"It's these damn shoes," he growled, pulling them off and tossing them out of the bathroom.

"I thought men liked women in heels."

Everett looked at me impatiently. "I like women – or more specifically, one woman – just the way she is. I don't need you to wear makeup or fancy clothes. It's not going to change how I see you." He stood up, satisfied with the state of my knees, and helped me down from the counter. "This," he said, running his fingers down my dress, "is perception. It's what my eyes see. But this," he pressed his hand to the center of my chest, just above the bust line of the dress, "is reality. I much prefer this. This," he said, pushing again, "this is what my soul sees."

I couldn't move my eyes away from him. My heart, the thing that I hadn't acknowledged all this time, swelled. It was my heart that was feeling all the things he did to me. The crack, the swell, it was my heart.

"Those things I said in the restaurant, what I said about you, it's all true. I can't lie. Sure, you're ornery and sometimes a brat. But you're good. You don't want to be, but you are. You're brave, and you stand up for yourself, even when you're wrong." He grinned. I narrowed my eyes. "But you stand by your opinion. You don't bend for anyone, not even me." His hands reached for my head, cradling it in his hands. He kissed me. And then he pulled away. "I do have a question though."

My head was tilted back, my eyes closed. I swallowed to relieve my suddenly dry throat. "What's that?"

"If fear triggered your memory, why hasn't it happened before?"

"I don't put myself in scary situations, I guess." I opened my eyes.

"But what about in Denver? When I pulled that..." Everett swallowed, seemingly uncomfortable with the memory. "When I pulled that man off of you. Why didn't your memory come back then?"

I thought about that moment, when I'd fallen and looked up at the sky. "Because the moment I felt fear, I remembered. I knew you were there, you called my name. I wasn't afraid, because I wasn't alone."

Everett's eyes were sad. I didn't like his sad eyes, I was realizing. I hadn't cared, not truly. And now I did. "What's wrong?"

I watched the muscles in his throat move as he swallowed. "I won't always be there."

"But you can try," I said. "You can try to fight it. You could have a long life."

Everett sighed and pulled me by the hand out of the bathroom, to the bed. He sat on the end and patted the spot next to him. "Sit by me."

I sat by him and watched him form his thoughts. "Have you ever seen 'Eternal Sunshine of the Spotless Mind', the movie with Jim Carrey and Kate Winslet?" he asked.

"I've heard of it, but I haven't seen it."

Everett pulled my hand onto his lap and held it between both of his. "Do you know what title means, where it comes from?"

I shook my head.

"There's this poem by Alexander Pope called 'Eloisa to Abelard' and it's based off the story of a woman named Heloise and her illicit love affair with her teacher, Abelard. Heloise/Eloisa and Abelard were doomed from the start. Her family believed he had bad intentions and they castrated him. The lovers were separated and Heloise was in such grief from it, from knowing that Abelard could no longer feel the same for her as she did for him. Alexander Pope described it in his this poem. I have it in my journal." He reached under his pillow and pulled out the journal. He flipped to the back of it, to the words he wrote on the back cover and handed it to me.

I read it aloud.

How happy is the blameless vestal's lot!
The world forgetting, by the world forgot.
Eternal sunshine of the spotless mind!
Each pray'r accepted, and each wish resign'd;

I looked at Everett, confused. "I don't know what this means."

Everett took his journal back from me. "It's told from Heloise, or Eloisa's, point of view. She begged, she prayed for forgetfulness. She was in anguish. She would rather forget than feel the pain. So in this section of the poem, she is happy because she's prayed for and received the gift of forgetting. The movie took the line from this poem, and it's about a couple who meet after having their memories erased of one another. They choose this willingly, to have their memories of each other erased." He set the journal by his pillow and stood up, pacing. "I've lost memories. I lost the good and the bad." He stopped pacing to look at me. "I lost memories of the trip I took with my family, the trip where everything was fine, right before it wasn't. I lost the memories from when we came home and my sister found out she was pregnant and my dad started sleeping on my grandfather's basement couch. I lost all of it." He sat back down next to me, grabbed my hand again and squeezed. "I planned this trip based on the spots I visited before, hoping it would trigger a memory and it would all come back to me, like fear did for you, tonight."

"And did it?"

He shook his head. "No. But something better happened. I created new memories. I danced with you in Las Vegas. I saw you take in the Grand Canyon and try to diminish it with words you didn't mean. I held you close to me while we stood in four states together, feeling your heart beat against mine. Giving you the hug you should have had years ago. And we sat under an arch and looked out over an area that was named for purgatory."

My breaths were shallow and I touched the space on my ribcage, where my new ink was.

He continued. "That moment was beautiful. You were beautiful." I had to turn my face away from him. All my feelings for Everett were materializing, and quickly, becoming solid and easily identifiable. He grabbed my face in his hand and turned me to face him. "It was sweet. It was a sweet moment for me," he said, staring into my eyes.

My chest hurt, my lips hurt, my eyes and my ears and my head hurt. I couldn't stop the pain. Couldn't stop the flood of feeling. And even more significant: I didn't want to.

"When you kissed me this morning, you did it with feeling, just like I asked," he said. His eyes stayed on mine, willing me to listen. "Another sweet moment."

I bit my lip to keep it from trembling. I opened my mouth but he put a finger up to it, quieting me. "Listen to me. If I had the surgery, there's a good chance I'd lose my memory forever, just like I did last time. This procedure would be more invasive, so I'd lose those moments. I'd be alive, but I wouldn't know who you were. I wouldn't remember how angry you were when I brought you to world's largest thermometer. I would never remember how it felt to dance with you in my arms. I would forget the moment I watched your eyes close at the Grand Canyon, how the sunlight lit up your features, making the Grand Canyon itself pale in comparison. I'd forget our bantering, and the sound you make when you laugh, even if it's scary as hell."

I laughed, a watery laugh, but a laugh nonetheless.

"See?" he said, smiling at me. "It sounds terrible. But look what it does to your face. You glow. I don't want to forget that. I'd forget the Four Corners, and the trip to Denver to meet Mira. I'd forget the way the blood rushed to my ears as I pulled that man off of you. The rage that filled me when I saw him knock you down. I don't want to forget that moment, because that's the moment I realized that you were important to me."

The first tear slipped from my eyes and I tried, futilely, to stop the rest.

"When you bandaged my knuckles and then we had sex in front of the mirror." I looked away at that, embarrassed. His fingers touched my chin and turned me to look at him. "I've told you that you look incredible when you come and you do. You're almost unearthly beautiful." He used his thumb to brush away the tear that slid down my cheek. "When we went on that tour through the canyon. I watched your face as I told you the history and then again when I told you to seal that view in your memory, so every time you looked at that photo, you'd remember how it felt, how it looked."

I knew I wouldn't forget that moment, not for the rest of my life.

"I'm not Eloisa. I don't want the gift of losing my memory. I want to remember it all, remember you. I would rather die with those memories in my mind, with your name on my lips, than have the surgery and wake up, forgetting the best times of my life, forgetting you. Ignorance isn't bliss."

More tears leaked from my eyes. I didn't know what to say.

"It's okay Parker. Be happy. You've given me happiness."

But I didn't want to give him happiness. I wanted to give him life, longer than the one he was on the path to live. I couldn't stop crying. The tears poured from my eyes and I nearly choked on a sob.

"Can I show you my tattoo now?" he asked softly.

I nodded through the tears.

He stood up, pulling off his shirt. My eyes slid up to the bandage just above the words on his ribcage. He slowly removed the bandage. It was my name, in bold block letters above the words, "This world has only one sweet moment set aside for us."

"You made a liar out of my tattoo, Parker."

I raised my eyes from my name on his chest to his face. "What do you mean?"

"I didn't get one sweet moment. I got handfuls of them."

I bit my lip again. I was still crying, but not as hard. "Do you want to see my tattoo?" I asked, choking on a sob.

"Of course I do."

"Help me unzip this," I said, turning around and holding up my hair.

He came up behind me and first placed a hand on the back of my neck. He squeezed gently on my neck before gliding his hand down to the top of the zipper.

When it was completely unzipped, I let my hair fall and turned around. I pulled the top of the dress down, clearing my breasts first. And then, after a deep breath for courage, I pulled it all the way down, pushing it over my hips to pool at my feet.

Everett was staring at the spot just under my left breast, on my ribs. He held a hand out for me and I grabbed it, thankful that he pulled me closer. His hand found the corner of the bandage. He looked at me, placed his other hand on the curve where my neck met my shoulder, and tugged the bandage.

I blew out a breath, from nerves, from the little lingering pain I still felt. He kept his eyes on me and threw the bandage behind us before leading me to sit on the bed. It was as if he knew, knew that the tattoo meant something more than just pretty ink on my skin. And then his eyes moved down and he sucked in a breath.

PurgatoirE

"Purgatoire," he breathed. His eyes moved up to mine. "The E is capitalized."

"The P and the E are both capitalized."

"Parker," he started, looking at the tattoo again.

"And Everett," I finished.

"Purgatoire. Purgatory."

I licked my lips. "It was the moment I started to feel again. You did that. It was my sweet moment."

He looked at me with feeling. And now I wasn't confused at what the feeling was, because I felt it too. It was the most solid feeling I'd ever felt, and the first time I'd ever felt it this deeply.

He stood up and leaned over me, kissing me, with feeling. When he gently laid me back on the bed, it was with feeling. When he kissed down my chest, he kissed me with feeling. Later, when he was inside of me, he stared into my eyes and his ice blue irises were warm, with feeling.

When Everett curled around me afterwards, his arm tight around my waist, he asked the question he asked the day before. But my answer had changed.

"Parker," he sleepily murmured against my neck. "Are you in love with me yet?"

I waited a minute, until his breaths were even and deep, signaling he'd fallen asleep.

"If I lied to you, I'd be breaking the rules. And if I told you the truth, I'd be breaking the rules."

Chapter 23

We woke up early the following morning and hit the road to New Orleans immediately. Everett's hand found mine across the console and held it. If the seven-hour drive taught me anything, it was that I never wanted to let go of his hand. My hand in his felt as natural as having another limb, and the loss of it would make my hand feel empty, for the rest of my life.

We strolled Bourbon Street together, holding hands. We ducked into little shops and walked across several blocks to have the famous beignets. We sat in City Park and people-watched. Everett made up stories about some of the strangers we observed. I laughed some more. It was coming more natural to me, though Everett still looked at me as if it was the strangest sound in the world.

While in a corner grocery store, Everett sent me a text, including an image of limes.

Asshole: Want some?

I laughed, knowing his name was still Asshole in my phone. Before I could reply, another text came through.

Asshole: I heard a noise. It sounded like a dying cat. Was that you?

I didn't feel anger or annoyance. A weight that had lived on my chest was lifted.

Me: And to think I'd considered changing your name in my phone. It still says, "Asshole."

Asshole: I never claimed to be anything else.

You know that moment you have, when you want to freeze time, right before everything falls apart? The awful thing is that you never know when that moment is. You look back on it and wish you'd committed more of it to memory. But you don't know that your world is about to tip on its axis.

For us, it was the moment we were back on Bourbon Street that evening, navigating our way through a sea of inebriated bar hoppers.

The air was warm and sounds from all the bars in the area were loud, messy noises, causing Everett to pull me into the middle of the street, away from the people swaying on the sidewalk. I pulled my tank top away from my chest to allow some air movement. Everett squeezed my hand three times and I let go of my tank top, looking at him.

"Why three?" I asked.

He looked at me and shook his head. Then, his eyebrows drew together and he put a hand by his ear, signaling he hadn't heard me.

I stepped closer to him. "Why three?" I asked again. I pulled away to look at him, but something was off about his expression. He was looking over my shoulder but I could tell he wasn't looking at anything. His eyes were blank.

"Everett?" I squeezed his hand. He didn't react. I looked around and pulled him over to the curb. "Sit down," I ordered, all but pushing him. His face was blank. And then his head turned to the left, came back, and turned to the left again. It was as if there was a rubber band, stretching his head to the left and snapping his head back straight.

"Everett," I said again. "What's happening?"

He wasn't looking at anything. His left arm lifted up and twitched, up and down. I didn't know what to do. And then he fell sideways to the sidewalk.

"Everett!" His entire body was convulsing, his eyes rolled to the back of his head so I only saw the whites of his eyes. I turned my head around, frantic. "Call an ambulance!" I screamed. His mouth was opened, but no sound was coming out.

"He's having a seizure," a woman said, crouching next to me. "Is he epileptic?"

I shook my head, watching him helplessly. Then he started grunting.

"Put his head in your lap, girl. There's too much glass around." I slid next to him, trying to put his head on my lap. The woman helped me, but Everett's spasms were getting worse, with his hands thrashing.

"Should I hold his hands?" I asked, my voice thick.

"No. Just wait. He'll come out of it." I watched her pull her phone out and call an ambulance.

Slowly, his seizing stopped. He blinked and looked at me. "Everett," I said.

I watched him open and close his mouth slowly, as if he was tasting something. But I saw recognition in his eyes, so I knew that was a good sign.

"He's coming out of it," I heard the woman say on the phone. I looked up at her gratefully but then her eyes widened. I turned back to Everett's head in my lap. He was convulsing again. His eyes were rolled back again and his body was thrashing so hard that I couldn't keep him in my lap.

"He's having another one," the woman said. This time, her

voice sounded more concerned than before.

Everett was making choking sounds at this point. "Everett," I whispered, my voice cracking. "Please, Everett." I didn't know what I was asking for. But a miracle would do.

By the time the ambulance arrived, Everett wasn't breathing.

I hated hospitals. I hated the waiting rooms. I hated that the water fountains were so far from the waiting rooms. I hated the smell and the sounds.

I hated that you had to wait to see a loved one. And I hated that I had someone in this hospital, a loved one. Mostly I hated that Everett wasn't here to see me hate everything. The girl who once embraced no emotions was now wrapped up in hate.

"You can see him now," a nurse in pink scrubs said. I tried not to sneer at her as I walked briskly past her. She'd been my nemesis when Everett had first come to the hospital and she'd barred me from his room. I'd been away from him for four hours at this point. I'd called his family and they were already on their way. But for now, it was just Everett and me.

I entered Everett's hospital room quietly, worried he was sleeping. My eyes saw a nurse in the corner, making notes, but I paid her little attention.

As soon as I came around the curtain, he was sitting there, in the bed, staring at me as if he'd been waiting to see me. He looked tired, completely spent, but he still had a smile for me. "Come here," he said, lifting the one free arm that didn't have tubes running through it.

I climbed in beside him, wrapping my arm around his waist, greedy for this, for him.

His hand touched my hair and he rubbed over it. "My precious."

I wanted to laugh and cry at the same time. "Everett," I said. Only, my words were a whisper. "Why?"

He held my hand in his, running his thumb over my knuckles. Even in a hospital bed, strapped to numerous machines, he was still soothing me. I'd always be broken. But being with Everett, I'd been okay being broken. He'd pushed me so hard, he'd smoothed out the sharper edges.

"Parker." It was said to grab my attention. His voice was weak, his speech was a little slurred, but he was still commanding. "I told you, I told you before this trip. I'm-"

"No." I nearly yelled it. The nurse looked at me with a sharp eye. "No," I said softer. "You're giving up. That's not a dignified way to die, dammit."

"I'm not giving up."

"Yes, you are." My voice was crumbling. The strength I summoned was noticeably absent. I swallowed tears, but they lodged in my throat. "You are, Everett. You can fight. You made me fight. You can, too."

Everett shook his head sadly. "Parker, listen. I fought for years. I've spent more of my life sick than not. I'm tired. I'm ready."

"I'm not." I choked this time. I brought my free hand up to my mouth. "God dammit, Everett. You made me feel. You made me want to live. You can't leave me."

He patted my hand with his hand. "I'm not leaving you, Parker. I need you to listen to me. Don't be a brat." I opened my mouth and he looked at me pointedly. "Listen to me. I wanted my one sweet moment. That's what this trip was about for me. But when I looked at you, watched the way your eyes closed at the Grand Canyon. The light lit up your face and your hair and all I could think about was how incredibly perfect, how incredibly sweet you looked. And then you opened your mouth and ruined it, but even still, it was all I could do to keep from kissing you breathless."

"I wish you had," I said, tears running down my face. "God, Everett. I wasted so much time,"

"Shhh," he urged. "Don't interrupt me. Remember that moment when you first laughed? I told you not to fall in love with me, and you laughed. I made fun of you then, but the way I felt when you laughed – I ached. You were so beautiful. It was the first sweet moment of my life. Knowing that I'd said something to pull you from the abyss of indifference."

I shook my head, opened my mouth to speak again but before I could, he spoke.

"Parker," his voice caught on my name, and my belly dipped. "You have no clue, do you? The effect you've had on me." He gripped my hand tighter, but his hand was still shaky. "I went on a road trip across the country, hoping to find one sweet moment somewhere along the way. Instead, I found them all in you. When we were in that canyon in Colorado and you fell. You were embarrassed when I carried you, when I fussed over your swollen ankle. I never cared, not for people, not the way I cared for you then. I think that's when I first started." He tugged my hand, making sure I was paying attention. "That's when I first slipped off the rocky edge, when I first fully embraced falling in love with you. It hurt, you know. Loving you. It hurts now. But I'd rather suffer through this pain in my final moments than suffer through being alone, from living a life unfilled. I don't want the eternal sunshine of a spotless mind. I want your laugh, your touch, and the way you kiss me. I want them to fill my mind. It's a lot of sweetness to live on."

I couldn't help it. A sob wrenched from my throat. "You are such an asshole, Everett," I said, hiccupping on a sob. "I didn't want to feel. I just wanted you to change your mind!"

"Well now you feel. And that gives me happiness. I want to see you hurting. I'd rather see you in pain than numb to everything, like you were when we met. I'm so glad I helped you feel again, Parker. That is the sweetest moment of them all."

Love, the emotion that should elicit healing, was in fact the most painful emotion of them all. It crept in when you didn't want it. Made itself at home, terrorizing your hormones with confusion. It made you more susceptible to pain, it weakened your resolve while simultaneously making you frantic with need. And it hurt. Not just mentally, but physically. My heart was aching, it was breaking, and I was so very angry with Everett, with love.

I wanted to punch him, to make him physically feel the pain I was emotionally feeling. Instead, my head fell to his chest on the bed and I sobbed. The tears were long suppressed, coming freely from my eyes. It was years of grief being released at once and it was the most overwhelming moment of my life. It was the first time I cried for anyone. It was the first time I loved anyone.

"Do you love me?" he asked. This time, I could answer without sarcasm.

"I hate you, Everett."

"Good."

I pushed my forehead against his chest, squeezing my eyes shut. "I hate you so much."

"Good," he said again.

I lifted my eyes and stared at him, anger, hurt, fear, and one more thing in my eyes. "I love you and I hate you and I am so fucking mad at you, Everett."

His hands were on face, cupping my cheeks and pulling me to him. He kissed me then. It was an I-love-you, an I-hate-you, and most of all, a goodbye kiss. Tears slipped from my eyes so freely, it was a never ending waterfall, slipping over our lips. Everett pulled back and then crushed my lips to his once more. Again and again. As soon as he felt ready to stop kissing me, he wasn't. His lips fell onto mine like gravity. But I couldn't be his gravity. I couldn't keep him.

It was excruciating. I finally pulled back and sobbed, my hands gripping his hospital gown. My eyes closed and I cried, my tears soaking his gown.

"I hate you," I said again.

"I know." His hand brushed my hair soothingly. "I'm glad you do."

"Why did you do this to me?" I asked. My heart was aching so intensely. I couldn't breathe. The pain wracking my body was worse than anything I'd ever felt.

"Because I want you to live. Your life is a gift, Parker. Live while you can. Smile, dance, see the world, fall in love-"

"Shut up!" I couldn't keep my voice down. "I already did fall in love, you asshole. You made it so fucking easy. I hate you, I hate you, I hate you." My voice broke on the last three words and I stood up, looking around. I couldn't think. My head and my heart were so full of pain that thinking clearly was not an option. I wanted to scream.

I looked at him, accusation in my eyes. "I wanted to spend the rest of my life with you." It was the truth, and it was painful to say, to admit.

"Isn't it enough to spend the rest of mine with you?" he asked, his eyes pleading.

"No. It's not." I rubbed a hand over my face. "I don't want to be in a world where you don't exist."

"But I will, Parker. You've made sure of that. I'll be at the Purgatoire River. Come here." He held his arms out for me and I climbed in his bed again, not wanting to ever leave. "I'll be here." His hand touched the spot my tattoo was on. "And most importantly to me, I'll be here." He touched my heart. "You're not ten below zero, Parker. Not in here. You're warm. A little broken, but warm." His lips pressed against my head. "And you'll have me in here. In your memories."

My lip trembled and I choked on a sob. "We never made it to the east coast. You wanted to make it to the east coast."

"Go there for me. Dip your toes in the Atlantic. Visit Central Park. People-watch."

I rubbed my eyes with the back of my hand. "I don't want to go there alone." I stood up and walked away, trying to get some distance.

"Don't you remember what I just told you? I'll be with you."

I shook my head. "It's not the same and you know it." I took a deep breath.

"Parker, I bought your plane ticket back home."

I stopped pacing, stopped looking around and brought my eyes back to his. "What did you say?"

"Your plane ticket home is in your email. You leave tonight."

"What are you talking about?" My voice was up several octaves and I saw the nurse move towards me.

Everett held up a hand to the nurse and then he turned to me. "I told you, if you fell in love, your ass would be on a plane. And it will be. In four hours."

I was speechless. I stared at Everett like he'd grown another head. I shook my head, over and over, back and forth.

"Yes," he insisted.

"I don't want to go." I placed a hand on my stomach and the other on my mouth. This pain, this was worse than anything. "I don't want to leave you."

"You won't." His eyes, though tired, were bright. His hand slid up to his chest. "I have your name on my chest now. When my heart stops, you'll still be here, permanently, on my skin." His hand slid off his chest and a look of peace came over his face. "It's a superficial representation of what's already on my soul."

I shook my head again. "I don't care. I don't-" I swallowed. I didn't think I was strong enough for this.

"I don't want you here for this, Parker. I don't want you to remember me like this."

I collapsed into the chair beside his bed and sobbed into my hands. This was more than I could physically bear. I lifted my head to see him again, my nose running and my tears tracking a hundred lines on my face.

"Come here," Everett said, his voice breaking again. He opened his arms and I climbed into the bed a third time. He wrapped his arms around me and held me tight, squeezing me. He was always pulling me to him. I wanted to pull him to me, to keep him.

"I love you, Parker. More than I've ever loved anything. I am so thankful for that text, so thankful it was you who replied. I'm thankful you drove halfway across the country with me. But most of all, I'm thankful for what you've given me. It's been the best time of my life. And it wasn't all the pit stops or the main attractions. It was you. It was always, only you."

I didn't think I would ever stop crying. My hands balled into fists against his chest. "Then fight, dammit. If not for you, fight for me. I need you."

"You don't, Parker. You're strong. You're a fighter. You're brave and beautiful and ornery and so many things. You don't need me."

I knew then, with absolute certainty, that nothing I could say would change his mind. He was done, he wasn't going to fight. I pushed my lips to his chest and squeezed my eyes tight. "I need to go then. Now." I held his hand and he squeezed three times. The moment he let go would be it. I'd lose a limb.

I tugged.

He let go of me, albeit hesitantly. I stood up and walked to the door. But before I reached the handle, I turned around.

Everett was right when he said I was stubborn. But I was right about this.

"Everett," I said. He lifted his head to me. His eyes were tortured, red-rimmed. "If you die, I'm the only one with our memories. But if you have the surgery, if you lived, you might lose them. But you'd be alive. I'd still have those memories. And I'd still have you."

And then I left, without looking back.

Chapter 24

Two months later

I received a box in the mail a few days earlier. The return address was Dallas and the sender was Bridget. But I couldn't open it. It sat in my bedroom untouched. It wasn't very big, but I was afraid of it. Loving Everett brought with it a range of emotions. I was a wreck. From anger to fear to happiness to love. I felt them all. And they hurt, all the time. Feeling things was painful. But if I had learned anything, it was that every bit of good came from a little bit of pain. I wouldn't be like Eloisa. I'd choose the memories of Everett and live through the pain. Because at least I was living.

My dreams were either replays our trip or an alternate reality. Where Everett lived. He wore all black and had a new scar on top of the old one and we spent a weekend in the Picketwire Canyonlands, a weekend in purgatory, together. That was my favorite dream, the one that made me cry whenever I woke up. Because my reality was often a nightmare.

Carly and Jasmine had invited me to go out with them a few times since I'd returned. But I couldn't. I was a different person in many ways, but I wanted to avoid people as much as possible.

That box in the corner of my room was a lot like me. Filled with Everett, but afraid to open up. It could collect dust in the corner of my room forever.

I testified against Morris Jensen. I sat on the stand, answered the questions from the county prosecutor. He pulled up photos of me from when I'd been brought to the hospital. I stared at those photos and ached for the girl I was when they were taken. Ached for the years of indifference I would embrace. I removed my suit jacket partway into questioning, to let them all see the scars that Morris Jensen left on my body.

I avoided looking at Morris the entire time. When the defense attorney questioned me, I answered all the questions, but Morris' fate was already sealed. If it hadn't been sealed by the DNA evidence under my nails, it was sealed with Mira's testimony.

She'd taken the stand, unhappily. When I'd returned to California, I asked her about the shot I'd heard in my flashback.

She'd looked at me with impatience, but also with resignation. "Yeah, I shot at him," she'd answered, pursing her lips. "He'd have died if he hadn't gone to the ER. So he fucked himself with that."

Mira had testified and her gun was used as evidence, confirming that the bullet found in Morris Jensen's abdomen belonged to Mira's gun. Mira wasn't charged with a crime, but she'd received a bit of heat for not coming clean sooner. I felt bad about that, but Mira shrugged it off.

"I'm moving anyway," she said as we left the courtroom.

"With Six?"

She looked at me like she was annoyed for me asking. But she was coming to see that I'd changed. I'd hardened a little. She teasingly called me a rat, saying it was more appropriate than mouse. And then she'd sighed. "Six has a lot going on right now. I'm not sure that I should hang around him." I didn't push her for more information, because that was practically a heartfelt confession from her in and of itself.

When I came home from the trial, I stared at that box in the corner of my room with contempt. And then my phone rang.

I didn't recognize the number, but the caller ID said it was Texas. My heart roared in my chest and my finger shook over the Answer button.

"Hello?"

"Parker." A woman's voice. I sat on the bed, overcome with emotion. I'd wanted to hear his voice. But this was likely the reason I couldn't.

"This is she."

"It's Bridget."

The breath left my mouth. "Bridget." I said her name with equal parts dread and hope.

"Can you come to Texas?"

My heart burned. "When?"

"Right now. I'll buy your ticket if you need me to-"

"No, I'm already coming," I said, not bothering to change my clothes. I rushed out the door with my purse in one hand and my phone to my ear. "Should I call this number when I land?"

There was a rush of relief in her voice. "Yes. Yes. Text me your flight details when you get to the airport."

I didn't ask for any other information. I didn't want to cry on the flight. I didn't want to be the object of anyone's interest. I only wanted to get to Texas as soon as possible. I could cry then, with confirmation from Bridget.

By the time Bridget met me in front of Arrivals at the airport, I was a wreck. She climbed out of the car and threw her arms around me. She was shaking and crying in my arms, so I started crying and shaking too, feeling a loss deep in the pit of my belly.

Everett was gone.

We held one another, limbs shaking, tears soaking our cheeks.

I wanted to scream.

By the time she pulled away, my entire face was covered in

tears. I couldn't see her, couldn't stop the flood from my eyes. As the tears slowly subsided, I inhaled in deeply.

I was wiping the last of them away with the back of my hand when I saw her face.

Or more specifically, the smile on her face. "Thank you," she said, her eyes brighter from the tears, the smile wider than I had ever seen.

My heart stumbled. "What did I do?" I wiped away more evidence of my grief as I felt the first glimmer of hope.

"Everett had the surgery."

I felt my knees grow weak and I grabbed a hold of her, desperate to stay standing. "Are you kidding?"

"No!" she exclaimed. "He had the surgery three days ago. His MRI scans look amazing. He's awake. He starts chemo to kill the cancer cells soon, but we wanted you to come. To see him."

My heart was aching. But it was the good kind of hurt. "How is he?" I felt my hands trembling. I'd been nearly brought to my knees with grief and then again with relief only a moment later. My body couldn't keep up.

Bridget knew what I was asking. And that's when I saw her smile slip. "He did suffer some memory loss. But it seems like it's just pockets right now. Not a specific duration."

I told myself that if he lost his memory, it'd be okay. I'd have it for the both of us – it's what I'd told him when I left the hospital in New Orleans. But if he was someone else, if this Everett wasn't my Everett, it would tear me apart.

Bridget broke a few traffic laws on the way to hospital, but I was thankful. I was desperate to see him. I didn't have a photo of Everett, so my dreams had been my refuge, my way to see him again.

When I arrived at the hospital, I followed Bridget down the corridor with shaky legs, pressing my hand against the wall for support. I saw Patricia, Everett's mother standing next to a man in a white coat outside of a closed door. Bridget stopped and introduced me to Everett's doctor. But my hands were itching to open the door, to see him.

The doctor turned to me, compassion in his eyes. "Parker. I want you to be prepared for what is about to happen. We don't know if this is short term or long term memory loss. We don't know how much he actually does remember. Memory loss is a tricky thing. He could regain his memories, but it might not be for some time. Or he might never remember."

"Parker," Patricia interrupted. "Everett doesn't know you're here. He doesn't remember you," her voice wavered. "You can walk away, right now. If his memory is completely gone, it will be like you were never here." Tears pooled in her eyes and she lifted a shaky hand to grasp mine. "No one would judge you."

I stared into her eyes, frosty blue like those of her son, who was lying on the other side of this door. I swallowed and then squeezed her hand. "I would. I would judge myself, for walking away from him. Even if I wanted to, I couldn't. I love him. I'm here, I'm alive, because of him." What was it about Everett's family that caused me to speak without a censor?

She smiled, her lips trembling as the first tear spilled down her cheek. "And he's here because of you. Thank you, thank you for saving him."

I pulled her in for a hug and swallowed the lump that had settled in my throat. "He saved me first."

And then my hand was on the door knob, turning and pushing it opened. The door opened with only a quiet whoosh. My eyes instantly found him, asleep on the hospital bed. His head was wrapped with thick white bandages and his left arm was resting across his abdomen, the wires coming from his veins resting peacefully against his hospital gown. One foot was sticking out of the blankets and my hands itched to cover it.

Instead, I walked towards the large window. The light flooded the room, making everything appear more alive. I looked back at the bed, took in Everett's warm complexion. He looked the opposite of how I thought he would. He looked peaceful, healthy. I knew, from what Bridget had explained on the ride over, that the doctors felt confident they'd removed the entire tumor. I felt relief then. It poured into my veins and into my bones, and I was nearly brought to the floor with it. I turned to the window, tears pooling in my eyes. I bit my lip to stop its trembling.

"Are you a nurse?" His voice was groggy, as if he was learning to use it for the first time. And the words themselves pierced a small piece of my heart. But it was his voice. It was Everett. I held on to that knowledge before I wiped the tears from my eyes and turned to face him, the window at my back.

He was squinting at me. I moved one step closer to his bed, but kept my hands clasped in front of me. "No," I said, slowly shaking my head. I took another step closer.

"Are you a doctor?" he asked, confusion on his face.

I shook my head and moved one tentative step closer.

"Are you going to a funeral then?" It was said with mild disdain. I let out a breath of relief. It really was him.

"No, I'm not going to a funeral." I was reminded then how I'd boarded the plane, thinking a funeral was precisely what I was heading to attend.

He gestured to my clothing with his hand, the hand that wasn't poked with needles. "What's with the fancy clothing then?"

I was close enough to sit in one of the bedside chairs, so I slowly lowered myself into one of them. I didn't let my eyes meet his. Instead, I just glanced around him. I knew if I stared into his eyes, I would fall apart.

"I just came from a trial." I brushed my hands down the black slacks, wiping away the sweat that had gathered on my palms. "I helped put someone, a bad someone, away for a long time."

"Good for you," he said. It sounded earnest. And it stabbed my heart again. I wanted to tell him all about it, to thank him for pushing me. For breaking the ice that I let form around me. For helping me remember. But I stayed silent and nodded, swallowing another lump.

"So..." he started, dragging the word out. "I'm guessing we know one another?"

My heart stumbled in my chest. This was harder than I'd expected. I nodded, not trusting my voice.

"Sorry. I am a bit forgetful these days." It was said with a laugh from him, and a wince from me. I looked down at the tiled floor and tried to think of what to say. "But there's good news," he said, his voice sounding hopeful. I lifted my head and finally soaked up some bravery and looked into his eyes. His eyes shined back at me.

"Your brain tumor is gone," I said, feeling happiness at that truth. "You'll start chemo soon, but you seem to be bouncing back better than expected-"

"I already know all of this," he interrupted. His abruptness hadn't changed. "I am more interested in what I don't know. Or, rather, what I don't remember."

I nodded. It would be a long road with him, especially if his memory never returned. We'd have to start from scratch. If his memory was permanently gone, he'd never remember how much he changed me, how far we'd come. I wouldn't let myself mourn for that just yet. I'd let it be enough that I knew, that I remembered. I would not fall apart in front of him.

"I'm told I brought this with me to the hospital," he said, reaching his IV-free hand under the sheets and pulling out a small book. His journal. I sucked in a breath. It was gray, the color worn and the material tattered, but I could see as he opened it and flipped through the pages, it was covered in writing. In drawings. My heart beat sped up as he turned the pages. He closed it and picked it up, tossing it to me.

I caught it clumsily, nearly dropping it. I heard him laugh from the bed and looked at him with a sharp look before remembering where I was, where we were. "Sorry," I said, pushing out a breath.

"Don't be."

I turned the journal over in my hands. 'PARKER' it said, in

bold letters on the cover. My hand moved to trace the letters, and my eyes closed as I imagined him writing each letter. The way his wrist moved with each stroke. Knowing that I was the only thing on his mind in that moment. It was a profound moment for me. The knowing. I was touching a piece of the Everett that remembered me.

"You must be Parker." His words were like a power-packed punch to the heart. "Your name is written on my notebook." My eyes opened, not without difficulty, and I finally met his eyes. The ice blue irises shined back at me. Eyes that belonged to another person, maybe even another soul. I looked down at the journal in my hands and kept running my fingers over my name. Maybe he had leaked a bit of his soul into these pages. "It's also written on my chest."

I nodded.

"They say that's bad luck," he continued.

I shrugged and met his eyes. "I had a part of you tattooed on me too." His eyes lit up with that.

I suddenly doubted myself. Could I do this? Could I start anew with this Everett? There was such calm between us at this moment, a calm that had never been present in our interactions before. I'd always been a ball of coiled fear, ready to run at a moment's notice. And after, I'd always been on guard around him, animosity thick in our every conversation.

"Don't." His voice was soft, but his words were firm.

I let out a heavy breath, releasing some of pressure on my heart. I looked into his eyes again. "Don't what?"

"Don't run." He narrowed his eyes, as if trying to compel me to stay with the force of his gaze.

I choked back a sob. He'd said those words to me so many times. Before I could say anything, he spoke again.

"You're not wearing the right shoes anyway."

The sound that came from my mouth was half sob, half laugh. My heart simultaneously ached and swelled. Could my Everett, my dark, funny, intense Everett, still exist without the memory of when we met? I had one true test. I lifted my eyes to his again. He was staring at me, but I didn't itch under his gaze this time. I ached for it, I relished it.

I leaned forward. "It's rude to stare."

One side of his lips lifted up in a smile. I sent up silent prayer to hear the words I hoped to hear.

God listened. Everett was still my Everett.

"I never claimed to be anything else."

Epilogue

10 months later

It was probably a dumb idea. I knew that. But it was worth trying. Or, that's what I told myself when I landed in Denver and waited in baggage claim for him after an early morning flight from California.

I looked around, looked at the people mulling around, waiting for baggage and hugging their loved ones. I ached a little bit. I ached all the time. I missed the Everett that lived in my memories. The Everett that lived now was in so many ways the same Everett. He still said rude things just to make me laugh. But he was confused a lot. I tried not to push him. I stuck around through his first round of chemo before heading home to California. Everett stayed in Texas, with his sister. She took him to his chemo appointments and to the gym as often as possible. The surgery had weakened him, but he was practically back to normal. His memory of me was still absent, and that stung a little bit. Especially when he remembered his life before me.

He'd called me from Texas a few weeks after the surgery and asked me if I knew Charlotte. His memory had left off being with her. I tried not to make gagging sounds in the phone, so all I said was, "Trust me, you don't like Charlotte."

Everett, to his credit, was committed to me. In the only way he really could be. He called or texted me daily. He asked me questions and I did my best to answer him. He read the notebook where he'd written things done, so he knew a lot of things about me that the Everett pre-surgery had known. He'd made comments on the picture he drew of me on the first page, the one of my profile, my head back, my lips slightly open. I'd laughed when he made the comments, saying how 'hot' it was. Once in a while, I flew out to Texas to visit him, but there was still emotional distance between us.

To be clear: we hadn't kissed. I knew Everett wanted to. But he seemed to respecting whatever it was that was holding me back. And the only thing holding me back was his memory. I was desperate for him to remember. I wanted that look he'd given me, the look with feeling. I wanted it more than anything. And I was still holding onto a shred of hope that he'd remember someday.

And that's why I was sitting in baggage claim after claiming my keys from the rental car company. My eyes searched the crowd for him. His hair had grown out again, though he kept it shorter than it'd been when we first met.

I missed the long hair. I missed a lot of things. And I tried my damnedest to push it from my head, to focus on what was important. Everett was alive. And he was strong. And he'd listened to me, when I'd made my emotional plea before leaving him in New Orleans.

So when I saw him emerge through the doors into baggage claim, my heart skipped a beat. And I walked towards him, my heart in my throat and my eyes shining.

"Parker," he said, holding his arms out. I went into his arms. This was my favorite place. He still felt the same to me, even if he didn't feel the same for me. "You haven't been hugged enough." It was something he'd read in the journal, but each time he said it, a fresh wave of tears started.

I pulled away first. "I have the keys to our Jeep. You ready?"

He angled his head towards the baggage carousel. "I just need to grab one bag."

"Oh, of course," I said, motioning him along. When he walked away, I missed Everett the asshole.

Everett had written a lot about me in the journal. But he didn't write about Picketwire Canyon or our tattoos. I wasn't sure why. He'd written about the Four Corners, about meeting Mira in Colorado, about how I'd kissed him with feeling in Texas. But it was as if an entire chunk of the journal was missing. He'd left his descriptions of each time we'd had sex, which was embarrassing for Everett to tell me about. It felt like a stranger was reading about our more intimate scenes. But I tried hard. I tried to accept Everett now. I tried not to mourn the Everett who remembered me. But it hurt.

Everett and I met up with the caravan for our trip through the canyon. We stopped at the petroglyphs first. I watched Everett look at them, waiting to see if he made the same comments the first time. He didn't. He just nodded and we returned to the vehicle, my heart a little heavier in my chest.

When we stopped for the arch, my heart started thundering. I grabbed my camera and walked around the car to Everett. "Let's go," I said impatiently. I reached for his hand instinctually and he clasped it. We looked at each other and our hands for a second. Everett scrunched his brow. It was the first time we'd held hands since I'd left him in New Orleans. But it felt right, right with the moment. So I tugged him, pulled him along with me.

As expected, everyone clambered up to the arch but I pulled Everett to the view that meant so much to me. "Don't look at the arch," I said.

"You're so bossy sometimes," he muttered.

"Get over it," I muttered back. This was off to a great start – with Everett calling me bossy and my temper short. "See this?" I asked, gesturing towards the valley in the canyon, the river that cut through it. "This is the Purgatoire River."

"Purgatoire." Everett tasted the word and looked at me with confusion. "Like purgatory?"

He was screwing up my speech. It was very Everett of him. "Yes. The Spanish explorers came through here first and their men had a rough time, so they called it a version of 'The River of Lost Souls in Purgatory'. And French explorers came through and renamed it the Purgatoire River, their name for purgatory. And then Americans butchered the pronunciation so they call this the Picketwire Canyonlands."

"Slow down, Parker," Everett said, looking at me like I'd grown three heads. "I didn't know I'd be getting a history lesson."

I gritted my teeth. I wanted to yell, "You imparted all that knowledge on me, asshole!" but I kept my mouth shut and breathed in through my nose. "Everyone comes here to look at the arch," I continued, using my thumb to gesture behind us. "But I like this view myself."

Everett looked back at the arch and then at the view in front of us. "I agree. I'd rather look at this than the arch." I wasn't getting what I wanted from him. I grabbed his hand again. He looked down at our clasped hands and up at me.

"What is purgatory to you?"

Everett studied me a minute, opened his mouth to say something but then closed it. Something was working its way behind his eyes. "A place to cleanse your soul before being admitted to Heaven."

My heart leapt. "Yes," I said animatedly. "One last stop before forever."

Everett was staring at me. I couldn't read his expression, but I wanted to continue. "Come," I said, pulling him up to the arch. Everett jumped up on the ledge below the arch first and reached his hands for me, helping me up.

"Hey," I called to a person that was taking photos of the view.

"Can you take a photo of us?"

The older woman in her khaki hat nodded and took the camera I tossed down to her. I blew out a breath and turned my head to Everett. I wrapped an arm around him and took his hand and pulled it on my lap, clasping it firmly in mine. My blood roared in my ears. My heart thudded painfully in my chest. I put my lips to his ear. "Everett, look out. Over the canyon, at the river. Look at all of it. Look at this view as this woman takes a photo of us." I squeezed his hand. "Everyone who sees this photo will see us, underneath this arch. But when you look at the photo," I swallowed emotion. "When you look at this photo, remember the canyon, the water, and all the beauty in front of us." I blew out a breath. "When you look at this photo, remember looking out at purgatory with me. While everyone else was looking at the arch, we were looking at that." And then I closed my eyes. A tear slipped, reminding me of how I'd felt when Everett had said those words to me. The fact that I'd felt at all. One year ago, we'd sat on this ledge together and I'd fallen in love with Everett. I ached for that moment. I mourned it. I mourned the Everett who'd taught me to live.

The hand in mine on my lap squeezed once. Then again. Then once more.

Three times.

I opened my eyes and saw Everett staring at me. His eyes were red, but soft. And his brow was furrowed. "Parker," he said, with recognition. With feeling.

"Everett," I said back. His name was strangled with fresh tears. Tears on top of tears. He touched my hair, slid a hand down my face, looking at me as if seeing me for the first time in forever, and then he cradled my face and kissed me.

It'd been a year since I'd felt his lips on mine. I'd thought about testing it after his surgery, to see if kissing me would reignite his memories. But I'd waited, stubbornly, hoping against all hope that he'd remember. That I'd kiss the Everett I'd fallen in love with.

I knew, from the way his lips pressed mine and by the feel of his thumb on my cheek, that this was that Everett.

I pulled back first and put my hands on his face. "You remember?" I asked on a choked sob, hardly able to see him through the tears.

He nodded, his thumbs on my chin. "Parker," he said again.

I brought my hands up to his wrists and squeezed. "I'm so happy," I said, laughing and crying from relief.

"You're laughing," he said, tilting his head to the side. "It sounds so weird."

I laughed and squeezed his wrists again. "You're still an asshole."

"I am," he confirmed. He blew out a breath, eyes wincing. "It's coming back to me so quickly. I can hardly keep up."

"It's okay," I said, wrapping my arms around his upper back. His arms wrapped around me and he hugged me, tightly.

"I'm so sorry," he muffled against my hair. He ran a hand down my hair, a move that was as familiar as it was deeply comforting.

"Don't be. Oh, Everett." I couldn't stop crying. "I'm so glad you're back. I've missed you."

Understatement of the year.

He held me while our hearts beat, for several minutes at least. Suddenly, as if a particular memory returned, his hand touched my ribs, where my Purgatoire tattoo was. "Why did you wait so long to bring me here?" he asked.

"I wanted you to be well enough to come."

He shook his head. "Did you get the box?"

My mind went to the box, the one still sitting in the corner of my bedroom, unopened. "Yes," I said, "but I didn't open it."

"Why?" he asked. "No wait," he said, holding up a hand. "I get it. But in the box are the Picketwire Canyon pages from my journal. And the photos."

"Photos, as in plural?"

"I took a lot of photos of you, when you weren't looking. I asked Bridget to send that box to you. I hoped you'd understand the reason, and bring me here in case it would trigger my memory."

"Huh," I said. "I feel kind of bad I never opened it."

"You could have saved yourself all this heartache, all this pain." He brushed my hair from my face.

"I don't mind the pain so much," I said. "I've found pleasure in the pain."

Everett smiled at me. "Good. It's good to feel." His fingers tugged on my hair. I smiled, a real smile.

"Smiles suit you. You should wear them more often."

"You suit me."

Everett hopped down from the ledge and put his hands up to catch me, as he had the first time. He pulled me to him for a hug. I clung tightly to him, thankful for the gift. Thankful for the Purgatoire River. Thankful for a text message that was sent to the wrong number. Thankful to feel, to be healed and broken at the same time by Everett.

"You're cold," he murmured. It was early June and early in the day, so I did have a slight chill.

"Ten below zero?" I asked.

"Nah," he said, pulling back and kissing my forehead. "Colder than that."

I laughed, pressing into him, into this kiss. Relishing this connection.

Everett pulled back and stared into my eyes, the way he had before. His hands clasped mine.

"Are you in love with me yet?"

I smiled. "Unfortunately. Are you in love with me?"

In answer, his hands squeezed mine. Three times. With each squeeze, he mouthed three words. "I. Love. You."

THE END

Bonus Scene

Everett's POV – the Picketwire Canyonlands

We were standing directly next to one another as I pointed out the petroglyphs. A few times, I looked over at Parker, watched her take it in. I wanted to peek inside her mind, to see what she was thinking.

She'd asked me earlier, at the gas station, how I was feeling. I'd told her I didn't know. It was true, to some degree. More accurate was that I didn't have words for this. In the span of a few days, she'd become someone I felt complex things for. All of that had come to a head the night before, when she'd cleaned my wounds in the bathroom of the hotel. And later, when I'd had the nightmare of the man that knocked Parker down. I'd stupidly tried distancing myself from her earlier that morning, pissed to be feeling anything for her.

And so I'd continued being an asshole earlier this morning, telling her to kiss me like she meant it. I was selfish, there was no other way to explain it. I pushed her and pulled her, ignored her and overwhelmed her. I knew I confused her, but I didn't give a damn. I wanted her to feel. It was as simple as that.

She turned to look at me, her eyes searching. I almost said something before one of the tour guides interrupted my thoughts, tore my eyes away from staring at her. "Now, you can find petroglyphs in many national parks around the country. Take the Grand Canyon for instance, has anyone been there?"

I hesitated only a second, glancing quickly at Parker. My lips curved as I spoke. "We were there a couple days ago." I felt her eyes on me.

The tour guide nodded, encouraging me to continue. "Did you explore it?" he asked.

I looked back at her, looking forward to what was about to happen. I aimed a thumb at her. "No. Parker called it a big hole in the ground, so we didn't stick around."

Like I expected, her eyes shot to mine, wide eyed with shock. I couldn't help but smile back. She self-consciously looked around, before she turned back to me and glared. "You're an asshole, Everett," she said, her cheeks coloring the most beautiful shade of red. My arm moved of its own volition, wrapping around her shoulders and pulling her closer to me.

"Do you love me yet?" I whispered, my breath at her ear. I felt my heart thud in my chest and the words I'd spoken became weighted as I realized what I wanted her answer to be. Shock pooled in my veins then, but I didn't let go.

She shoved away from me, muttering "Definitely not," as she walked back down to the car.

The thud in my chest became a punch, a solid one. I winced a little, not expecting my body's reaction to her answer. I knew I was an asshole. Part of my reason for being an asshole was because it was easier to be one, to keep people at arm's length. I was dying. I had to deal with the disappointment my mother and sister felt every time I told them I was taking this final journey.

But the bigger reason I was an asshole was the cancer. The surgery years earlier had removed the tumor and my tact. Gone was the Everett that had been the life of every party. In his place was me, this person who spoke harshly, sometimes by choice and other times because it was in my nature.

The funny thing was that with my mother and my sister, I was very mindful of how I spoke. Careful not to hurt. But with Parker? I didn't censor myself as much. I very much wanted to hurt her. To know that I could, because then she'd have to admit that she too was feeling whatever it was that was building between us. If I could hurt her, pull her from her tomb of indifference, then she was feeling something. And not just something, but something for me.

When we reached the stopping point for the arch, I collected my thoughts as I grabbed the camera from my backpack in the backseat. Parker went ahead of me, with the group up to the arch. I watched her for a moment, so completely committed to keeping her thoughts locked inside that head of hers that I nearly forgot what my mission was.

I caught up to her a few yards from the arch. "Wait a second, Parker," I called, placing a hand on her shoulder. "Turn around."

She turned around and I moved so I was standing behind her, my hand still on her shoulder. I inhaled the scent of limes that followed her. "That's the Purgatoire River," I said, motioning out to the view in front of us.

"Picketwire. Purgatoire," she said. I could tell she was working it out in her head.

"Yes. Spanish explorers called it their translation of "The River of Lost Souls in Purgatory" after having a tough go of it. French trappers later called it the Purgatoire River. The pronunciation was bastardized when American Explorers came through, and so this canyon was called Picketwire." I leaned down, bearing a little more weight on her shoulder and put my lips to her ear. "Everyone comes here to see the arch, but I think the arch is the fortunate one, to have this view, a view that was named for purgatory." It was the truth.

I always told people I didn't remember this, didn't remember the Picketwire Canyonlands, from the trip I took pre-surgery. And while it was true, it wasn't completely true. I remembered the parts I'd studied in advance, the arch and the dinosaur prints. I had the vaguest memory of watching my family climb up to the arch while I stood in this spot and stared at the valley below, thinking about the possibility of death. Thinking about Purgatory. Heavy stuff for a teenager.

I wanted Parker to see it, to understand.

"But isn't purgatory a place of suffering, a place you have to atone for your sins before being admitted to Heaven?" she asked.

I wanted to connect with her. Maybe by touching me, she'd feel it. She'd get it. I needed to speak more deeply to her. I wrapped my arms around her waist and pulled her back, into me. "How very Parker of you to think of purgatory so negatively." I leaned in so close I could kiss her temple. "I prefer to think of it as a place to cleanse, to purify your soul before heaven." I pressed a quick kiss there, unable to resist being so close and not tasting her skin. I closed my eyes and breathed in her lime scent. "And is there a better place to see while you're waiting for your forever in the afterlife?"

She seemed to relax in my arms so I held her for a moment, letting the warmth of her body soothe me.

"Come," I said, reaching in front of her and grabbing her hand. I pulled her up the hill as the last tourists started to depart. I reached a hand out to one of them and asked him to take our photo.

I jumped up on the ledge below the arch and pulled her right up next to me. My heart was beating loudly in my chest and I summoned the words that I hoped would speak to her soul, that would help her understand the significance of this moment. "Look, Parker," I said, point out in front of us. My voice sounded gruffer than usual. I swallowed. "Look at this view as this man takes this photo of us." I turned to look at her, put an arm around her and pulled her close, so nothing, not even air, separated us.

I put my lips to her ear. "Everyone who sees this photo will see us under the arch. But when you see this photo, you'll see the canyon and the water and all the beauty in front of us." Everything else around us dropped off. All I saw was her. She was in my arms, her short breaths becoming the only sound I was aware of, and her scent wrapping us in everything that was perfect about her. "Remember that, Parker. When you look at this photo, remember looking at purgatory with me. While everyone else was looking at the arch, we were looking at that." I felt the ache then. I'd been trying to speak to her soul. Instead, I'd succeeded in speaking to mine.

She turned her head tentatively, so she was looking at me. Her eyes were wide, vulnerable. Her lips trembled. My lips touched hers and my hands moved to hold the sides of her face, my grip tight. This kiss involved only our lips, but there was no doubt that my heart was tangled in that mess of flesh.

Fuck.

I pulled back and stared at her, wanting to see her reaction. She still looked vulnerable. But she had a secure lid on her emotions, so I swallowed uncomfortably. "Let's catch up to the group," I said, jumping down from the arch in a fall that was more graceful than the one my heart had just done.

I wouldn't ask her if she loved me again. Not unless I knew, wholeheartedly, the answer. Another "No" would be like a knife to my soul.

As a self-published author, reviews mean the world to me. If you decide to leave a review after reading this novel, please email me a link to your review on Amazon and I will send you a signed TEN BELOW ZERO bookmark.

whitney.barbetti@gmail.com

Acknowledgments

Sona Babani, my best friend for fifteen years, if you haven't figured it out yet, I based a lot of Parker on you. You wanted to be Mira, the bad ass, and you are. But you're also Parker. Kind, observant, thinks-she's-cold-hearted Parker. Parker whose soul is beautiful, like yours. Remember what I told you, when couldn't decide between the sunflower seeds that had shells and the ones without. You've wasted a lot of your life on people who don't deserve you. Fuck those shells. They don't deserve your effort. Eat the seeds, straight up. You deserve them.

It wouldn't be my acknowledgements if I didn't thank my husband for being awesome. Also, thanks for disappearing for three weeks so I could channel all the missing you I did into this book. To my beautiful sons, I love you so much. Please sleep more than four hours a night so I can write my next book much faster.

Thank you to my family for your support. You all know who you are. There's too many of you, and too many miles separating us. I can't wait to hug you all.

To Wilma and Jessie Bristol, and Tracie Ingram, for all your support. You three are like family to me. I am so thankful to have you in my life.

To Angie VanLeuven, Rebekka Sampson, Ashlee Grimmett, Candi Rash, Kelly Hoover, Hilda, Salgado – my fellow Army wives and soldiers. I love you all so much. Thank you for your support, for reading my drafts, for sharing the crap out of my books, for your votes on my cover options, and for being excited with me. You humble me with your love. Thank you.

To Debbie Snyder, another fellow Army wife and one of my closest friends. Thank you for pimping out He Found Me so much.

Thank you for all your support during AT, when I was going out of mind trying to finish this book and also get sleep. I love you!

Christine Janes! I miss buddy reading with you. Thank you for telling me over and over how much you loved this story, and how you thought this novel would do so well. Everything you said propelled me to finish this novel in thirty-four days. I wouldn't have done that without you.

Karla Sorensen, you are an angel. I feel like I've know you much longer than I actually have. Thank you so much for your chapter by chapter feedback of Ten Below Zero, and your guidance and tips. I would have missed out on a lot of good stuff if it were not for your 'grain of salt' advice. You, my dear, are BASEBALLS.

To all my friends, I so appreciate every share, every email, every word you've spread about my novel. Cindy, Megan, Joni, Samantha, Jennifer, Karen, Hailey, Ashley, Ashley, Cecilia, Jessica, Heather, and Jamie. Thank you from the bottom of my heart.

To the early Goodreads members who read He Found Me and told their friends to read – Anne OK, Em, Bibliophilia, Christie with Smokin' Hot Book Blog, and Jennifer Kyle – thank you for taking a chance on me. I appreciate you all so very much.

Thank you to Jade Eby, for rescuing me, and for humbling me. You are so sweet and kind. I wish nothing but good things for you in your success as an author. You've already excelled as a human. I am forever grateful you went out of your way to message me. Click, click, click.

Thank you to Lex Martin. You have no idea how far-reaching your post was, the one you shared about my novel. Thanks to you, I found a beta reader who sent me the most amazing email after reading the copy of my novel you advertised. Thank you for being so supportive and offering to share about He Found Me in your group. I've made some really great friendships already thanks to you.

To Najla for another amazing cover. I would never go to anyone else. You are a beautiful human being.

Thank you to the reader reading this. Ten Below Zero is an emotional read, but there's a reason for that. If this book moved you, I'm happy. I don't rejoice in the tears of strangers for the reasons you may think. Everett wanted Parker to feel. I firmly believe in reading books that make you feel. You should never read books that are easy to put down, mine included. Read books that make you think, that make you feel. Read books that impassion you, that enlighten you. Don't be afraid to hurt. You'll be stronger for it. Loving and healing are intertwined, and with both comes pain. You can't love without pain. You can't heal without pain. Don't be afraid to love, to hurt, to heal. Embrace it. Be stronger for it. Be a compassionate human because you've hurt before.

The whole entire point of Ten Below Zero is to allow yourself to feel. In feeling, there's healing. There's love. And that love is within you.

Thank you to the incredible soul who inspired this story. The regret I feel is now palpable and it lives among these pages. Saying I miss you is the most inadequate thing I'll ever say.

That is why, for Christ's sake, I delight in weaknesses, in insults, in hardships, in persecutions, in difficulties. For when I am weak, then I am strong.

- 2 Corinthians 12:10

Also by Whitney Barbetti

He Found Me (He Found Me #1)
He Saved Me (He Found Me #2)

Made in the USA
Charleston, SC
21 May 2016